A Quilting of Scars

"Black writes with a wonderful sense of place, as she takes the reader back to a 'not so' gentler time. A comfortable, yet suitably disturbing read about secrets and the ever-present of the past."

~ Robert Rotenberg, author of *One Minute More*

"At once a searing portrait of rural life at the turn of 19th century Canada, profound family drama, and a dark mystery, Lucy E.M. Black's *A Quilting of Scars* takes the reader on a tumultuous journey from the ashes of a tragic fire to the revelation of secrets and recriminations that burn just as deeply."

~ Anthony Bidulka, author of *Going to Beautiful*

"*A Quilting of Scars* by Lucy E.M. Black is a gorgeously textured story of the brutality and sorrows of submerged identity and trauma. Set in the early 1900s in rural Ontario, Black's writing is stylistically cinematic and thematically universal. Her masterful use of the historical fiction genre serves to amplify human behaviour, allowing us to take it out of our current context and place it in an uncluttered setting that is free of contemporaneous issues and distractions. The effect is a deftly-crafted character-driven narrative that's as breathtaking as it is shattering."

~ Hollay Ghadery, author of *Fuse, Rebellion Box* and
Widow Fantasies

"In the tradition of Donna Morrissey and Emma Donoghue, *A Quilting of Scars* highlights Black's deft proclivity for painting a Canadian setting so real readers can taste and touch it. This backdrop is the careful canvas wherein she marries the beauty of place and story with an undercurrent of pathos, deep characterization, and a profound empathy for staggering questions of humanity, identity and even faith. Achingly relevant, Larkin Beattie forces us to confront a broken and tragical mirror that in its most lyrical and challenging moments has the propensity to heighten our collective compassion."

~ Rachel McMillan, bestselling author of *The Mozart Code* and
The Liberty Scarf

A Quilting of Scars

A Novel

Lucy E.M. Black

INANNA

CANADA

*Publisher's note: This book is a work of fiction. Names, characters, places and
incidents are either the product of the author's imagination or are used fictitiously,
and any resemblance to actual persons living or dead is entirely coincidental.*

Library and Archives Canada Cataloguing in Publication

Title: A quilting of scars : a novel / Lucy E.M. Black.

Names: Black, Lucy E. M., 1957- author

Identifiers: Canadiana (print) 20250209020 | Canadiana (ebook) 20250209039 |
ISBN 9781989689899 (softcover) | ISBN 9781989689936 (EPUB)

Subjects: LCGFT: Novels.

Classification: LCC PS8603.L2555 Q55 2025 | DDC C813/.6—dc23

Printed and bound in Canada on 100% recycled paper.

Now Or Never Publishing
901, 163 Street
Surrey, British Columbia
Canada V4A 9T8

nonpublishing.com
Fighting Words.

We gratefully acknowledge the support of the Canada Council for the Arts
and the British Columbia Arts Council for our publishing program.

To the Larkins of this world…

Blue Heron Books
62 Brock Street West
UXBRIDGE ONTARIO
905-852-4282
www.blueheronbooks.com

Sun Oct19-25 12:49pm
Inv: 418481 W 00

Qty	Price Disc	Total Tax

9781989689899 Quilting of Scars,A
| 1 | 26.95 | 26.95 |

| | Subtotal | 26.95 |
| | a GST 5% | 1.35 |

Items	1 Total	28.30
	Cash	30.30
	Change	2.00

GST/HST 868450529

So full of artless jealousy is guilt,
It spills itself in fearing to be spilt.
                —William Shakespeare, *Hamlet*

Cemetery Hill, April 10, 1909

Today was a breeding day. Larkin Beattie and his horse were due at the stables by ten. Culloden, a dark bay stallion, sixteen hands high and five years of age, was a proven foal-getter. One of his colts had already taken a first at Georgetown.

Limping slightly, Larkin crossed the kitchen to the cellar door and made his way carefully down its steep steps. He took in the stench of stagnant groundwater leached from the soil, now moistening the stone walls with a dank musk, like stale urine. The spring earth pissing away the last of winter. A brief skittering betrayed the presence of mice fleeing his intrusion. Larkin reached down to draw out what he sought from the deep slatted crates and then returned to the kitchen, apples and carrots bulging his pockets. A habit born of years trying to detract from his height meant that he slouched forward as he walked.

He unhooked a barn coat from the peg, and as he pulled it on, he moved outside into the stinging chill. The groom he'd hired was waiting by the wagon. Larkin climbed aboard, his rheumatic leg dragging only a little.

Finally, he settled himself on the seat, took up the reins, and urged the two drays forward. The road to Eryn was easy; it wasn't long before he relaxed into the wagon's rhythmic bouncing and jostling. The snow and ice had mostly melted although patches of white could still be seen deep in the thickets, protected from the sun. Fenton, the groom, sat behind him. As was his custom, the groom faced to the rear, towards Culloden, who was tied to the back of the rig and trotted along serenely behind it. The drays, Pirate and Thunder, were used almost entirely for farm work; they kept an even pace but not an especially rapid one.

As he drew closer to Eryn a horseless carriage passed by; Larkin had to hold the reins tightly to keep his drays steady. He heard

Culloden snorting and looked over his shoulder to see that Fenton had jumped off the wagon and was soothing the anxious stallion. Then, once the stallion was calmed, Larkin went back to calculating his potential earnings for the day. At eight dollars per single leap, he might collect twenty-four dollars in total. With only a few more showings he'd soon have the ready money to purchase a motor car.

When the fairgrounds at Eryn hove into view Larkin turned onto the dirt drive with a growing eagerness. Culloden was a superb creature, and letting him stand for mares had been profitable. Fenton led the stallion into the turnout while Larkin tended to the drays. Culloden looked well in the morning light, his brushed coat gleaming; he was as fine a specimen as anyone could imagine. Bill Dempsey, stationed already at the fence, let out a low whistle as he watched the powerful animal entering the enclosure.

Larkin greeted Bill and took a position on the fence beside him. Then, when a mare was led to the turnout, Fenton came to stand with the small group of gathered onlookers.

"He's going to the party!" called one of the spectators. Larkin watched calmly while Culloden pranced towards the mare with a determined gait, his neck arched and his tail raised. The mare responded with a combination of kicking and posturing, her tail held firmly down. Then, as Culloden approached more closely, she got aggressive, squealing and nipping at him. Now the stallion retreated, pawing and stomping the ground, rebuffed but still interested. Moments later he approached again, with soft nickers and whinnies. The mare squealed louder this time and attempted to bite him.

"She's playin' hard to get," said Bill. "Just like my ol' lady."

Larkin nodded sagely.

Undeterred, Culloden nipped at the mare's mane, shoulder, and flank. These advance-and-retreat forays continued for over an hour, the group of men quietly observing.

A change suddenly took place when the mare lifted her tail and expelled a strong stream of urine. She presented herself to Culloden by backing towards his head and shoulders. Culloden responded by sniffing and nuzzling her and then by licking her flank and posterior. The men watched as the penis dropped and became firm. When the erection was complete, Culloden mounted the mare with his head pressed against her flank. Then he planted his legs firmly and moved in more closely. Deep, shuddering thrusts followed while the crowd watched the flag of the stallion's tail and listened to the characteristic grunts and squeals.

Culloden dismounted quickly and sniffed the area briefly before defecating. His neck and head were raised and he rolled his upper lip back as he inhaled, displaying his teeth. The onlookers could not help but think this was the look of a self-satisfied male, proud of his endeavours. Some of the men shifted uncomfortably.

"Well, that's done the deed then," said Bill, pulling out his wallet and passing Larkin eight dollars. Fenton hopped the fence just then and led the mare away, leaving Culloden to graze not far from the enclosure.

"How long ya plan on leavin' 'im?" called one of the men.

Larkin turned to see that it was Thom Granger from over in Rockwood. "An hour or more. I like to space 'em out. Need to make sure folks get their money's worth."

"You think he's having a good time?"

Larkin laughed. "He's havin' a good time, all right." At that, Larkin held out an apple. When Culloden came near the fence and suctioned it from his hand Larkin patted him gently and whispered, "Well done, boy."

Fenton was paid to watch the horse while Larkin headed off with the other men for lunch at Nestor's Restaurant just down the road. Larkin had a chicken pie and a pot of tea. He did not order dessert when the others did, as he liked to watch his pennies. That was his way, cautious and steady. Buying Culloden, and the others before that, had been the only impulsive decisions of his life. Larkin loved horses. He didn't break them and he didn't ride them, he just loved the look of them running proud in his pasture.

After their plates had been taken away Bill Dempsey leaned back in his chair and pulled a chew out of the little pouch he carried in his pocket. Larkin watched as Bill's tongue moved the tobacco around in his mouth, eventually sucking it through his teeth, one cheek bulging prominently with its mass. Tiny drops of golden brown saliva appeared on his lower lip and sprayed outwards when he spoke. "Drove past the old Skinner place day before," he began. "Shame no one's doing anything with that land."

Larkin stiffened a little at the mention of the Skinner place. He nodded in silent agreement.

Thom Granger answered. "Good land that. Sandy loam, I reckon."

"Nah. Got some clay in it," said Bill. "What do you think, Larkin? Your place being close by."

"Ours is good loam all right." Larkin's voice was thin. "But there's a streak of clay runs through and a little seam of sand over by Currie's." His companions took in the information and the amiable conversation continued. Larkin was relieved when the waitress came to announce the amounts they owed, thus breaking up their chinwag. He was eager to get back to Culloden and the discussion had made him uncomfortable.

Culloden serviced four mares in Eryn that day. Larkin typically stopped after three but there were four in estrus waiting and the last farmer, Jeb McCormick, an old friend from school days, was prepared to risk success. Larkin gave him a two-dollar discount in the event that the mating did not take. Thirty dollars minus the groom's salary and the cost of his lunch meant that Larkin had cleared twenty-seven dollars for the day.

As he and Fenton drove back to Cemetery Hill, Larkin ran columns of numbers in his head, trying to calculate how close he was to the amount required for a McLaughlin horseless carriage. A dealer had come through Collingwood the year before, and when Larkin saw the vehicle he conceived of the immediate notion that he must have one. Despite being thrifty, he relished the idea of being among the first in the township to own such a thing. He saw himself driving up and down the road to the village, slowing down to keep from shying horses. Waving to neighbours. He would offer rides back and forth along the concession from his farm on Cemetery Hill to Murton, a straight run of two and a half miles.

Larkin had long ago acquired a considerable sum when he sold off the last of his beef cattle. That, along with what he made renting grazing land, was more money than he'd ever known. One afternoon, twenty-three years before, he'd been walking around the weekly market when he saw a beautiful colt prancing about in a little corral and thought, *would I ever like to see that horse run*. And he bought him right there and then. Paid cash.

It was his first breeding stallion. Larkin named him Bedivere, after one of King Arthur's knights. Ever since then, every one of his horses had been named after someone or something that Larkin had found in the encyclopedia set. He liked to sit quietly of an evening and puzzle through an entry in one of the books, endeavouring to teach himself something new.

Larkin had never been a scholar, but in midlife, after his parents had passed and he was alone in the large empty house, he yearned for company. And so it was that he'd taken to dusting off the encyclopedias and propping a volume open on the table while he ate his solitary supper. The set was mostly intact, his father having bought them at a sale when Larkin was still a boy. Volume MUL-PER was missing; Larkin could no longer remember whether he'd lost the volume or his father had purchased the set incomplete. There was plenty of learning to be had between AAC to MUL and RUS-ZWI, however, so he wasn't much troubled by the missing book.

Larkin already had enough money in the bank to cover the cost of a horseless carriage, but he wasn't for touching that in case it was needed for something else. The figures he was tallying in his head were the sums he'd tucked away in mason jars around the house. Some were in the cellar hidden behind old sacks, and some were in the backside of dresser drawers. Hidden under a quilt in his mother's cedar-lined hope chest stood four jars, each one holding a hundred dollars. Larkin calculated that he could soon travel to Collingwood to place his order. Money was a mighty thing, he reflected, givin' people power for all sorts of foolishness.

It was near seven when Larkin finally arrived home that evening. After seeing off Fenton he settled the horses, checked in on the other animals, and thought about his day. It had been a rather fine one. Culloden had performed well. But Bill's comment at lunch niggled at him. Even after all the years that had passed he still didn't like talking about the Skinners.

Using both arms he heaved the barn door shut, feeling the strain of the effort in his muscles and in the slight tightness of his chest. Larkin was fifty-one now, almost the same age as his father was when he'd died a quarter century before. And in the last while Larkin had been thinking about his own mortality. About how the past could feel more present the further away you got from it.

Larkin turned and stood motionless, looking at the dark that hid the open fields and beyond them the dense bush surrounding the farm. He was remembering.

Entering the house from the back door—the only door that ever got used—Larkin walked straight into the kitchen. The room astonished anyone who saw it for the first time, painted as it was entirely in a shocking, rosy pink. It had been his Ma's choice, and she'd loved it. His Pa had done it up for her one winter before Larkin was born. The shelves, the cupboards, and even the chairs were painted to match.

"It's a wonder," his Pa once said, "that she dint want the floorboards done as well."

Larkin had laughed. "Shush now, Pa, you'll be givin' her ideas."

He kicked off his boots impatiently and headed upstairs to his bedroom. There he moved across the floor in his stocking feet and knelt down stiffly beside his bedstead. Reaching beneath the overhang of the quilt, he withdrew a flattened flour sack from under the bed. Then, leaning heavily upon the mattress, he pushed himself upright and made his way downstairs again to the kitchen, where he lay the sack and its contents upon the table.

Seated now in a chair thick with paint, he pulled the sack closer. He glanced around quickly. Then, slowly and tenderly, Larkin inserted his hand into the sack and drew out a large scrapbook, its deep blue cover marked at each corner with a delicate pattern of winding vines. Hesitating for only a moment, he

opened the cover and pressed it down before him. Larkin nodded, as if to acknowledge a familiar friend. Finally, he began to
read the yellowed bits of newspaper that had been carefully glued
to brittle, unbending pages.

The clippings came from *The Murton County Chronicle*.
Beside each was the date, written in his mother's flowing hand,
the ink faded now. The first was dated August 8, 1871, almost
forty years back.

FIRE BLAZES IN MURTON!

Volunteer firefighters were out in full force Sunday night
two miles west of the village after neighbours spotted a
blaze. The coroner's office has stated that two bodies
were found in the burned-out farmhouse while another
man is under doctor's care with serious burns to his hands
and feet. The fire department continues to investigate.

Then, on August 15th:

SKINNERS LAID TO REST

Funerals were held in Murton for Silas and Elgin
Skinner. Both men, father and son, died on Cemetery
Hill the night of August 7th. The Skinner farmhouse and
barn burned to the ground on the same evening. On the
night of the fire, flames from the barn were seen to soar
sixty feet in the air. The funerals were well attended by
community members who recalled the Skinners as "nice,
old-fashioned folk." They were laid to rest in the Murton
Memorial Cemetery. A luncheon was held following the
service at the United Methodist Church Hall.

And February 13th, six months later:

MURDER IN CEMETERY HILL!!

Investigators now confirm that they are building a case
for murder concerning the suspicious deaths of two men
in a farmhouse fire near Murton. The community was

shocked to learn that Silas and Elgin Skinner suffered
stab wounds prior to the tragic blaze in which the family
home and barn were consumed six months ago. A thirteen-year-old boy was badly injured in the fire. He has
not been charged with any wrongdoing but remains
under the watchful eye of the police.

Larkin sat back from the table and groaned softly. Paul
Skinner—the thirteen-year-old who'd remained carefully
unnamed in the story, the younger son of Silas—had been his
childhood friend. He hadn't seen or heard from him for twenty
years. In their youth, however, they had a closeness he'd not
known with anyone else.

Closing the scrapbook, Larkin slid it back into the flour sack
and stood stiffly. After pushing aside the chair, he stepped across
the kitchen to stow the sack in the sideboard. The face of the
north wind puffed at him from the wooden chair's pressed back.
He grimaced at the carving as he hobbled from the room.

It was a bright-lit night with the moon almost full, casting a
white glow inside the house. Larkin looked around at his surroundings and smiled. Sure, it was too large for an old bachelor
living alone, but it was where he'd been born, and felt as much
a part of him as did his legs or arms or feet.

He'd been told that his Pa had ordered the fine red brick
from a brickyard near the town line, and that the men had
dragged skids of it across the county as soon as the ground froze
hard. The windows and quoins were of a soft butter-yellow
brick, edging the structure with elegance. Apparently, his Ma had
always wanted a "bay winder," and so Pa had managed two of
them, one on top of the other.

The house was built tall, three storeys high, with steeply
pitched gables. His father had been a tall man and didn't want to be
stooping over in the rooms. The ceilings on the main floor were
fifteen feet high, ten feet on the second, eight feet on the third.
There were two parlours, one at the front of the house and one at

the back, providing an escape from the blistering sun depending upon the time of day. Upstairs were five bedrooms as well as a little room for washing up and personal conveniences. The third floor had never been finished; it remained an open, expansive attic with unspoiled views stretching across the countryside.

Larkin especially loved the third floor. As a boy he would climb upstairs during a storm to hear the rain pounding overhead. He took a secret delight in being seated close to the raging tempest while the house protected him from the elements. The attic was where he often played his solitary games, wondering what it would be like to have a brother or a sister to share in his childhood.

Another baby in the house was not meant to be. His Ma's stomach was swollen from time to time with a promise of sorts but nothing ever came of it. When he was young he had wondered aloud, "Why doan Pa reach in and pull it out by the leg like he do with a calf?" When his folks heard this he was given only a vague answer about "God's timing" that made no sense to him.

Larkin's family were Methodists and went to church Sundays along with attending the picnics and other socials. His Ma loved teatime following the services. The ladies would all stand together sipping from mismatched china cups while the men stood outside with their pipes or their chew, indulging the womenfolk by leaving them be. Larkin and his Pa often waited an hour for his Ma to finish up before joining them. On the drive home she would merrily tell them all the news, laughing easily at small jokes or amusements.

Larkin was less keen on the entire going-to-meeting experience. Being scrubbed up from head to toe, wearing itchy woollens, and sitting still for an hour or more always seemed torturous. And after all that waiting, being bored even longer while his Ma undertook her socializing was plain tedious. The only part of the whole proceeding he actually enjoyed was seeing her face lit up and happy when she got in the buggy afterwards and started prattling. His Pa liked it too, he could tell. He'd shift on the seat so she was close and look at her proud, like she was a new lamb just finding its legs.

The kitchen had been pink for over fifty years now. The colour had not much faded. And although there were scrapes and chips off the chair legs and the walls and cupboards were looking a worn, Larkin didn't feel the need to waste money in repainting. Besides which, he liked that the place still had all his Ma's touches. It was the same in the front parlour and the rest of the rooms. Ma's wallpaper still covered the walls. Her crocheted covers remained in place on the arms and headrests of the furniture. Ornaments and figurines and empty vases were now lined up in military precision on the sideboard. Larkin was frightened to think of what might happen if he cleared away some of the frivolous bits. A dismal thought had taken hold that, if he ever dared dispose of his Ma's treasures, the resulting hollowness of the place would haunt him forever after.

It had been for this reason that he denied the women from church his mother's dresses after she'd passed, insisting that it was not yet time to part with them. In truth, he could not have borne the thought of someone else fingering the fabrics and cutting them into fragments. As Larkin walked through the house at night, he found himself comforted by touching the familiar pieces. He liked to think that if his Ma were looking down on him, if that were possible, she'd be proud of how he kept things up. The top of her dresser, for instance, still held her comb and brush, along with a bottle of rosewater fragrance which she used only on handkerchiefs. For a time, after her passing, Larkin had allowed himself to unscrew the cap to sniff it. He'd put a stop to such an indulgence once it struck him that he might inhale all its contents. He needed her scent to linger.

Returning to the kitchen, Larkin sat down heavily at the table. The money from Culloden's siring needed to be put away, but he felt too weary to do much of anything. He stared at the sideboard. Although he knew what it contained, he felt both drawn to the scrapbook and repelled by it. All these years later, the events still hit him hard. The three of them had saved the clippings under the sugar bowl and mused together about the cause of the fire. By unspoken agreement, when the stabbings were revealed, they never mentioned Paul's name.

The inquest that followed a year after the fire had been a wholly new experience for Larkin and his folks. The three of them had attended the entire week, even though Larkin had only to testify on the first day. On that day his parents sat together near the back of the room. Larkin was glad to have them there. He figured his Pa would verify anything he said, an assurance that filled him with a shaky kind of mettle.

Still, it had been intimidating. Someone had murdered Silas and his older son, Elgin. That much was for sure. And someone had set the fires to cover it up. That was also for sure. The real questions were: Who wanted Silas dead? What happened to Elgin? And was there anyone present besides Paul? The inquest never did answer those questions.

Sergeant Cian Quinn had gone all around the township interviewing folks and collecting ideas, but he didn't turn up much. People mostly kept their opinions to themselves. No one wanted to speak ill of the dead. Larkin *had* to speak during the inquest, of course, but that was only because he was under oath and needed to tell the *whole* truth. He had instinctively felt that it was equally important to be selective about what he told. There would have been a hanging. That was also for sure.

Larkin's folks had taken Paul in after the fire, bedding him down in the parlour. A week later, Doc Mather recommended that Paul be moved to Collingwood for treatment. The burns on his hands and feet were acute, and needed more medical attention than he had the experience to provide. Although the closest hospital was in Toronto, Mather said he had a colleague in Collingwood with a practice whose office was close to the shipyards. This gentleman had apparently become quite a specialist in the treatment of burns using something called nitrate of silver.

Larkin's Ma and Pa had discussed the matter, with his father being the first to speak. It was the deep timbre of his voice that had drawn Larkin's notice. They were in their bedrooms late at night, but when Larkin lay with his ear next to the stovepipe, he could hear them clearly.

"It will be costly," his Pa said. "Who's to pay for it?"

"I heard that folks were dropping off clothes and food for the girls and widow. There's been nothing here, though. It's as like they already declared him guilty."

Him. Larkin knew his Ma meant Paul.

"No one's come except the doctor," his Pa remarked. "And Cian."

"We'd not think twice if it were our Larkin. And the pair of 'em are so close."

"What if he *is* responsible for what happened?"

"That's not ours to decide. Look here, I found it in Matthew. *'I was hungry and you gave Me food; I was thirsty and you gave Me drink; I was a stranger and you took Me in.'* This is our answer, Edgar. It's in the good book."

"Yes. All right, Ellen. You doan have to convince me. We need to figure how much is needed. Doc said at least two to three weeks' treatment."

"How much for the hotel?"

"Sixty cents a night, maybe more."

"As much as that?"

"Yes. And the doctoring?"

"Fifty cents a visit plus the cost of any cures."

"And he needs to eat."

"If he buys his own food, it won't be so dear." His Ma paused. "Twenty-five cents a day?"

"Fourteen nights at the hotel, fifteen days of food, and maybe four visits to the doctor?"

"Yes, something like that, Edgar…"

"I figure sixteen dollars and change. If the doctoring costs more, or the hotel, he'll need extra."

"We have it in the tin."

"Get it out in the morning and some food, and an extra sweater and jacket. My old boots will work. They be big on him, but he'll want room for thick socks and the bandaging."

It took a while to convince Paul of the plan, and longer again to help him dress and get into the buggy. Larkin's Ma had packaged up some biscuits and a couple of sandwiches and had kissed him lightly on the forehead at parting. Larkin could see that Paul was overcome and did not know how to respond.

By noon that day Larkin, his Pa and Paul had arrived in Collingwood and secured a room at the North American Hotel. The grand structure, positioned on the corner of Huron and Hurontario Streets, was within easy walking distance of the medical hall. Mr. Beattie paid the hotel nine dollars and ten cents for a two-week stay.

Paul, fatigued from the journey, looked as though he might easily collapse. Pain marked his pale colouring, leaving dark circles under his eyes and blotches on his face, not unlike an apple with scold. He was wearing a set of Larkin's clothes which were baggy on him and an old jacket of Mr. Beattie's which was also too large and nearly reached his knees. He had difficulty walking in the oversized boots and shuffled his feet painfully. Larkin's Pa gently pressed the princely sum of a further eight dollars into Paul's bandaged hand, enough to cover food and medical expenses for two weeks.

Paul was ashamed, Larkin could see, by the need to accept charity. "I promise, Mr. Beattie," he said, his voice grave, "I'll find a way to repay you."

Larkin's Pa shook his head firmly. "When you get the chance, son, I reckon you can do the same for someone else."

"You'll tell my Ma where I am?"

Placing his large hands softly on Paul's shoulders, his Pa looked into Paul's eyes and said, "I will son, doan worry."

Witnessing such gentleness had stirred and humbled Larkin. He was vastly proud of his Pa that day.

Once, when Larkin was about six, he'd scooped up a baby robin fallen from its nest and brought it to his father. His Pa had taken the nestling in his cupped hands and held it delicately. "Go see your Ma," he instructed. "I think she may have something for you." Larkin had set off in the direction of the house, but partway there he turned back, wanting to watch his Pa restore the bird. By now Pa was standing by the rain barrel. Suddenly, he plunged his hands deep into the water and held them there. Shocked, Larkin had run towards him. His father lifted his clasped hands out of the water, high above the figure of his small son who was pounding him with clenched fists. Quietly, his Pa explained. "Its neck was broke, Larkin. I did what needed doing."

His Ma reinforced the message when a sobbing boy flung himself at her minutes later. "Your Pa is a godly man, son, and you have to know that he'll always do the right thing even if don't make sense in the moment."

There was a time when Larkin thought as how, when he had children of his own, he'd try to be just the same as his Pa—good and gentle and kind. That he never did become a father was one of a handful of regrets that had unsettled him over the many years since. Things had not come together the way they were meant.

It had never occurred to Larkin that the difficulty lay in his manner of being passive and somewhat withdrawn. Instead, he attributed his continued bachelordom to the dark secrets he carried and the unforgivable trespasses of his youth. He held to the certain belief that anyone who got close to him would sense his sinful past. And so, as a result, he had never intentionally sought the company of a marriageable girl, or signalled to any that he was serious about courting. The girls in turn mistook his reserve for disinterest, saving their guiles and charms for rather more willing prospects.

His mother had dropped hints from time to time, to which Larkin would answer vaguely, "Be best if such a thing were to happen more natural-like." But still, it came as a bit of a shock to one day realize that he was forty years old and living alone in an oversized house with empty bedrooms, and that there were no longer any candidates for marriage.

There *was* Lizzie Sanders, of course, who had also never married, but she was walleyed and had bad breath. Back when he was still in his twenties Larkin had bid on her basket once at a church picnic. Their lunch consisted of brown sugar sandwiches and apple pie made with last year's apples, all dried out and tough. Larkin was careful to keep his distance from her after that.

He found it remarkable how one simply got busy with farming, and how that led to another thing like his stallions, and the days passed, and the seasons changed, and then one suddenly realized that one had become thirty and then forty and then fifty. And that the things you took for granted, and the things you assumed would happen, had somehow passed you by when you were unaware. Life had moved on ahead of Larkin while he was still waiting to grasp it.

It was like the fire, he thought. One thing just led to another thing. Most folks knew Silas Skinner was sheep-stealing. When lambing season was at its pitch Silas would sneak around in the night, helping himself to newborns. Anyone ever asked him about it, Silas would blame coyotes for filching the little ones. A couple of farmers even sat up all night with their guns, waiting to get a shot off at him, but somehow, he always knew when there were folks around and he'd slink off without a fresh snatch. Word was he had a nose like a bloodhound.

Larkin blamed Silas for setting in motion the events at Cemetery Hill. It was a hard thing to blame the dead but he knew for a fact that Silas had brought about his own fate. Besides, it was all so much easier to withstand by giving the blame of it to Silas.

It had begun with George Larmer's girl, Minnie. Pauley was sweet on Minnie. According to him, she was the prettiest girl he'd ever seen. Not that they were sparking or that he'd declared his feelings; he just thought as how she was special.

One day at church, near the end of July, Minnie showed up with this tiny runt of a lamb that was nearly two months old. Her Pa and everyone else had figured the runt's chances weren't good. Its Ma had rejected it and one of the other sheep had head-butted it into the air, trying to kill it. But Minnie had rushed in and rescued the little thing and was determined to see it through. She'd been bottle-feeding it and carried it everywhere in a wooden crate filled with straw and an old piece of towelling. No one thought much about it at the time. Girls do things like that sometimes. When it began to bleat pitifully during the service, a red-faced Minnie excused herself and took it outside to leave it in the shade, under the Larmers' wagon.

What people remembered and talked about in quiet whispers was what happened next. When the Larmers went to their wagon after church the little lamb was gone *and* so was its crate. While it was possible that a coyote or a dog had been bold enough to take the lamb, where the crate had gone remained a mystery.

But Larkin knew. He knew because Pauley told him. And Pauley was so ashamed of his Pa that he gave the crate to Larkin, and Larkin broke it into small pieces and burned them in the stove. Both boys had sworn never to tell. But Pauley never forgave Silas for what he'd done. And even now, after all these years, the knowledge of that first awful secret made Larkin feel as though a small hard ball had lodged in his chest and kept him from breathing normal.

Secrets can ruin a man, thought Larkin. There were many times when he wished he'd never been friends with Paul Skinner. Other times, Larkin thought as how it was his lot in life to be the keeper of secrets, and he took pride in holding close the ones he knew. It was uncanny how changeable such feelings could be, even when they ran so deep.

And Larkin had feelings aplenty. Since his Pa had passed twenty-four years back he didn't have anyone to talk to regular, and things inside got all stoppered up. He caught himself talking to the horses sometimes. That weren't so bad, he reasoned, as they're mighty smart and always sense what it is I'm feelin'. The trouble was they couldn't answer back, and that made for only a one-way conversation.

Larkin didn't think he was lonely, exactly, but on occasion he knew when it was necessary to drive to town and get his thinning hair trimmed or pick up some fresh bread or other supplies at the Mercantile. He could feel the need building in his throat and his gut when it was getting to be time. Then, when he'd sidle up to acquaintances in town or stand at the sales counter and engage in banter or the always-important discussions of weather and crop conditions, there'd be a freeing gush of words. And on two Sundays a month, Larkin would clean himself up and drive to the Revival Café in Murton for his supper. For thirty-five cents he was served a slab of meat, soup, potatoes, a side dish, pudding, and coffee. Even with a small tip, he figured it was pretty good value.

Larkin didn't like to be reckless with money, and so he restricted himself to limited outings each week. He made an exception to the rule for his birthday, Christmas, and Easter. He'd stopped going to regular church services when his mother passed. It didn't feel the same without her. Larkin remembered childhood Sundays when she'd wet his hair and comb it flat before leaving the house. He had a cowlick at the front and it would bounce up like a coiled spring when his hair dried. His Ma was always licking her fingers and trying to press it back down. Larkin touched the top of his head self-consciously at the remembrance.

I dint rightly appreciate those times, was what he told himself. It was only now, looking back, that he realized how fortunate he had been. His parents were honest, kind, and generous, and as far as he knew they were as stuck on each other as married people could be. They tried to give him the best of everything. But more than the pocket knife he received for his birthday or the musket for Christmas, it was the smaller stuff that came back to him. Fishing for trout and salmon in the Beaver River and catching smelt in the crick out back. Camping with Pa out on one of the islands, just the two of them. Hunting ducks and turkeys and deer. Trapping rabbits in snares. Sliding on Brown's pond in the winter. So many memories that made him smile.

There was hard work, too: picking rocks, haying, clearing trees and brush, blasting stumps, planting potatoes, digging post holes, fixing fences. But somehow, remembering those days of punishing labour, the memory that was foremost was his Ma's voice saying as how "God loved a cheerful worker." Larkin wasn't sure where she got that idea from, sure as blazes not from someone lifting hundred-pound rocks out of the field, but she held on to it, and he and his Pa knew better than to ever complain. A woman does that, thought Larkin. She sets her mind on sumpen and makes everyone else take notice. It's not that he had a great deal of experience with women. It was simply the conclusion he'd reached after seeing some of his friends married. Those women just took things in hand and made their men mind.

Larkin still had that musket. It was probably an antique now. He hadn't been hunting for years. He remembered the excitement and pride of holding it for the very first time; he couldn't wait to go outside with it. The heft of it in his arms made him feel like a man. His Pa took him to practise his shooting in a clearing at the edge of the woods. They tramped through the snow together, Larkin pushing ahead eagerly, his father smiling indulgently while he puffed a little to keep up. When they reached the edge of the bush Larkin set off into the deep snow, aware that they were quickly losing light in the gloaming.

His Pa watched as Larkin carefully rehearsed everything he'd been taught. First, he lowered the musket to his chest and placed it in half cock. He poured a tiny measure of fine black powder into the pan, which he then shut firmly. Next, glancing at his Pa for confirmation, he poured more powder down the front, added the lead ball, and emptied the rest of his powder charge on top. He used the ram rod to tamp things tightly against the base. Finally, he lifted the musket into position and braced it firmly against his right shoulder. Pa stood behind him then, his strong arms helping to support the weight of the musket. He spoke down to the top of Larkin's head, telling him how and when to position himself, take aim, and pull the trigger.

The recoil startled him. He fell back against his father and lost his footing. Larkin was mortified but his Pa didn't seem to notice. Larkin was better prepared the second time, with his body more firmly planted, but still, the blast unsteadied him. They were both quiet as the explosion reverberated against the calm wall of the woods.

The last time he'd seen the musket it was in one of the bedrooms. He'd noticed some pitting around the nipple from corrosion and felt guilty knowing that he hadn't greased the bore before putting it aside. His Pa always used bear grease for this job but the stench was awful and Larkin hadn't ever got himself to the Mercantile to see whether something else might be available. It was one of those little tasks that got lost in the bigger picture. Keeping up with the house and buildings, feeding himself, managing the small garden, looking after his horses and the handful of chickens plus a couple of old milk cows—these were the things that filled his days.

In the latter part of his parents' time, Annie had been around to help his Ma with anything that needed doing. When Annie left to get married, he'd hired a succession of girls to come in two days a week, but they were more trouble than they seemed worth. He hated having to show them through the appointed rooms and to explain, in detail, his expectations. That sort of disclosure felt unnatural to him and he was embarrassed by it. And he didn't much like the idea of strangers touching his Ma's things or having them rearrange the way her bits were set out. And when they looked at him, he was never sure what they were thinking. Was it pity for him being alone in the great, fine house or was it envy? Were they inventorying the contents or were they appraising him? The not knowing made him shivery.

There were two or three men he called on regular for help with farm work, mainly plowing, haying, and the other strenuous jobs. Most of the land was now rented to the Dempseys, but Larkin still worked twenty-five acres for his own needs. There was a veterinarian in Murton these days, Doc Chester, and he came around to inspect the cows for signs of bovine tuberculosis and blackleg and other ailments. Larkin had read the pamphlets

Doc Chester gave him on such things and was proud to know that his two remaining cows were regularly screened. It cost him a little for every visit, but Larkin reasoned that it was a way of protecting his investment.

And Doc Chester also came for the horses. He had an eye for them. When he finished checking the cattle, he and Larkin would often lean on the pasture fence and watch the stallions grazing or running. They were a thing of beauty for sure, and it filled Larkin with gladness to watch them so free and fine. When Larkin would pull up some long grass and hold it out, calling, "Have a sweet bite," they'd come over and nuzzle briefly before suctioning the grass from his hand.

Those rare moments of quiet companionship with the Doc meant something to Larkin. The farm had been all-consuming for so long that he'd pretty much lost touch with others.

Larkin stood up slowly from his chair. He walked over to the sideboard; and then, bending slightly, pulled open its door and withdrew the flour sack again. Returning to his place at the table, he sat still for a moment, summoning the will to proceed. Finally, he inserted his right hand and tenderly withdrew the scrapbook once more. Opening it gently, Larkin bent over the pages, turning them until he came to the one he was seeking.

The *Chronicle* story was dated August 23rd, 1872.

DAY ONE OF MURTON CORONER'S INQUEST!
A large and sombre crowd gathered outside the Pine Street School in Collingwood early this morning. Despite the weather, neighbours, well-wishers, and the curious waited in the rain for two hours before being allowed to enter.

An expectant hush fell when fourteen-year-old Larkin Beattie was sworn in. The honourable Judge Harold Campbell, recently retired from the bench, presided. Seated to one side, eight gentlemen from the surrounding counties were assembled as a jury of peers.

Well-known prosecutor Finlay Taylor, acting as the Coroner's Counsel, led the questioning with vigour, striding backwards and forwards in front of the bench, bellowing his questions in a voice that resonated richly within the room. The onlookers were spellbound by the testimony of young Beattie, who described in detail the events of August 7th as he knew them.

No charges have been laid in the fire that claimed the lives of Silas and Elgin Skinner.

What follows is a partial transcript of young Beattie's statements to the court.

"May it please your Lordship, the Court will require the first witness to stand. Thank you. Please state your full name and address at the time of the events in question."

"My name be Larkin Ryan Beattie. I live on Cemetery Hill and that's where it took place."

"Thank you. Mr. Beattie, what is your relationship to Mr. Skinner and his family?"

"Silas Skinner was my Pa's age and we was neighbours. My Pa said as Silas dint have a decent bone in 'is body. He was a real mean sonofabitch."

"Mr. Beattie, the Court takes a dim view of that type of language and I must ask you to refrain from using it again."

"Sorry, sir. I'm aimin' to speak plain."

"Please continue."

"Only a certain type of man kicks a dog, and they say Silas was born kickin' and he just never stopped. Kicked dogs and kicked his kin. And Silas, he dint need liquor to be mean; that's just the way he was."

"Please confine your remarks to the questions as I ask them, Mr. Beattie. Do you understand?"

"Understood, sir."

"Thank you. Now will you please describe your relationship with Paul Skinner."

"The Skinners had a big spread on the west side of the Line and we was across from 'em. The Skinner place was always a sorry sight—their sheep weren't never sheared nor the tails docked. Down the road a piece is the cemetery. There weren't no one else on the hill 'cept those already buried. Paul Skinner was my friend. We mostly called him Pauley. Doan know why exactly, to tell truth. He's like a scared rabbit most days. But he is some smart. He can do figurin' and sums like no one else. Our teacher, Mr. Braithway, treated him special. Said he had the makin's of a real scholar. Well, that weren't never gonna happen. We all knowed it. Pauley would work on the farm as soon as ever his old man could pull him from school. Pauley already swilled pigs and helped milk every mornin' and had to run hard so's not to be late. He always pushed in just as Braithway was closin' the door, breathin' heavy, and he'd bend over like it hurt to stand up straight. I never seed anyone work that hard just to gets someplace…"

"*Continue.*"

"Pauley never did bring a lunch pail. I reckoned it would slow him down when he was runnin'. But my Ma always made sure I had plenty. Pauley and me would share my sandwiches. Good weather we sat outside on an old log behind the school, and bad weather we ate at our desks like everyone else. Pauley was shaggy like our old dog, Bella. Nothin' ever fit him right and he had a mess of hair that never stayed combed. No one ever said, though. And if someone ever threw a pencil or reached for sumpen near him, he'd duck down quick like he was afraid. After, he'd tremble fer a spell, like a caught kit.

"Like I said, I used to fix on Pauley. And the first thing I used to see was these giant black spots in 'is ears. My Ma wouldn't let me out a the house like that. She'd take the brush and scrub me up like a tattie. 'Bein' poor's no excuse for bein' dirty.' That's what she had to say about Pauley. But I dint care. Some days he favoured his arm like he fell or sumpen else. I never asked and he never said."

"Thank you for your detailed description, Mr. Beattie. Now I wonder if you might reflect for a moment on how Paul Skinner got on with his father."

"There was one thing I remember real clear. We was on our log eatin' tomato sandwiches an all a sudden he looks at me and he's cryin' and he says, 'I hate him!' And he says it real mean like he's angry and I figure I know what he's sayin'. And I give him the apple from our barrel and I doan take the first bite... And sumpen else, too. Another time we was playin' baseball with George Larmer and Bill Dempsey, an George hit a good one, an Pauley an me was both runnin' for the ball an Pauley's shirt came untucked, and the wind blew it up over 'im an we all saw his back had marks criss-crossin' like a patchwork. I told my folks about what I seen and my Pa said 'Silas must be free with his belt.' And he and my Ma looked serious and they told me it was real important to keep what I saw to myself and to stay away from the Skinner place. But they dint need to tell me, I already knowed it."

"Mr. Beattie, I understand that Silas Skinner came to your school some time before the fire. Is that correct?"

"Yes, sir."

"Please tell the Court about that visit."

"It was scorchin' hot and we was in our last week of school an there was these big exams we was doin'. Mr. Braithway been hollerin' for us to take 'em serious. But the heat made our arms stick to the desks an you could sit there and feel the sweat peelin' down your legs. And then Braithway told us if Paul or anyone else did real good they might maybe earn a scholarship for a college or university. So we was all tryin' but it were hot and the only thing comin' through the winders was that sweet smell of first cut.

"All a sudden the room went real dark and we looked out and saw the blackest clouds ever and they was sittin' low. And then a chill wind blew through

makin' our papers fly off our desks and float round the
room, and then cold, winter-cold hail started poundin'
down. And we all looked round and saw as how everyone was scared, knowin' the cut would be ruined. And
no one said nuthin' while Braithway rushed around
shuttin' the winders and makin' sounds about us gettin'
back to work. But there was an awful hush in that room
like we was waitin' for sumpen to happen next.

"An I swear I was lookin' at the door before it
opened an in came Silas all soaked, and he yelled Paul's
name and came at him madder an a wet hen. Paul tried
to back away but he got trapped by a desk, and Silas
tackled him and laid inna him sumpen fierce. 'I tole you
to stay home and finish the cut! You ain't nuthin' but a
worthless shit.' Sorry, sir. Beggin' your pardon."

"Continue."

"Silas yelled 'I'm gonna teach ya to mind me!' An
every time he said sumpen he finished with a couple a
punches, and then he started kickin' 'im, an Pauley
covered his head with his hands an rolled around on
the floor tryin' to avoid his Pa's boots. Braithway
looked like he might shit his self but he took off his
specs an put 'em on the desk, and he went to Silas and
tried to hold 'im. But Silas was in a fury, and he turned
around and socked Braithway so fast and so hard that
he went 'cross the room and landed on his arse against
the stove, with his head makin' a loud crack. We was
all scared. Some a the girls rushed to Braithway an
started makin' a fuss but no one went near Paul or
Silas. And Silas, even he looked sobered up when he
saw Braithway knocked out and a puddle of blood
startin' on the floor, and he yelled at Paul to 'Get up!'
and he took off out a the room, an Paul galumphing
after him.

"And then I got up and ran after him, shoutin' his
name, but Paul dint turn round and so I went home and
found my Pa. It was rainin' fierce but even so Pa hitched

up the wagon and we drove back to the school and Pa sent everyone home. And my Pa picked up Braithway and put him in the back a the wagon and we took him to town. People said as how Silas near kilt Braithway and what a mean murdering bastard he was. Pardon, sir. And when September came there was a new teacher but I was done with my learnin' and that's what I know."

"And did you speak with Paul Skinner after that?"

"Well Pa ran beef cattle an when I was done my schoolin' I helped with the farm. We had sixty acres of bush still needin' clearin' and crops to plant, and the cattle to feed an water an so I had no occasion for foolin'. But there were times we went to town for the Mercantile or feed store and I went to the dances and plays an entertainments and saw lots of people but I never saw Paul or Silas. They must a got Paul's brother to do their town chores 'cause nobody else seen 'em neither. Paul had one older brother, Elgin, and a pair a sisters. The girls went to school but nobody much saw Mrs. Skinner nowheres either, an Elgin stopped schoolin' a couple years back. People said maybe his Ma dropped 'im when he was a baby but I reckon he more'n likely got hit too hard or got kicked in the head. I thought what a shame Pauley never finished those exams and got hisself a scholarship. I never met no scholar before. And that's what I know."

"Tell us about the fire."

"Yes, sir. I was in the pasture, puttin' down fresh hay for the horses, and they was jumpy-like, with their nostrils snufflin' and then they started runnin' round and round an whinnyin' like they never do, and I had a feelin' they felt sumpen. I went and got my Pa and he looked round for a bit but he dint see nuthin'. And we went inside and washed up for supper an after we went back to finish chores. We put the horses in and they was still twitchy and worked up but we dint know why."

"Continue, please."

"Well, I was asleep in bed and I woke up 'cause there was a bright light at my winder and I looked out and saw fire. My Pa was waked up too and we got dressed and ran outside an across to Skinners to see what was what. And when we got there we was out of puff from runnin' hard, and the house was burnin' with flames shootin' high up past the roof. The barn was already gone with only some beams left standin'. The smell of burned sheep was so bad it made me want to puke some. We had to stand back from the house, maybe a hunnert feet or more. My Pa held me back with his hand and we walked backwards together. The fire so hot it felt like my face was burnin' and I had a notion that the fire was chasin' after us. And we dint say nuthin' cause it was a fearsome sight. And I ain't never seen such a thing before."

"And tell us what happened next."

"After a bit my Pa says as how we should try to see round the other side. And we made a big circle so we can come up on the backside of the house. And the smoke was chokin' us and that fire was still hard at it. And when we come round to the back of the house, we sees somethin' movin' maybe a hunnert feet away. An Pa runs towards it an I run too, and when we get close, we sees it's Paul, and he's kneelin' in the dirt, moanin' and cryin' and covered all over in blood and dirt. And he's holdin' his hands out and they are fierce burned with the skin off 'em like raw meat. And it's a starry night and it's cold and hot at the same time.

"So my Pa goes to pull Paul up and Paul cries out, and we both settle in under 'is arms and we half drag 'im and half carry 'im back to our place and Pa lays 'im out on the kitchen table. And my Ma comes downstairs, and when she's finished lookin' 'im over she sets to wrappin' 'is hands in cotton. And Pa makes Paul drink a slug of whisky and he offers me some too, and then he takes the wagon inna town to get the doctor."

"And tell us what, if anything, did Paul Skinner say to you about the fire."

"When my Ma left the room, I sat with Paul and I told 'im we was goin' to take real good care of 'im. And he turns 'is head to look at me, and he closes 'is eyes, and he says, 'I started it, you hear? *I* killed 'im.' And I takes a minute and asks him, 'Was everyone else in bed?' And he says, 'Ma and the girls were away visitin'. They been gone a week. Just me an Elgin and Pa home.' And I thinks what a good thing the others warn't there. And then I think how strange the fire burnin' the barn and the house, on account there bein' a big piece a distance between 'em."

"And what do you think he meant by saying, 'I started it. I killed him'?"

"I doan rightly know. I thought as he was sayin' he had an accident and started the fire."

"The bodies of both Elgin and Silas were recovered from the fire. The coroner says they died from multiple knife wounds. Do you know, or think you may know, what happened before the fire?"

"I doan know 'bout no *knife* wounds."

"Maybe you could tell us what happened next, after the night of the fire."

"The Doc came and he checked on Paul. I heard him tell my Ma that she done a good job. The Doc had linseed oil and lime-water liniment. He said it looked like Paul tried to grab a knife by the blade and the cut went deep in his thumb. He was covered all over in bruises. I seen 'em when Pa and I lifted him inna the tub. Every time anyone touched 'im, like when my Ma went to comb his hair, he whimpered some."

"And did you encounter any other members of the Skinner family after the fire?"

"Mrs. Skinner and the girls come back after the fire and first they stayed in town but then they moved to the Plowrights. I heard the girls went back to school like nuthin' happened. Mrs. Skinner came one time to call but she stayed in the kitchen with my Ma and never did check on Pauley. Like she forgot he was there or sumpen. It seemed queer. I know Paul heard her talkin' 'cause he got all quiet. He got stoppered up after. I tried to get 'im to come outside with me a spell but he wouldn't and finally I just had to leave 'im. Pauley stayed with us about a week and then one day Doc Mather says as there was a doctor in Collingwood who was good with burns. And me and my Pa left him be in a big hotel close to the shipyards."

"Go on. What happened next?"

"Nuthin' happened."

"Is there anything else you can add?"

"Doan think it."

Day two of the Murton inquest will proceed next week. It is expected that Paul Skinner will testify. Expert witnesses are also expected to make statements.

Larkin sat back in his chair and closed his eyes. He remembered it all. Every word. The trauma had not dissipated nor the recollections faded over all the years in between. There had been the sweet smell of beeswax on the highly polished wood when he gave his testimony. There had been the scrutiny of onlookers, the feel of wool from his good Sunday suit catching against his long underwear, the burning flush that crept up his neck while people stared at him. He remembered pulling at the cuffs on his jacket sleeves. And he remembered the reassurance of looking across the courtroom and seeing his Pa nodding his head as his words came tumbling out.

He hadn't seen Paul in the crowd that day. Larkin had thought he might be there and had fretted to himself about what to say if there was a chance to be alone with him. Then, afterwards, he worried that he'd said wrong things in court. Later, he asked his folks, "Do you think Paul would mind any of them things I said today?"

"Course not," replied his Ma. "You only spoke what was true."

"But did I make Silas out too bad?"

His Pa answered next. "You're not responsible for what the world thinks of Silas Skinner, son. You answered the questions straight up and clear. There's others would've said worse." Larkin's Pa sat down at the end of the table and held out his arms so the three of them could hold hands while they recited the blessing.

"Be present at our table Lord. Be here and ev'rywhere adored. Thy creatures bless, and grant that we may feast in paradise with Thee."

Larkin remembered there being fresh bread on the table and a pot of thick lamb stew. Or at least, he thought he remembered this detail. Maybe it wasn't lamb stew and his mind was just putting in the specifics because lamb stew was one of his favourites? They maybe had something else to eat that night, but in his heart he'd convinced himself that it was lamb stew and fresh bread, with rice pudding for dessert. Sometimes he questioned his entire recollection of events. He'd ask himself repeatedly what was *really* true.

The night after his testimony had been one of those times when he *almost* told his folks the whole story. They were always ready to help a neighbour or kin. It only followed that they wouldn't see him in trouble without trying to help.

He *almost* told them but then he didn't. It was better for everyone, he reasoned, if they didn't know. They would want to help but it would be hard for them to hold their heads up once they knew. And his Ma was always so big on telling the truth she would insist he tell Sergeant Quinn, and things would just get messy from there.

Still, he often thought about how he might start. "Ya know how Pauley was all covered in marks when we seen him? Well, the thing is, his Pa done that. And he done worse. On the day of the fire, I seen Silas and he was…"

But Larkin could go no further. He could not give voice to the unspeakable, even in his head. Besides, it was Pauley's secret and he'd sworn to keep it. Larkin knew that the very telling of this one thing would result in Pauley hanging.

He remembered wanting to say something the night it had happened. But no matter how much water he drank that night, he still felt parched, his thickened tongue stuck to the roof of his mouth, his dry, chewed lips cracked and split, the horrendous truth writhing deep down in his gut, sickening him with shame at the acts of evil and depravity.

The kind of care that had blanketed his own life was unfamiliar to Paul. But for Larkin, the certainty of steadfast love filled him and was deeply felt. It was nothing you could put your finger on but it was real just the same. Unlike Paul, who mostly acted like a scared animal, always running someplace or hiding in a shed or up a tree. He *could* make up stories fit to make you wonder, though. And there were just so many things he knew. Things he read in books borrowed from Mr. Braithway, and things he puzzled out for himself. He would a made a scholar, all right.

There was a time, Larkin remembered, when they were hawking around in the woods out back, checkin' snares and runnin' around. They were eight years old. Larkin's Pa had tied strips of red flannel around some pine trees and had told Larkin he wasn't ever to go past those trees alone. And when Larkin saw the flannel strips, he told Paul they needed to turn back and why. But Paul said, "We ain't alone, Larkin, we're together." And even though Larkin knew that wasn't what his Pa meant, he followed Paul further through the trees until they were completely lost in the dense growth. They wandered around kicking at sticks and climbing over deadfall till they finally sat down, thirsty and tired.

It was early October, with nightfall dropping in suddenly, bringing with it damp, chill air. Both boys were wearing only light jackets with no mittens or hats. It didn't long before they were shivering. But Pauley pointed up at the sky and said to Larkin, "If we can find Polaris and keep walking straight, we'll be going north and be home in no time." So he and Larkin got up off the ground and walked back through the woods, confidently following the North Star. While they walked, Pauley pointed out the adjoining Little Dipper and the Big Dipper and told Larkin about other constellations that could be seen at different times of year. Pauley told him there was a horse, a bull, a crab, and more. Braithway had lent him a book on stars and Paul had been reading about them.

Larkin hadn't ever heard about such things. His Ma had simply told him that the stars were holes in the sky that gave them a small glimpse of heaven. He could *almost* see what it was Pauley was pointing to but mostly because he was in awe of Paul's superior knowledge and simply trusted him.

The boys had been walking for some time when Larkin heard his father's voice, calling.

"Larkin… Larkin!!! Where are you, Larkin?? LARKIN!"

A second voice was also calling. "Paul, you out there? Paul! Boy, you best get home NOW! PAUL!" That was the voice of Elgin Skinner, Paul's older brother.

Larkin and Paul had looked at each other in relief and ran in the direction of the voices. They didn't have far to go before they saw lanterns, held by two tall figures. Larkin ran to his Pa, who put down the lantern and picked up his son and held him close. A few desolate tears had slipped out and Larkin's face was messy with them and a bit of snot besides but his Pa just held him tight and kissed him over and over again without putting him down.

Larkin looked up from his Pa's shoulder at one point and saw Elgin giving Paul a couple of hard wallops. Paul was trying to explain about Polaris but Elgin wasn't listening. He held up his lantern and told Paul to "Get along home!"

Larkin had heard the stories about Elgin. After Elgin quit his schooling, folks all around somehow knew that he couldn't read or write and that Mr. Braithway had once suggested he might have trouble learning. Word was Silas had dropped him on his head when he was a baby to make him stop crying. Whether that had really happened or not, people didn't know. But they knew Elgin had a mean streak like his Pa, that was certain.

One time, at the Blake place on the other side of Murton, Elgin proved the point. The Blakes had a large sheep operation—a pretty nice-looking spread with a pair of fancy gate posts at the road. The posts were thick columns of rubble stone neatly cemented together and topped off with big round stone balls; Mrs. Blake even whitewashed the balls so that they caught the light and stood out in the dark. The story was that the Blakes had lent the Skinners one of their rams—a particular ram called Hercules that was highly sought after for local breeding—for one full week in exchange for two ewes or one ram lamb come spring.

After the lambing the Blakes waited for their lambs to be delivered, but by the time fall came it was obvious that Silas was in no hurry to make good on his promise. So, Mr. Blake drove over to the Skinner place and spoke with Elgin. Elgin said Hercules hadn't done his job and that they didn't owe Blake any-thing. Mr. Blake insisted that he be allowed to speak to Silas directly or else be allowed to look in on the lambs. Elgin got nasty and threatened to cut the balls off Blake's useless ram if Blake didn't leave right smart.

A couple of days later the Blakes noticed that the balls on their fence post had been removed. The message was clear. "Mess with Skinners and we cut your balls off." It was a story that lost nothing in the telling but reinforced a general sense in the community that Elgin was Silas's spit.

Larkin had put his head back down against his Pa's coat and didn't complain when his Pa picked up the lantern and carried Larkin all the way back to the house; his legs were wrapped tight-ly around his father's waist and his arms curled securely around his neck. Larkin smiled at the memory.

Even as far back as that time, he'd known that Paul didn't have the same kind of family he had. Mrs. Skinner sometimes took her children to church, even though Silas never attended. Larkin's folks went regularly. His Pa said, "It were a simple thing to count your blessings and thank the Lord for 'em. Folk who don't go to church are folks who doan know what to be thankful for."

Larkin felt guilty thinking about this now.

The Reverend Presley Baxter warn't exactly his cup of tea, so to speak. More concerned about the offering plate than he was in anything else. That was Larkin's take on it anyhow. When the Reverend had come to make arrangements for his Pa's funeral and burying, he managed to put Larkin right off. Larkin considered himself to be a fairly easy-to-get-along-with individual. But the Reverend Presley Baxter got under his skin like a tick on the back of his neck and aggravated him no end.

Larkin was prepared to concede that he'd been pretty shaken by his Pa's death. It was a shocking event to find your Pa face down on the bedroom floor. Doc Mather said, "That was the way of heart attacks, they're silent and sneak up on you with no warning." So, Larkin admitted that, given the shock of it, he wasn't feeling particularly sociable when the good Reverend showed up. Larkin had laid his Pa out in the front parlour in preparation for the undertakers to come for the embalming. That was some new thing Mr. Morris, the undertaker, told him was the way of fixing the dead before they was buried. "It were meant to keep things sanitary," he said.

Anyway, Pa was laid out and Larkin was trying his best to take it all in. He was pacing the centre hall, back and forth, just trying to calm himself and make a plan, when the front bell rang. He wasn't expecting visitors just yet, and went to the door surprised that someone was using it instead of the kitchen door like most folks. Standing there looking all shiny and smart was the Reverend Baxter. His hands were folded around a Bible which he held in front of his privates like a holy shield.

Larkin opened the door and the Reverend walked in, spinning his head from side to side, taking in the rooms and the furnishings like he was writing a report. "Did you and your father live here alone, Mr. Beattie?"

"After Ma passed, it was the two of us only."

"This is an awfully fine house for a bachelor to be living in on his own."

"It is."

"Do you have someone to cook and clean for you?"

"Sumpen like that."

"I don't suppose you might have some tea and perhaps a light refreshment?"

"We can go to the kitchen. I'll scare up sumpen."

"That would be fine."

Larkin had led the way with the good Reverend following behind. Larkin saw that the Reverend Baxter was continuing to glance in all directions, apprising himself of the details of his surroundings. Larkin resented the intrusion but readied a pot of tea and cut thick slices of the jam cake Bill Dempsey had dropped off.

The Reverend helped himself to a generous slice of cake and washed each bite down by sloshing a mouthful of tea around in his mouth before swallowing. It was the sort of thing Larkin's mother would have scolded him for, had he done so as a youngster.

"I suppose you will wonder at my visit?" began the guest.

"You're here about my Pa's service, I reckon."

"Oh, yes. Yes, of course. About that. I'm sorry for your loss, Mr. Beattie. We can discuss the details in a short eventuality, if you don't mind." He stopped to plunge his fork into the cake and to swig another mouthful of tea. "I hear you never married."

"No."

"A shame that. Being all alone. An unusual choice. The book of Genesis does say 'Be ye fruitful, and multiply.'"

"It warn't a choice so much. It never happened, is all."

"So, you *were* interested in marrying at one point?"

Larkin coloured to hear the implication in his words. He felt his throat, face, and ears flushing red. He stammered out a response. "I suppose. I would a liked a son."

Larkin waited while the Reverend eyed him over the top of his tea cup. Mercifully, when he spoke again it was on a different subject. "I'm visiting all my congregants this week, you see. Our church has never had a bell, Mr. Beattie. Can you imagine a church without a bell? It's a deficiency that must be addressed. Bells are rung in the event of fires, or wars, or invasions. And to welcome the flock to worship, of course. Our community is in desperate need of a church bell."

"I thought you was here for my Pa."

"Of course, of course I am. I thought we might accomplish the two things at once. I felt sure you would want the opportunity to contribute to the bell. Everyone I ask is contributing a little something. It doesn't have to be much. Although I must say," he added, looking around pointedly, "you do seem to be rather comfortable."

"You expectin' a war or an invasion?"

The Reverend stopped chewing and looked confused. "I beg your pardon?"

"I asked if you was expectin' a war or an invasion, and that's why we need a bell."

"Me? No! Of course not. But it's best to be prepared, don't you agree?"

"'Bout my Pa's service," interrupted Larkin. "I want it done proper. Nothin' too fancy. We'll have it here. Morris's men will bring the coffin tomorrow when they've finished it. Day after would be good timin' for the service. The hearse will move 'im to the graveyard for prayers there."

"Thank you, Mr. Beattie. It sounds as though you have made all the necessary arrangements." The Reverend Baxter took a deep breath and launched into the rest of his sales pitch. "Wouldn't it be a fitting remembrance to your father to make a generous contribution, in his name of course, to the purchase of our bell? I'm sure that would make your father very proud."

Larkin quietly counted to ten before responding. He knew his Pa would think no such thing. Pa warn't the sort a man who took pride in *things,* especially for himself. He took pride in actions. And he wasn't for letting folks know about a good deed. He just did them and kept quiet about it. "Maybe you could tell me, Reverend, what you charge for a funeral service and a buryin'? I suppose I could add sumpen extra."

All these years later, Larkin was still angry at the money Reverend Baxter had extracted from him. The cost of a nice oak box, with good hardware and dovetailed joints, custom made by Trott's Undertakers & Cabinetmakers, had been only four dollars. The Reverend Baxter had charged him twenty dollars for the service, the committal, and the bell. It's not that Larkin resented spending the money; it's that he resented the money-grubbing.

Even if Larkin had been inclined to return to church and, even if the Reverend hadn't rankled him and given him reason not to go, it was hard to know what he personally believed about religion. His Ma had been pretty clear about what she believed, and his Pa seemed to go along with it, as he did most things. But Larkin wasn't certain what he thought. Sometimes when he looked around him, he felt sure that some force far smarter and more powerful than himself had worked out all the details of creation. And at other times he thought as how religion was just a bunch of hooey folks made up to make themselves feel better.

The thing of it was, he understood that people in other countries had different religions. So how could everyone be right at the same time? Paul had told him about a god called Zeus and another one called Poseidon. It was a bit confusing how they all fit into the picture. Paul tried to explain it but he hadn't finished reading the book and wasn't able to piece things together in a way that helped Larkin understand how it worked. Even around Murton, Prenticeville, Collingwood, and Barrie there were Roman Catholics, Methodists, Presbyterians, Mennonites, and Church of England congregations. How did that make any sense?

The church bell, long after it was installed, was a constant source of irritation to Larkin. He liked the sound of it all right, but the recollection of what had happened to finally put it in place troubled him.

Everyone had waited, with great anticipation, for the bell to arrive from England. When it finally came, arrangements had to be made to transport it from Collingwood to Murton. That took some doing. The men rigged up eight horses to Jeb McCormick's heavy wagon to pull it. And George Larmer ripped something deep inside his shoulder trying to help push the bell when it began to slip off sideways from the crude ramp they'd hastily assembled.

All the men in the community were gathered at the frame church the day the bell was to be hung. Larkin had gone, too. He figured as how since he'd paid for a big piece of it, he might just as soon make sure the thing got put up proper. And he was a little curious. He didn't recall ever hearing a *big* bell ring before, not in a church or anywhere else. The Catholics in Collingwood were said to have one, but Larkin hadn't heard it. It was going to be a first for the people of Murton.

When Larkin arrived at the church, he saw that the women and children were clustered around tables outside setting up a luncheon. Larkin eyed their offerings with anticipation. It wasn't often that he had the opportunity to sample that many pies and cakes.

He noticed Annie Barker in the crowd. It had been only a few months since she'd quit her job to get married to a widower with children. Larkin hadn't expected how much of a hole she would leave in his life. Between his Pa dying and Annie quitting, the house had suddenly become empty and nothing was working right. Larkin saw that she was wearing a new dress and was holding hands and laughing with a little girl. It stopped him dead still. She looked pretty and he hadn't ever noticed that before. And he never saw her laughing like that neither. He wondered at the change. Was it getting married that made the difference or had he just never looked at her?

Although George Larmer now had his arm in a sling, he was clearly the one in charge. Larkin looked around for the Reverend; he didn't see him among the group of men hard at work. Then, after a few moments, he spied the crowish figure fluttering about with the women, drinking tea, his pinky finger extended in an exaggerated show of elegance.

Larkin scoffed to himself and returned to the heavy work. They'd laid a series of short logs on the ground and were using them as rollers to push the bell and its housing the distance from the wagon to the church, and would do so once again when they were inside, advancing it carefully forward until they were underneath the opening for the wooden tower.

It was slow, arduous labour. Some of the men were removing the logs and repositioning them while others were straining to push the bell across the uneven ground. George kept shouting "Heave men, heave!" at regular intervals over the quiet grumbles and softly uttered curses of the rest. Larkin, right in the thick of the toiling crew, felt a little scandalized by all the profanity so close to the church. The Almighty himself may well have had a few choice words to dedicate to the endeavour, but somehow such blasphemy seemed an affront. He found himself colouring with the shame of it.

After much effort, the bell was finally positioned under the hole the men had cut to open up the empty bell tower. An actual bell had never been part of the church's design, and so the men had first puzzled out a plan and then assembled all the bracing and timber they would need for the headstock. Two of the younger men, Mattie Evans and Bill Dempsey's son Luke, had climbed up the inside to reinforce a sturdy frame—one intended to support the bell while allowing the wheel to spin freely so that the toller and clapper could do their jobs. Larkin looked up into the bell tower at one point and saw Mattie swinging merrily from the newly installed crossbeam. "We're testing it out for load bearing!" Luke shouted down as he sat astride the beam, gesturing at the athletic movements of his friend with a laugh.

The men working alongside Larkin glanced up at the boys and smiled. A little tomfoolery in the midst of hard work wasn't a bad thing. And that bell sure was heavy. It was good they were checking that it would hold the weight.

Finally, after Luke and Mattie had clambered down from their perch, the men decided to have lunch. The women had put together a hearty meal featuring sandwiches thick with tomato and horseradish, buttered tea biscuits, and smoked oysters wrapped in tiny slivers of cold pork. There were plates filled with pies and cakes, and pitchers of lemonade and cold milk were being served along with hot tea. Larkin sat down with his friends and took his nourishment, the likes of which he'd not enjoyed since well before his Ma had passed. The niceties of well-cut sandwiches, thinly sliced date loaf, and thickly iced and decorated cakes were a rare treat to Larkin, who missed the care with which such things were done.

Annie came over to him while he was seated. She brought him a thick slice of apple cider pound cake, generously covered with powdered sugar. "I saw you sittin' here, Larkin, and remembered how you liked this cake."

Larkin reached up to take the proffered plate. "Thank you. It was always mighty fine."

"You look good, Larkin. You takin' care a yourself?"

Larkin flushed at the personal question. "I am. Things is pretty quiet at the farm."

"I sure do miss your folks, Larkin. They was good people."

Larkin nodded, unsure how to respond. "You married now?"

She smiled happily in response. "I am. That's my little girl." She pointed at the child he'd seen her with earlier. "She's six. Her brothers are with their Pa today."

Larkin attempted a smile. "This cake sure looks good."

"I 'membered as you liked it."

She stood for a minute longer, but when neither of them could think of what else to say, he looked down and began on the cake. Annie dipped her head and quietly drifted away.

She'd been a more than passable cook, and ever since she'd left, Larkin had struggled to make meals. He did have a standing invitation to share a dinner with George Larmer and his family, and George's wife was always welcoming, but she didn't go in for baking much and her suppers were often boiled potatoes and pottage. Lots of it, too, and the company was fine, but the heavily salted, unidentifiable ingredients didn't agree with Larkin's stomach. Then there was Bill Dempsey's wife, who was a good cook as well as a good baker; Larkin was always glad when he ran into Bill and got asked back to his house for a meal, although it had been a while. Bill and George were both old schoolmates of his and, like Larkin, both had taken over their family farms. Larkin was glad of their friendship even though he'd never let them in too close.

After an hour, George Larmer stood up, patted his not-inconsequential stomach with his good arm, and announced loudly, "Well men, I'm not nearly as hungry as I was!" The women all tittered at this while he went on to thank them for a "mighty fine meal." Larkin observed the Reverend at one end of the table, his chipmunk cheeks puffed out, evidently taking his fill before the leftover sweets were wrapped up and returned to their baskets and boxes.

The men regrouped inside the church and stood together looking at their task. Mattie volunteered to take one end of the heavy rope up into the tower to thread around the beam. The men would then grab hold of the other end and pull slowly while the bell, tied to Mattie's end, would be raised in the air and fastened into place. It was a straightforward job, but no one was looking forward to the actual pulling. The bell was excessively heavy and their arms already burned from having pushed it such a distance.

George Larmer signalled to Mattie. The men watched in silence while the young man climbed the ladder as high as it went and then pulled himself up into the tower; where he manoeuvred himself further upwards until he could toss the rope across the top of the new crossbeam. The rope missed its target the first couple of throws, but Mattie was able to pull it back into his hands and toss it again and again until it finally landed across the top of the beam. Now only a short piece of rope was left, suspended downwards. Mattie needed to grab it and climb back down holding the end of it in his hand.

Those closest to the tower looked up, focusing on Mattie while he swung himself out into the opening, reaching for the rope. The space wasn't twelve feet across but the rope was resting farther from Mattie than he could easily reach. There was a thirty-foot drop downwards should he fall. The men were tense as they watched him stretch and strain to grasp the rope. Then, in a bold manoeuvre, Mattie let go of the upright beam and eased himself onto the crossbeam, finally securing the elusive rope. Only when he began to climb safely downwards did the group of men break apart and resume their chatter. Larkin realized that he'd been holding his breath along with everyone else. A grinning Mattie jumped down the remaining six feet or so and the men let out a small cheer, clapping him heartily on the back.

George Larmer directed the men to take the rope end and wind it around the middle of Luke Dempsey, who was to stand at the front of the line. Luke was a sturdy fellow with a strong body accustomed to the rigours of farm work. The rest of the men stood behind Luke, well spaced out, and grabbed hold of the rope as well. Most had remembered gloves and seized the rope tightly even though they weren't yet pulling on it. A feeling of apprehension kept the group solemn.

George stationed himself beneath the tower, as it was his job to tell the men when to pull. Mattie and a couple of others stood at the ready with their tools; once the bell and its housing were in position, they would scale the inside of the tower and secure it to the beam—something that would have to be done speedily and carefully, since the men couldn't manage to hold the suspended bell for long. With twelve men lined up to do the job, the church doors had been propped wide open, giving them room to walk backwards to the outside of the building once the operation was underway. The Reverend, meanwhile, was standing near George's elbow, anxious to observe the proceedings but apparently unwilling to help.

At George's signal, the men began to pull. Larkin remembered that much, and he remembered the feeling of being a small part of a collective effort. It was a good experience, working closely with men he'd known all his life. As they pulled and strained, the bell rose slowly from the floor. Larkin tried not to look, concentrating instead on keeping his footing. As one, the chain of men walked slowly backwards, struggling to hold the airborne bell. Gripping his piece of the rope as tightly as he could, Larkin set his jaw and clenched his teeth. The bell was at roof height now, and George was shouting, "Easy men, easy, she's going up through the hole—take it steady!"

The pain in his arms was fiery. Larkin was glad to know they were almost done. Half the men were now outside; Larkin, near the front of the line, was still indoors. Without warning, the rope went slack. Before Larkin could see what had happened he heard the crash. The men rushed forward at once. Luke was writhing on the floor, the rope still tied around his middle, one of his legs wedged under the bell. It had fallen heavily and broken through the floor of the church. A splintered mess of wood planks held up Luke and part of the bell.

Bill Dempsey ran to his son and knelt down beside him. "Luke, boy, how are you?"

Luke didn't respond. It was quickly apparent that he was in shock.

"Son, you all right there? We'll get you out, in a minute now."

Larkin and some of the others kicked at the broken planks so that they could jump down into the hole. They worked swiftly. Luke's breathing was jagged—they knew they had to free his leg quickly. Someone rode for the doctor. In the background, Larkin was aware of voices crying and screaming. "For God's sake," someone yelled, "keep the women away!"

Larkin and four other men were now standing in the hole, attempting to use the broken planks as a fulcrum to tip the bell enough to release Luke's leg. Bill Dempsey was holding his son's shoulders and head against his own body, crooning quietly to the boy. The men worked furiously, grabbing what they could and shoving it under the bell with all their strength. Finally, after what seemed an interminably long time but was likely only several minutes, they succeeded in using a thin log as a lever and were able to slightly tip up the heavy bell. Bill and a couple of others pulled Luke free and laid him down flat on the floor.

Luke was by now unconscious and had taken on a greyish pallor. His pant leg had been ripped; someone reached down to tear the fabric entirely away. Luke's calf was split open exposing muscle, tissue, and bone. The foot was partially severed. Blood was quickly seeping everywhere. The men stared in dismay. The leg had been badly crushed and was swelling quickly around the knee and thigh. Pools of bright purple were visible under the skin and grew larger even as the men watched. "Raise the leg!" shouted one of the men. "Slow the blood down!"

"It's too badly crushed," said another.

"If we move him the foot will come off," warned a third.

The group looked at Bill for a decision. His eyes were glittering with tears as he shook his head slowly. "I doan know," he said, miserably. "I doan know what's best."

"We should splint it," offered Larkin, "and then raise it. I'm not sure if that's the right thing but it might help."

Bill nodded. He was now bent over Luke and weeping openly. The men had succeeded in keeping the women outside, but Luke's mother was wailing at the doors: "I want to see my son... let me see my Luke!"

Finally, one of the men went to the doors and let her in. She ran towards her husband and son and knelt beside them on the floor, sobbing and shaking. A couple of men meanwhile had torn two thin planks of wood from the flooring and were busy positioning them underneath Luke's leg. A length of cotton, rapidly torn from something, was used to make a splint. The men handled the foot as gently as possible, binding it tightly with cotton strips in an effort to stem the bleeding and hold it in place. Someone handed Larkin a couple of tablecloths and he rolled these into balls which the men helped him wedge under the leg, raising it slightly above his torso. Luke had roused briefly and moaned but fainted again.

"How long for the Doc?" was the question most whispered.

Doc Mather arrived within the hour. To save time he'd come without his carriage and ridden his horse hard. He unstrapped his medical bag and hurried inside the church, everyone stepping back to give him space to work. He noted the splinting and the elevated limb and nodded briefly. "Good job here, men." Then, looking around at the assembled, he asked if anyone had whisky. When a surprising number of small flasks were produced, he pointed at Bill Dempsey. "Give the man a drink. His wife, too. Then take her outside to wait with the women. This is a man's work." No one challenged him.

Reaching into his bag, Doc Mather withdrew a metal syringe and a bottle of morphine. He injected Luke's arm and massaged the vein gently with two fingers to help the infusion course through the body. Satisfied that Luke's pain would be slightly diminished, he slapped Luke's face and tried to rouse him. "Did he hit his head in the fall?"

"We think so."

"Not sure."

"Dint see, it happened so fast."

"What *did* happen?"

"The knot on the rope holding the bell gave way, and the bell fell. Luke was at the front of the line and it pulled him through the floor."

Doc Mather nodded. "Then he may also have a concussion. I need to look at that foot. Bill, can you manage there, holding him? I can't have him moving."

Bill nodded by way of response, and Mattie Evans walked over to stand behind Bill, ready to help if needed. When Doc peeled the cotton strips back, now quite sodden with blood, Larkin had to swallow to keep from retching. Even in remembering, the familiar tingling sensations had started running up and down his arm. His chest felt tight and he was trying hard not to run from the room.

"The foot has to come off, Bill," Doc said quietly. "It's barely attached as it is. Our best chance of saving the leg is to amputate the foot."

They had all been expecting the news but hearing it out loud, in the finality of spoken words, felt chilling. It was decided to move Luke to Doc's surgery. The conditions there were sterile and Doc felt they needed to protect against infection and gangrene. Once Luke was laid out in a wagon, Bill and his wife climbed in beside him and the sombre group set off.

Larkin walked away from the church and the distraught women and was sick to his stomach. Then, when he was able to breathe normally again, he stayed to help repair some of the damage inside as best as could be done. The Reverend Baxter was carrying on about the ruined floor and saying what a shame it was the bell wasn't hung. Larkin deliberated smacking him in the mouth to shut him up but decided he was too weary to make the effort.

As Larkin drove home afterwards, he thought about the accident and how quickly something so simple could turn bad. He knew the Dempseys must be having a terrible time and felt sorry for his friends. He remembered how awful it was when his Ma first got so sick. It would be a setback if Luke couldn't work on the farm.

Once home and inside his own kitchen, Larkin looked around at the dismal state of things. He'd left dishes in the tub, a fry pan on the stove, and last week's papers on the table. He was hungry but there wasn't anything to eat that didn't require work. He was out of bread and biscuits and didn't have any leftovers.

As he made his way upstairs, he remembered the taste of Annie's delicious cake. Her appearance had surprised him. She had a very nice shape in that new dress, and she looked sweet and happy. Pretty, even. Why had he never seen her, noticed her like that before? Had his Ma's big aprons covered up those appealing mounds and curves?

After he undressed and got into bed, he tried to imagine what it would be like to lie next to her. He fell asleep wondering why things always needed to change.

It was some weeks later before the men finally finished the job of hanging the bell and repairing the floor. Reverend Baxter flitted around uselessly, admonishing the men to "Be attentive with *my* bell" and stating the obvious: "We need to be more careful this time!" But no one had the energy or will to respond. It was a gloomy, dispirited group that laboured at their tasks, all of them preoccupied with thoughts of Luke Dempsey, who was still recovering at Doc Mather's. The Doc was fighting hard to save the leg, and word was that Luke's pain was terrible.

A special dedication service was held to bless the bell after it was finally installed. Reverend Baxter began his remarks by congratulating himself on having proposed the idea of a bell and having worked so hard to raise the funds. No mention was made of the folks who'd given generous donations or who'd toiled to install it. Larkin had shifted in the pew uncomfortably, waiting for the sermon to commence.

The sermon that followed was classic Reverend Presley Baxter. Larkin still remembered most of it. He had a way of recalling such things in detail:

> A church without people is simply an empty building! A bell on a church summons its people to church. Its ringing signals that services will begin. It inspires the faithful to come together to worship in the house of God. A bell is a voice that stirs our conscience and reminds us that we must heed the call of God. A bell is the treasured voice of a community. It will ring out informing us of disaster, of fire, of funerals and weddings. We must always heed the call of our bell and always come together when it rings!

But for Larkin the bell had cost Luke Dempsey his foot, and was the cause of George Larmer's permanently damaged shoulder. The bell, according to this reckoning, had cost a great deal more than money, although the amount of money was not insignificant.

~

Larkin suddenly sat up straight in his chair, startled by something, likely the sound of his own snoring. Rubbing his hands through his hair, he stood up and walked around the kitchen feeling panicked. What time was it? Had he fed the animals? It was black all around him, in the house and outdoors, and it was cold in the kitchen. The wood furnace must have gone out.

After lighting the oil lamp on the table with stiffened fingers, Larkin was able to check the time on his Pa's pocket watch. Twelve forty-five. Long past his regular hour for retiring.

He shuffled over to the wood box and withdrew a few pieces of cordwood along with smaller lengths of kindling. He set these on the Findlay Oval and opened its iron door. A bed of ash lay inside, thick but not too thick; there were some embers in one corner that would help. He inserted the wood, stacking it the way he'd long since learned, and struck a match to a paper twist. Then he placed the twist inside and bent down to blow. He needed the flame to catch. He stood there, folded over and blowing, watching the embers brighten and the flames start to dance and snap across the bark. Finally, the fire caught. Larkin stepped back to shut the door so that the stove could do its work. Then, wearily, he filled his arms with wood and descended the cellar steps to stoke the wood furnace.

Upstairs again, once the stove was well lit, Larkin retrieved the milk pail from the cold room, filled a little saucepan, put the pan on the stove, and left it to boil. A cup of hot milk would warm him up from the inside, he thought. Standing at the stove, tending to the milk so it wouldn't scald, he thought of his Ma standing right there beside him.

Larkin closed his eyes and summoned the look of her in a brightly patterned house dress, a big apron covering her front. Her apron pockets were always bulging with wooden pegs for the laundry or with socks she was darning. She carried a scented handkerchief in her dress for dabbing at her neck and wrists when she was warm and her hair was sticking to her dewy skin. She was not a tall woman, shy of five feet maybe. But to Larkin, she was an imposing presence. She could be right fierce with him and his Pa, even as much as she was mostly soft and gentle. When she got her dander up about something, they were apprised of her position in short order.

Larkin made sure to keep the stove polished the way she liked it. It had been a source of pride for her. She particularly loved the little warming oven up top; when he and his Pa would come in from outside, she'd often pass them a biscuit or bread roll she'd kept hot for them. Larkin looked down now and saw that the milk was getting a skin: time to take the pan off the heat. He'd already left it too long. He skimmed the skin off with a knife and set it aside on a plate to spread on a slice of bread later. No point wasting the goodness in it.

After pouring the warm milk into a thick mug, Larkin returned to the table and sat down to drink it. The warmth was comforting. The stove was now generating a great deal of heat, and Larkin luxuriated in his surroundings. The scrapbook lay open on the table, just as he'd left it. He was closing its pages to return it to the flour sack when he saw the name Cian Quinn.

Cian, an Irishman, had been the Murton police sergeant for many years. He was already an experienced copper when he'd arrived from Toronto where he'd worked along the waterfront. Respected by the community, he was generally thought to be a well-intentioned fellow, despite his being Irish.

All the Quinns had flaming red hair and chalky white skin, looks that set them apart from the locals. Being Roman Catholics, they had to travel to Collingwood for their religious services. Only a few other Catholics lived in Murton, and people found their church affiliation suspicious. Nobody wanted Fenian troublemakers in Murton. So, although the Quinns were well enough liked, they were not completely trusted.

The town had hired Sergeant Quinn to be the official authority in the area, but the unstipulated expectation was that he'd exercise that power in "small doses." Folks preferred to work out most things on their own. The fire at Skinners was different, in that two men were dead, but over the years there'd been many examples of locals not welcoming an authority figure.

Once the train came to Murton, for instance, men learned of the ready money to be had selling timber. At first the locals had felled their own trees and hauled them to the railway yard for shipping. Larkin and his Pa had joined the community effort, with each man marking off how many trees he brought in. McGuffin, who also worked as town clerk and was believed to be precise in his accounting, kept a tally in a ledger and split up the payment when it came in. It was a fair arrangement and everyone was glad of some extra cash.

But then one of the canniest men in the group, Harold Currie, decided he might just help himself to some trees off Crown land, as the distance to the train was far shorter and he could use the time saved to fell more trees. Everyone knew that logging on Crown land was allowed only if you'd purchased a permit, and that even with a permit, you were allowed only six trees.

The trouble started when Sergeant Quinn was riding by the government section and glimpsed a wagon and horses tied up just inside the woods. The Huron peoples were permitted to collect deadfall and hunt and fish on the land, but no one else. At least not without a permit, and Cian knew he hadn't issued any permits. So he tied up his own horse, climbed the simple wire fence, and made his way to the wagon. The sounds of someone felling a tree could soon be heard. Rushing forward, he was just in time to see a giant pine, maybe one-hundred feet tall, coming down towards him. Quickly reversing his course, Cian had tried unsuccessfully to run out of the way. As it was, the very top of the tree fell on him, knocking him down and pinning him to the ground while he shouted and swore: "Jesus, Mary, and Joseph! Help!"

Harold Currie heard Cian yelling and turned around to see what had happened. The legs of the sergeant were visible, kicking furiously from under the branches. Discerning that the sergeant could not be much hurt, given the colourful language and vigorous struggling, he hesitated for only a moment. Knowing that if he stopped to help he'd be charged and fined for illegal logging, Harold jumped in his wagon and drove swiftly away through a carefully constructed break in the wire that just happened to be close by.

Cian, meanwhile, was wrestling himself free and heard the sound of the wagon making its escape. That did nothing to improve his humour. "I could ha' been kilt, an te scoundrel is away an leavin' me te me own misfortunes!" He was unhurt save for some deep scratches and a broken wrist. After Doc Mather bandaged him up, Cian declared war on illegal logging and announced his intention to find the man who'd left him trapped under the tree.

Round and round the township he rode, questioning everyone and inspecting their wagons. While folks sympathized with him, and thought the worse of Harold Currie in this instance, to a man they buttoned up tight and wouldn't tell Cian a thing. It was at times like these that they pulled close together. There was "them that belonged" and there was "them from away," and no matter how long he lived in Murton, Cian would always be from away.

Things proceeded apace and gradually became somewhat unfriendly. In an effort to find the man who'd left him trapped under the tree Cian began a rigorous inspection of all the farmsteads in the area. While doing so, he found the whisky still being run by the McCormick brothers which he promptly smashed to bits. It was said that Jeb McCormick wept to see Cian savaging their equipment but stood dolefully by to observe the proceedings, hands in his pockets. His brother Abe, meanwhile, ran to the barn and climbed up into the granary to make sure the jugs and bottles were still hidden safely and covered with burlap and a thick layer of straw bedding.

When word spread that Cian was on a tear, Harold Currie got worried. Not all wagons look the same, and it was possible that Cian might recognize his. Harold knew that if he painted the wheels or the box Cian would see the fresh paint and become suspicious. Finally, in great desperation, Harold dismantled the wagon, hiding the pieces around the farm. His wife was none too pleased with this strategy as they did not own a buggy and it left her without the means to drive to town or to church. Ada Currie was made of good farm stock and there was nothing particularly delicate about her. Rumour had it that when she realized what her fool of a husband had done to the wagon, she gave him a good clip on the ear and a piece of her mind to go along with it. No one envied Harold that. Some said he had nothing but cold suppers to eat and a cold bed besides until the wagon was fully restored and refurbished for his Missus.

The farmers continued logging in their off hours, although Cian now took to inspecting the record book McGuffin kept— and if any man was credited with more than five trees in any given week, Cian would interview him. How was it possible, he'd ask, to fell a tree a day and still run a farm? It's not that Cian begrudged them the extra income logging provided, but rather his continued pique that they wouldn't reveal the identity of "the man who by Jesus almost kilt me." An event that Cian, perhaps not unreasonably, continued to take as a personal affront.

The men felt the aggravation of the log inspections; Harold Currie felt the effects of his wife's ill humour; and all mourned the loss of the McCormicks' still. The scant inventory saved in the granary was soon gone, and the tubing and parts needed to build a new still were not readily available. Jeb or Abe would gladly have gone to Collingwood for the required pieces. But Jeb's wife, Sarah, was a teetotaller, and she enlisted Abe's wife, Enid, in her mission to end what she considered to be the brothers' nefarious business dealings. All the men in the county blamed Harold for this unfortunate turn of events.

Larkin smiled and then laughed out loud to himself remembering Cian's clandestine visit to their own farm. He and his Pa were limewashing the inside of the barn when they heard an unholy commotion in the yard. It was late fall, and although the light was fading quickly, they hadn't yet gone in for their evening meal. When they heard shouting in Cian's unmistakable brogue—"Jesus, Mary, and Joseph!"—they went rushing out to the yard to see what the matter was. The first thing they saw was Cian running from the driving shed, his legs and arms pumping. Following him closely and attempting to nuzzle him from behind was their cow, Lily.

Lily was an old Jersey they kept for milk. More pet than farm stock, she was allowed to ramble around the farm at will, much like Bella, the family dog. As Cian ran straight towards the men he collided with Pa's pail of lime, which splashed up and over him. "Holy mother of God, it's te devil hisself burning me!" yelled Cian. "What in te love of God?"

Lime burns being no laughing matter, Pa quickly helped Cian strip off his clothing and led him into the kitchen where Larkin's mother washed the sergeant down and dressed the worst of the burns. Larkin, meanwhile, had stayed outside to tidy the unfinished painting job and complete the evening chores. When he did go in, he found Cian seated at the kitchen table wearing some of his Pa's old clothes and recounting his tale of woe. "I been lookin' round at te wagons, as you know, intending as it is te find the scoundrel as away an left me when I was near kilt by the tree. So I was away lookin' at your wagon an seen it warn't te one an of a sudden there's hot breath on te back of me neck an someone pressin' up against me hard, an they kept breathin' an pushin' without speakin' a word, an I moved quick beyont. That's a fret."

Larkin saw his Pa fighting back a smile, but his Ma grinned widely and pointed out the window to Lily, who was now standing beside the porch waiting for her treat. Ma always kept a bowl of vegetable peelings for her, and every night at mealtime the Jersey would wait patiently at the porch for the little enamel bowl filled with leavings. "There's your heavy breather," laughed Ma, "waiting on her bowl."

Cian had at least the good grace to look embarrassed before standing up smartly. "I'll be off an away, I will yea."

Larkin closed the scrapbook for a second time and slipped it inside the flour sack. Folding the flap neatly down, he carried the package back to the sideboard where he tucked it away.

Then he carried his empty mug to the dry sink and sloshed it around in the tub of cold soapy water. A thin white film remained inside which he wiped at using his forefinger. He wouldn't trouble to pump and boil more water to clean it properly just now; instead, he'd wait until he had more dirty dishes to wash. The cistern in the cellar was full, he knew, and the pump easy to hand in the kitchen, but the economy of water and soap was a long-established habit. Nothing was ever wasted at the farm.

Reminiscing over the scrapbook had made Larkin both melancholy and restless. He moved through the darkened house now, lamp in hand, searching for a distraction. The front parlour with its doilies and trinkets lurking in the shadows offered nothing of interest. He perched on one of the pink upholstered chairs for a moment but stood up again. After opening the china cabinet door he peered inside but could make out only general shapes in the dark. Concerned lest he break something, Larkin shut the door again with a satisfying little click and turned the tiny key to secure the lock.

Moving to the upright piano, he sat down on the stool and lifted the curved wooden lid protecting the keyboard. With his two pointer fingers, he plunked out a few random notes. Even to his ear the sound was discordant.

Old Lester Daley used to travel around and tune pianos, but it had been some years since Lester had passed. Larkin remembered seeing him unpack his leather satchel, laying out the specialized tools on a piece of folded flannel. Over time Larkin had learned the names of the different tuning levers and forks, the homemade mutes, the tip wrench, the strip of wool felt Lester used to mute the strings while he was working. It was a delicate and lengthy operation.

Lester had shown him how to turn and set the tuning pins in order to adjust the tension in the strings. Larkin learned that these need to be adjusted once or twice a year to keep the piano in pitch. Lester had been an accomplished pianist before moving to just north of Murton. He'd even toured with a little group of classical musicians, putting on recitals at town halls and theatres across the United States and Canada. The group fell apart when the baritone soloist married Lester's first cousin and decided to stay home to farm.

When he was finished his work, Lester would carefully wrap his tools and put them away in his satchel. Then he'd motion Larkin's mother to come closer before he sat down to demonstrate the improved tuning.

At her request, Lester would play for them. Sometimes Pa would hear the music and come in to listen while Beethoven's *Moonlight Sonata* or Debussy's *Clair de Lune* was played with a light touch that filled their world with soulful magic.

"I declare," Larkin's Ma would say when he was done, "that piano never sounds half so fine when I play." Lester would graciously acknowledge the compliment and then stay for tea before taking his leave.

His Ma had tried to teach Larkin to play when he was a child, but Larkin didn't have a musical bone in his body. The notes on the music scores confused him and made him tense. For a time his Ma would sit beside him at the piano every day after school and make him practise for half an hour. But Larkin was always anxious to get outside and help his Pa with the chores. He felt confident there, sure of himself in a way he never felt inside.

The brick house, built just before Larkin was born, was beautiful and had every convenience that could be afforded at the time. His Ma loved it, and was rightly proud of how well the rooms were fitted out. The furniture in the front parlour had been ordered from Trott's of Collingwood; the room was kept for special occasions only. He and his Pa never felt as comfortable there as they did sprawled out at the kitchen table. His Pa used to joke that old man Trott got his plans mixed up when he was making the settle and thought he was making a hard coffin instead. Ma would cluck softly in disapproval at the slight and pat the pink upholstery protectively.

Larkin remembered that detail when he ordered his Pa's coffin from the younger Mr. Trott many years later. He fixated on the idea of having the coffin lined in pink upholstery to match the settle, but Mr. Trott said as they no longer carried such material. Larkin suspected that he just didn't want to accommodate such an unusual choice.

Still, because he believed his Pa would be resting in the box for all eternity, Larkin remained determined to make the coffin comfortable. As he'd aged his father's hips and knees had begun to ache; in the winter he'd taken to cushioning the wooden kitchen chair by placing a square of sheepskin on it. So now Larkin scrubbed the square clean with soap and hot water, left it out in the hot sun to dry for a day, and then brushed it till it was soft and fluffy. When Mr. Trott and his assistant appeared with the coffin, Larkin instructed him to lay the sheepskin down underneath his Pa.

Mr. Trott looked exceedingly unhappy with the eccentric instruction—the box was already fitted out nicely with a pale blue lining—but Larkin insisted. Reluctantly, the assistant removed some of the upholstery nails and carefully slid the sheepskin under the lining to make a thickly padded bed. He then refastened the lining and laid out Edgar Beattie in cushioned comfort.

Larkin was pleased with the effort. He'd recognized in himself the need to keep busy with something during his distress and knew that this fixation was only one in a series of similar small thoughts he would act upon. Although his father did not often indulge in liquor, the occasional dram of McCormicks' whisky (the brothers had once again set up their still) was not something he would decline. Larkin had a small bottle of it set aside and slipped it into the box when no one was present to see.

The funeral would be held in the house; friends and neighbours had offered to take care of the luncheon afterwards. Larkin left its preparations to the womenfolk and spent as much of the day as he could outside with the animals. When he went to the barn, he looked around instinctively for a glimpse of his Pa. He caught himself doing it and was shocked at the abrupt sense of loss that hit him. Tears streamed down his face in a private convulsion of grief. He attempted to push them away with the heel of his hand but succeeded only in rubbing the sadness deeper into his pores.

It's a funny thing about funerals, thought Larkin. Everyone comes round and brings food and tells you how sad they are. "Sorry for your trouble" gets repeated countless times. But death makes folks twitchy. And no one likes to talk about the actual dying part. It's as if they're afraid it might hasten their own departing. And Larkin was aware that he *wanted* to talk about it. He wanted to talk about the shock of finding his Pa. And he wanted someone to acknowledge the huge hole in his life that had just opened up. He had many questions but no one to ask them of. For instance, if your soul flew up to heaven the instant you died, how come we paid our respects to a coffin and the empty shell of a body? Why was that?

Even after all these years, Larkin still didn't understand the way of it. It was a natural process all right, he knew that. Life on a farm teaches you about birthing and dying. That warn't the troubling part. It was the *how* of dying that seemed a puzzle. How could you be living and breathing and working hard one minute, and the very next minute be lying face down dead? How does that happen? How come some folks gets a warning, like his Ma, and others just drop down dead like a stone?

Larkin worried about this from time to time. He worried about his horses, especially. Who would feed them? How long would it take for anyone to notice that his time had come and he, too, had dropped down dead? How long would the horses wait before someone came to check on them? He thought about this mostly in the evenings when he was finishing the last of his chores. He always saved the horses for last so that he could enjoy his time with them. They seemed to sense his need and whinnied softly when he came near.

Culloden liked having his ears rubbed; he'd even bow his head and nudge Larkin in the shoulder to remind him of that fact. Larkin would reach up to softly stroke his velvety ears while Culloden nickered, his breath hot against Larkin's neck.

Of his two mares, Guinevere and Merlyn, Guinevere responded best to having her mane brushed. Larkin would first run his hands through her mane to make sure it was free of knots, burrs, and tangles. Then he'd pick up the mane brush and start at the ends, brushing in a downwards motion as he worked his way up in increments. The closer he got to the top, the thicker the hair growth became. Sometimes the thicker mane hid a snarl he'd missed. Larkin would feel gently for these with his fingers, prying them apart carefully. When he was sure the knots were all out, he'd brush the thicker mane from underneath, still working downwards, until the mane lay soft and feathery. Guinevere would often blow in his face afterwards, expressing her satisfaction with the attention given. This small exchange always made Larkin smile.

And it was then that he mostly thought about death. What if I were to drop dead right now? he'd ask himself. It wouldn't be such a bad way to go, standing here with my horses. But who would rub Culloden's ears or brush Guinevere's mane?

Larkin tried not to brood about his own demise, but there were related matters he occasionally pondered. He wondered if Silas had been too far gone on whisky and meanness to realize what was happening when he was killed. And he wondered about Elgin, too. Had he already begun to turn, as Paul had implied, into a crueler version of his father? Was it true, as the locals whispered, that only blackness lay in the hearts of the Skinner men? Which one of the two had died first? Was there an explanation for the sequence of events that made sense? These were questions that Larkin knew must have answers. He could have asked Paul, but the burden of being the keeper of secrets was already weighty and he hadn't been sure he could take in any more. The not-knowing sometimes troubled him.

Two weeks after leaving Paul in the hotel, Larkin and his Pa had driven back to Collingwood to check on him—only to discover that he'd already signed out. The clerk wasn't sure where he'd gone. "The boy with burns? He left. Maybe three days ago? Said he was broke. I sent him to the shipyards. They're always looking for workers."

"Where would a lad like him stay?" asked his Pa.

"There's shanties down by the wharf and docks. Some bunk there."

Disappointed, Larkin and his Pa left the hotel. "We should have come sooner," said his Pa. "I could have given him a few dollars."

Larkin didn't respond. What troubled him most was knowing that Paul was friendless in this busy place—a place where throngs of people filled the streets and shops, hurrying about at what seemed a frantic pace.

His father suggested they inquire at the harbour before returning home. He approached several of the men working on the dock, calling out to them and asking after a boy with burns. The men stopped their work long enough to shake their heads.

A foreman of sorts appeared to be striding about with an air of self-importance. Larkin's Pa walked up to him, introduced himself, and asked after Paul. "I wonder did you see a young fella, shorter than my boy but the same age? He would have been looking for work. Burns on his hands and feet that might not be healed." His Pa waved in Larkin's direction and the foreman glanced over, taking in his height and scrutinizing his appearance.

As Mr. Beattie spoke the man had been chewing a toothpick, nodding along. Now he removed his toothpick and gestured vaguely with it towards the wharf. "Gave him some errands for a five-cent piece. He was eager enough for the silver but the lad could barely walk and weren't no use to me."

"Thank you. I understand." His Pa returned to Larkin's side looking downcast. "We should have come sooner. I doan know where he is."

"Maybe we could try over there?" Larkin pointed at an imposing lake ship stationed in its berth. Men were scrambling all over its hull, each of them busy at something. Several men were dangling from ropes above the waterline, some were hammering, others were blackening the surface with brushes. With the docks not considered particularly safe, Larkin had only ever driven by them before and so was intrigued by all the unfamiliar sights. "What are they doin', Pa?"

"Worms get in the wood when it's wet and bore holes through. The ships come here to be repaired. The men are replacing the worst of the exterior planks and will coat them with tar when they're done. It helps with waterproofing and keeps the worms out."

The sounds of men hard at work filled the air with cussing and the kind of language that let you know it was a rough part of town. And it was said that the only ladies who ventured there were those of "low morals." When Larkin noticed the brightly coloured outfit and strange yellow hair of a woman sauntering back and forth along the wharf, his father put his hand on his shoulder and turned him physically around so that she was no longer in view. "That one's trouble, son, best look away."

When Larkin twisted his head back for a final glance, he saw her lifting her foot up on a box, displaying a black-stockinged leg. Now his father gripped his arm and led him to another section of the docks altogether.

"Do you think Paul will be here, Pa?"

"Likely. It may be he found work at the silos or with the builders." His Pa looked at him searchingly. "He knows where we are, Larkin. He could come home to us if he wanted."

"Should we keep lookin'?"

"For an hour only. We need to get back for the chores."

"What will happen to him?"

"I doan know for sure. I reckon life will call on him to be a man before he's finished his growing."

Larkin loved that about his father. He loved that he answered difficult questions honestly and didn't try to whitewash things. He said what was what and spoke straight and plain.

They walked to the silos together and asked more men there. Along the way back they approached another grouping, and then another. No luck anywhere. Paul seemed to have leaked away into the swarm of workers and had become lost in the commotion.

Later that fall, Larkin and his folks attended the Collingwood Agricultural Society Fair. His Pa had given him some money of his own and Larkin was eager to see what he could spend it on. So, when his parents, intent on watching the cattle judging, agreed to meet him later by the horse pull, Larkin hastened away to the tent where refreshments were being sold. He'd seen people carrying large apple fritters and wanted very much to try one.

On his way through to the tent he got a glimpse of a boy who looked vaguely familiar. His hair was long and unkempt and his clothes, particularly an overlarge jacket, looked filthy. Larkin stopped. While he watched, he saw the boy's gloved hand reach for an apple fritter then scurry away without paying. Larkin followed him. The thief had an awkward gait and was loping unevenly.

Larkin quickly outpaced that lope and then stopped right in front of him, blocking his path abruptly. Paul looked surprised, then embarrassed and awkward. Larkin moved forward to greet him. "How are you?" Then, before Paul could answer, "Where are you livin'? Are you workin' somewheres? Pa and I came to find you at the hotel but you was gone. Did the doctor fix you up?"

"Your Pa was awful good to me. I do jobs around town. Run errands mostly. I do all right."

"Let's find my folks. They be over by the horse pull now."

Paul hesitated. "I doan want your Ma seeing me like this."

"She won't care, Paul, honest she won't. They be pleased to see you."

"I got to go. I have work to finish."

"What kind of work?"

"I can't stop, Larkin." Paul turned to move away.

"Wait!" Larkin reached into his pocket and handed Paul the coins his Pa had given him. "Take this."

Paul looked at the coins Larkin had pressed into his hand. "Larkin Beattie, you're the best friend a fella ever had."

"Come home with us. My Pa will help you."

"I ain't got no home, Larkin. You know that."

"Stay with us a spell."

"No one wants me. Everyone thinks I'm to blame. I got to go." And with that, Paul disappeared into the crowd.

Larkin hadn't told his folks about seeing Paul on the day of the fair. Weeks later, though, it seemed to him that he couldn't avoid it.

His Pa had driven to Murton to pick up the mail and brought home a letter addressed to Larkin Beattie, Cemetery Hill, Murton, Ontario. Larkin couldn't remember that he'd ever received a letter before. His parents watched him while he opened it. Inside was a piece of paper folded around something hard. He unfolded the paper carefully and saw some coins. Without reading the note, he knew Paul had sent it. His parents were watching him curiously.

Larkin offered the dollar to his Pa and began his explanation. Not wanting to read the note in front of them, he folded it back up small and slid it into his pocket. His parents had a few questions about Paul and why Larkin had thought to keep the sighting of him a secret. Larkin didn't know how to account for himself. People round about had talked about Paul. They were all convinced he'd somehow done it. Larkin just didn't want more discussion of the topic. Nor more of the whole truth to come out.

Larkin's face must have betrayed his discomfort. His father glanced over at his Ma then handed him the money back. "I gave you this to buy yourself something special. You used it to help a friend instead. That makes us real proud. You keep it now, son. It's yourn."

Later that night, when Larkin was finally alone, he stood by the window in his room and held the note up to the moonlight to read. It was short and written in a messy, uneven hand. *Larkin, I owes you this and more. Your friend always, Paul.* Larkin tucked the note away and kept it as a kind of charm. The note was now in the flour sack along with the scrapbook.

His bond with Paul was something Larkin had tried to puzzle out over the years. He felt protective of him, and yet a little in awe of him, too. He also felt indebted. But besides this was an element of fear. Paul had a quick temper and could occasionally be violent and cruel. With only a few words, he could destroy Larkin's life. Larkin felt vulnerable and largely defenceless against such power. Still, he was aware that he held some small slight advantage of his own, in that he knew some of Paul's deepest secrets. The truth was that they were entwined together like a stick of barley twist.

~

Larkin spun slowly around on the piano stool and stood up. Piled neatly on top of the piano was a stack of sheet music anchored down by the metronome. Larkin hated that device. His mother had set it to swinging whenever he'd attempt to play a piece of music. He knew he was supposed to keep time with it, but somehow the easy fingering went too quickly and the difficult fingering went too slowly and he could never make it come out right. He wasn't fond of piano practice, and yet he'd kept trying, just to please his Ma.

Moving towards the centre hall, Larkin hesitated but then entered the back parlour which had mostly been used by the family when they were alone. Pa would sprawl out in an old armchair, his Ma kept her darning and knitting in the room, and Larkin was allowed to play on the floor when he was young. It wasn't a large room but it always felt comfortable when the three of them were together. There was a fireplace on the outside wall; Larkin's Pa had built a little bookcase that stood to one side of it. His Ma's books were all lined up neatly on the shelves. She took pride in her modest library and loved to read on those rare occasions when she had time to herself. "If you have a book, Larkin," she would say, "then you have a friend for life."

Sometimes, when Larkin would ask about other countries, or what it must be like to travel to faraway places, his Ma would say, "There are books in the parlour, Larkin, you can read all about these things if you want to. *Gulliver's Travels* is a book you might enjoy, or *The Pilgrim's Progress*, or *Robinson Crusoe*." His Ma was a great one for self-improvement and was always encouraging him to read.

But Larkin had never liked to sit still long enough to do such a thing. His Pa read the papers once a week, and Larkin understood the necessity of doing that. "It's important to keep up with news" was what his Pa said when he unfolded the large sheets and began to scan the pages for something of interest. Still, Larkin would always much rather be outside, working or doing.

Things had slowed down inside of him as he'd grown older. Like the sap in the sugar bush when the temperature warmed up near the end of the season, was how he thought of it. He had more patience now and was calmer in himself.

Larkin bent over his mother's bookcase and selected a volume randomly. Placing his lamp on a side table, he looked at the spine first. *Concordance*. He opened the front cover and was surprised to see an inscription. *To Ellen Joy on the occasion of her birthday, with love from Matthew. 4th June, 1852*. Larkin settled himself on one of the room's upholstered chairs and casually flipped through the pages. A fine piece of folded paper fluttered to the floor in the gloom. Larkin held the lamp closer, picked it up, and placed it on his knee. It appeared to be a page from a letter. The small, tissue-thin sheet was yellowed and brittle. Larkin unfolded it gingerly, smoothed it out as best he could, and squinted at its contents. The handwriting, he saw, was rather large and rather loopy.

23rd November, 1871

Dear Mrs. Beattie,

You maybe no that my sister and me and Ma are living with Uncle Roy over in Angus way. We been here since after the fire. My Ma's been taken down sick with stomach troubles and we're aiming to restore her. She's been fratching about our brother and wants us to find him. Uncle Roy told us

Larkin read the page twice. *Since after the fire.* Then he carefully refolded the sheet and slipped it back into the book, his heart thumping a little more quickly. He sat back for a minute and waited for it to level out. Why had just this one page been saved?

Larkin found his mind veering away to the inscription in the Concordance. Ma had spoken of a Matthew, a cousin of hers he'd never met. He couldn't immediately recollect how they were cousins, nor the names of all six uncles on her side of the family. Ma's father was named Alex, he knew. And there'd been an Uncle Lloyd, an Uncle Duncan, an Uncle Archibald, and three others. He'd never paid much attention to family histories or the names of distant relatives, and now that his folks weren't around to remind him, he didn't remember who belonged where. There was a family Bible with names and dates written down but one of his Ma's sisters had it. Larkin couldn't recollect which one. Maybe it was his Aunt Shirley out near Riseborough, but she like as not had already passed and left it to someone else. He couldn't remember whether she was married or if she'd stayed at her teachering.

Larkin sat quietly for several minutes contemplating his Ma's family. Uncle Archibald he well remembered. An oversized man with a barrel-shaped chest and a booming voice, he was a family favourite; Ma had always made a fuss of him whenever he came to visit. He had a wife, a petite bird of a woman who would perch on the edge of the furniture and look as if she might take flight if she was startled. His Ma treated her like she was something fragile, and would bring her cups of tea in the best china cup and saucer.

Once, he remembered, his Ma had gone to stay with them for a spell because Uncle Archibald's wife was in a "delicate condition." That was the way such things were talked about back then. Throughout the country, Larkin knew, womenfolk were often called to assist with childbirth and sickness and any other kind of trouble that might come along. His Ma would go off on such business and not return home for two or sometimes three weeks. He and his Pa would manage well enough, that was no matter, but the rightness of things was disrupted. The three of them needed to be in their places for home to feel right.

His Ma was gone a long while but she came home finally, after the baby was born. Larkin couldn't remember what the baby was called or if he ever knew. He guessed it was his cousin. He knew he had a whole heap of cousins on his Ma's side but didn't know who they all were or where they were living.

From the letter's date, he figured his Ma would a been fifteen when she received the Concordance. Before she'd even known his Pa. His folks met at a social, he knew that. But he couldn't remember the occasion. The one thing he did remember was that his Pa had started attending Sunday school and church after they met because his Ma played the organ and he wanted an excuse to see her. And he pretty much kept up the practice, too, even after she passed, because by then it had become a habit.

He once showed Larkin where he'd carved their initials into the back of a church pew: EB+EFB surrounded by a tiny heart. Larkin was surprised.

"What did Ma say when she seen it?"

His Pa laughed. "She said yes, is what. I asked her to marry me after I done carving it an she said yes."

"You asked her in a church?"

"Figured I needed all the help I could get. Dint know what she'd say."

"An she said yes?"

"She did."

Larkin couldn't remember a time when he saw his Pa lacking in courage. The idea of him being scared to propose tickled him a little.

It also plucked at his heart. He and his Pa had loved Ma something fierce. It was a hard thing to watch her in such pain at the end without being able to provide relief. Larkin had been just nineteen. For weeks when her time was near, he'd walked around feeling like someone had punched him hard in the gut just thinking of her upstairs suffering. At the last she stopped eating, and it was all they could do to help her with a little water or broth. Even though she was lying there in the bed and they were holding on to her hands tight and talking to her, she just faded away.

Larkin swallowed hard with the memory of it. His Pa had moaned in his grief, the deepest, most wrenching sound Larkin had ever heard. He knew right then that there'd be no comforting him, so he left him alone with his Ma and walked outside to the yard.

He walked and walked, but no matter how far he went he could still hear the sound of his Pa's mourning. Larkin spent that first night in the barn asleep, finally, on a bed of straw. The animals' snorting and deep breathing provided comforting sounds.

He felt differently about such things now. Although he'd wish both his folks still alive and well, he wouldn't want to see his Ma suffer again the way she had done. You couldn't wish folks back to face such an ordeal. And his Pa, well, his Pa hadn't suffered; he'd had what folks called a "good death." The thing was, Larkin was pretty sure that even with the surprise of dying so sudden like, his Pa would a been awful glad to see his wife in the ever after. And that thought comforted Larkin.

Thoughts of death generally made Larkin feel morose. He returned his Ma's Concordance to the bookshelf and stood up. He would go upstairs and ready himself for bed. Taking the lamp, Larkin ascended the steps and stopped at the top landing. Just the other day he'd left an apple basket there to be filled with old clothes. The ladies in the community were having a quilting bee, with the results auctioned off as a way to raise funds for a new hall. There'd be a beef supper and a square dance. Larkin wasn't too fussy on the idea of all that socializing, but Mrs. Daley had asked him to contribute some old clothes and he had agreed.

Larkin's clothes were mostly hanging on hooks in his bedroom. He picked up an old shirt and looked at it critically, wondering if it was the sort of thing Mrs. Daley wanted. Thinking about some of the brightly coloured quilts he'd seen over the years, he didn't trust that his old checked shirt was the thing.

Hesitating briefly, he went into his parents' bedroom and held the lamp up high. His Ma's dresses were still hanging on hooks behind a little curtain. With his free hand he pulled the curtain back to survey the selection.

He didn't really want to donate any of them, but he was aware that this was the sort of cause she would have supported, and so he reached one down and hung it over his arm, then a second and a third, and a fourth, and a fifth, until finally the hooks were bare. Then he walked over to the bed and laid all the dresses flat, intending to fold them tidily for the basket.

The first dress was a summer print, its faint pink stripes filled with tiny yellow flowers. He folded, then bunched, and in the end rolled it into a lumpy bundle. The second one had a white collar and big white buttons with a funny kind of knobby thread running through the purple and white checkered material. Larkin remembered her wearing it.

He'd started folding and then rolling it into a second bunched-up parcel when he heard the faint sound of something crinkling. He straightened the dress back out on the bed and saw the pocket. Feeling inside, he withdrew a brittle piece of paper. It had been folded into a little square but looked very like the page he'd discovered in the book. Carefully, Larkin set it aside on the bed. Then he methodically folded, rolled, and bunched the remaining dresses into soft mounds which he placed inside the apple basket.

Larkin picked up the letter and the lamp and gently nudged the apple basket with his foot until it rested once more on the landing at the top of the stairs. Then he went back down to the parlour, set his lamp on the side table, reached for the Concordance, and flipped through its pages until he found the first page of the letter. Unfolding the new piece he'd discovered, he compared the two sheets and their handwriting. They were definitely the same.

He sat down on the settle, slid the lamp closer, and placed both pages next to him, side by side. Then, to approach the matter properly, he read the first page once more:

23rd November, 1871

Dear Mrs. Beattie,

You maybe no that my sister and me and Ma are living with Uncle Roy over in Angus way. We been here since after the fire. My Ma's been taken down sick with stomach troubles and we're aiming to restore her. She's been fratching about our brother and wants us to find him. Uncle Roy told us

And then the second:

that he ain't welcome here and that he sent him away the couple times he already come. So we thought as how you live close by, you might of seen him on the old place or round about. We no that him and your boy were friendly and wondered if any of you

had news of how to get word to him. Ma is right poorly and we
think she needs to see him. We no too when Ma went to see

They fit together but were still not complete. A third page, at least, was still missing. Larkin shivered. This letter must have been written by one of the Skinner girls. *We no that him and your boy were friendly.*

He refolded the two pages carefully. What would make the sister think Ma might know something about where Paul had got to? What did she mean by *We think she needs to see him?*

The letter had been written in 1871. The same year as the fire. But why would they have waited so long—three months— to look for Paul? Had they even *tried* earlier? Were there other letters? Larkin felt the need to know. Carrying secrets for so many years had been a burden. For someone with less of a conscience, or a different type of constitution, perhaps what Larkin knew would not have seemed such a difficulty. But for him it had been a torment and had exacted a heavy toll.

Resting his head in his hands, Larkin closed his eyes and tried to conjure a picture of Paul's sisters. There were two of them. And they weren't particularly pretty. They mostly wore their hair knotted up in plaits and had a horsey look to them, with plain faces and big teeth. One was named Ethel but the other's name was gone. If he didn't think about it too much, it might come back. He'd never known a Skinner girl to write his Ma. His Ma and Mrs. Skinner were not companions. His Ma was friendly with lots of women, mostly from church, but Mrs. Skinner wasn't one of them. Paul's Ma didn't attend church all that regular. In fact, she mostly kept to herself. She came to the house just that one time he knew of, after the fire.

Larkin stood up and paced, glancing out the window as he passed. It was a still night; all was quiet outside. The moon and starlight provided faint illumination in the otherwise sapphire-black sky. The colours of darkness were pronounced and in them he saw the outline of familiar shapes: the just barely budding trees, the split-rail fence, the corner of the tool shed, the chicken coop. All were laid out clearly in the shadowy silence. What wasn't clear, and what he now had a burning desire to know, was whether another page of the letter was concealed somewhere else in the house.

Surely it wasn't happenstance that the pages had been separated and then tucked away in different places, out of sight. That they'd been *hidden*. For so long Larkin had carried around questions he couldn't ask anyone. And now, somehow, in the midst of what was becoming a long, restless night, he felt the letter might give him a clue.

One by one, in the flickering light, he removed his Ma's books from the shelves and took hold of their covers to shake out the pages. Some of the titles stamped in gold on their spines were familiar, others were not. He smiled to remember how much joy his Ma had in stealing away with a book for a short spell. She always had a touch of guilt about it and would even apologize when she was seen, as if reading was slothful. It's not that his Pa had ever tried to make her feel that way, it was just the way of her. And those were the only times Larkin ever remembered seeing her hands idle. Mostly they scrubbed or baked or cleaned or knit or mended or sewed. Only when she was reading a book did she sit quite still, her face smooth, all of her calm.

Having shaken all the books by turn, Larkin slumped into a chair and considered. One page was in a pocket and one page in a book. It stood to reason that she'd tucked away another page in a different kind of location. Larkin stood up and looked around the room with a critical eye: nothing looked as though it might be hiding secrets. He scanned the front parlour. The sheet music? He leafed through the pile—most of it was church music but there were also some popular tunes: "By the Sad Sea Waves," "I've Left the Snow-Clad Hills," "The Wedding March." He opened each of the paper folders carefully.

Nothing. Larkin stood motionless, considering. In his mind he walked through every room in the house, surveying each in turn, searching for spots that may yet lie unexamined, that may just hold what he was so intently wanting to find.

Finally, his shoulders slumped. He'd lived in this house his entire life; there wasn't an inch of it he didn't know. The books, the pockets, the sheet music—those were one thing. No other such possibilities presented themselves.

Defeated, Larkin took up the two folded pages. Then, walking directly to the kitchen, he went to the sideboard and reached for the sack that held his scrapbook. The least he could do was secrete the pages away for safekeeping.

The book opened to a page bearing another *Murton Chronicle* report. It was one he'd read many times before.

DAY TWO OF MURTON MURDER INQUIRY

All those present as the coroner's inquest resumed were deathly silent when the name "Paul Skinner" was called aloud. Heads turned to watch as a thin young man in an ill-fitting suit entered the courtroom. With his eyes on the floor, Mr. Skinner navigated the short aisle towards the judge's bench and stopped still, waiting for direction. A clerk of the court led him to the wooden podium where he was quietly sworn in and seated.

Lead prosecutor Finlay Taylor began the proceedings in earnest by bellowing, "Good of you to join us, Mr. Skinner! We understand that you have only recently returned from town!"

What follows is a partial transcript of the interview on the second day of this much-anticipated inquest.

"Mr. Skinner, would you be so good as to describe to the Court the events of August 7th as you know them?"

"I can't say that I know much… I can't remember."

"You do remember the fire, Mr. Skinner, do you not?!"

"I heard 'bout it and 'bout my Pa and Elgin. But I don't remember it."

"You sustained injuries in that fire, did you not?!"

"Yes, sir, so I been told."

"But you claim not to remember how you sustained those injuries to your person?"

"I do not remember, sir."

"So tell me, Mr. Skinner, how do you explain the injuries you received?!"

"I been told I escaped the house when it was alight and that Pa and Elgin didn't get out in time."

"In time for what, exactly, Mr. Skinner?!"

"In time to escape from the fire."

"And how do you propose that your Pa and Elgin could have escaped the fire when they were already dead before the fire started?!"

"I... don't know."

"Mr. Skinner you appear not to know very much. I wonder if you can tell me who else was at the farm on the day of the fire. Was there another person there with a knife, perhaps? A very large knife, I'm told. A knife that was used repeatedly to stab both your father and your brother?"

"I don't know."

"Will you tell the Court anything about that day, Mr. Skinner, or are you deliberately obfuscating? Is this a ploy to avoid your personal responsibility? Are you the man with the knife, Mr. Skinner? Did your father fly into one of his drunken tempers and attack you, and did you grab a knife to defend yourself? Did Elgin intervene in the fight and try to take the knife from you? Or was it the other way around? Did Elgin stab your father and you grabbed at the knife and fatally stabbed him in a struggle? Tell the Court, Mr. Skinner! Tell me!"

"I... don't... know."

In a dramatic end to the questioning, Mr. Skinner appeared to collapse and was carried from the room by two clerks of the court.

Larkin closed the scrapbook slowly, making sure the letter fragments were tucked securely inside.

His family had been present for Paul's questioning. He and his parents had also read the account in the paper when it came out. The inquest was the talk of the community while it was underway, and although Larkin's parents had tried to shield him from much of the drama, there was no escaping the gossip and speculation.

The whole thing was over in a week. Then they had to wait several weeks more for the judge to submit his report. The Beatties read the final verdict in the paper: "Inconclusive," the judge had written. "Insufficient evidence," he went on to declare, detailing his findings using big legal words sprinkled with a few others that they assumed were Latin or maybe Greek.

It didn't matter. Local judgment had already condemned Paul as the murderer. The community was united in the belief that Silas's sons, like their father, were fiends. The stories continued to grow until the name Skinner became synonymous with all things diabolical.

Larkin had remained upset about Paul. He worried about where he was living, how he was managing. He wondered if he was lonely. Sometimes when Larkin bit into an apple or a sandwich he'd have a fleeting memory of sharing his lunch with Paul at school. Those flashes of tender intimacy stirred a longing in Larkin that he could not describe and that filled him with a familiar sense of deep regret and shame.

As Larkin sat at the table thoughtfully, recollecting that time, he gradually became aware of the sound of a wind starting up outside. The kitchen was a little drafty, he realized now; he could feel cold air stealing in from the window and the door. The pink gingham curtains were undulating faintly. From the feel of the drafts, he knew the wind was coming from the northwest. Those were always the coldest winds, the ones that did the most damage. If a gale blew up hard, he could lose some of the wooden shingles. He'd lost some in the last storm but had been waiting for warmer weather to climb up and replace them. You didn't want to be slipping around up there in the winter months, especially with such a steep pitch. As his Pa had always said, "The steeper the pitch of the roof, the longer it lasts." Even if the sun was out, you needed hard-packed ground to plant your ladder on. Larkin worried about the roof as he listened to the blowing outside and then further worried that if sleety rain should follow the wind, he might also have leaks. He hated the thought of that. He hated the idea that he might not be keeping the house up the way his folks would have done.

But life was like that, he reasoned, full of compromises. You want to do the right thing but you're held back from the doing of it by competing priorities. He *wanted* to climb up there straight away and fix those shingles, but he also knew the risk. Luke Dempsey's accident had always been a keen reminder of the importance of safety. The doctor had managed to save his leg, and Luke had travelled to Toronto some months later to be fitted with a wooden prosthetic foot. He managed all right with one crutch after that, but was unsteady and couldn't walk too long without needing to rest.

And compromise was what Larkin had to deal with regarding the murder. He'd *wanted* to tell the whole truth at the inquest but was too scared of what would happen to Paul. *And* he'd wanted to tell his Pa about the secret but felt too ashamed and didn't know how his Pa would manage the hearing of it. And when he *had* tried to tell, the words just wouldn't come. And so, he'd kept his part of the story, along with the other secrets, close inside.

The summer they were both eleven, Larkin and Paul had ventured closer to the swamp and farther away from home than ever before. And it was down by the marsh that they found the remains of an old hunting cabin. Although the roof had begun to collapse inwards at one end and the door and single window had long since been liberated, the log walls were still in place. And when the boys entered the cabin, a sheltered room of sorts was still standing. With most of the chinking between the logs having perished, summer breezes swept through the enclosure, making it feel airy and pleasant. He and Paul had spent days clearing out debris, patching the roof, and sweeping the floor with leafy branches they'd pulled from a nearby thicket.

The entire place smelled of decaying vegetation and water-logged wood. The earth was peaty and moist and the dank water had a strong sulphur smell. Their shoes were always soaked through when they visited. And yet they both felt as if they'd discovered a private kingdom—a place where they could play the last of their childhood games and embark on imagined adventures.

Some days they were mounting an exploration to the East Indies or the North Pole, while other days they were kept busy defending their country from an American invasion. Larkin's Ma would fill his lunch pail with sandwiches and biscuits, and when each boy had done his chores he'd race across the fields and through the woods until he reached the cabin. Then, once they'd both arrived, they would devour their feast on a fallen tree nearby, surveying the empire of their murky marsh and planning all manner of quests and journeys. The cabin was their private sanctuary.

One day, the last day Larkin would ever visit the cabin, he found Paul huddled up inside when he arrived, curled into a ball and crying. Larkin sat down beside him and awkwardly patted his shoulder, trying to make out what had happened. When Paul sat up after a while, Larkin was shocked to see an angry welt across his face that had broken through the skin. Larkin reached out to gently touch his cheek, instinctively trying to infuse the wound with gentleness.

"What happened, Pauley? Your Pa do that?"

Paul nodded.

The boys looked at each other sombrely. Larkin's Pa had never laid an angry hand on him and he couldn't feature how a father could do such a thing. Paul, though—Paul didn't know any different.

"You think we should tell someone, Pauley?"

Paul shook his head. "I sauced him back, Larkin. He told me to do sumpen and I sauced him and he took off his belt and walloped me."

"What did your Ma say?"

"She didn't say nothing, or she'd a got it worse."

"He wallops your *Ma*?"

"Alla time." Paul began to cry again, slumped against Larkin, who embraced him and began to make shushing noises. Paul nestled in tight against his chest, then reached his scrawny arms up and embraced him back. After a time of shared misery, Paul unbuttoned his trouser front, and taking Larkin's hand in his, guided it towards his privates.

And somehow the two boys ended up lying alongside each other, their clothes abandoned beside them, Paul resting peacefully in his friend's arms.

Larkin closed his eyes against the anguish of the recollection. He'd watched the sunlight dapple patterns on Paul's thin white limbs. His fingers had traced the cruel marks and bruises left on his back and shoulders and buttocks. He'd cupped his hand around Paul's most intimate places and felt the tickle of the fine blond fuzz against his own skin. Both boys had watched their peckers swell and grow hard with pleasure. They had caressed the secret places wordlessly, looking steadily at each other as they did. It was a profound bonding, one they never spoke of again.

But thereafter Larkin could never bear the aroma of hard-cooked eggs. Even the smallest whiff of sulphur would take him back to the smell of the marsh and to that time.

Larkin had lived on a farm all his life. He knew what animals did. But before that afternoon he'd never experienced anything sensual in relation to his own body. Being touched and stroked in that intimate way had felt delicious—and yet, even as they were enjoying each other, Larkin had worried. He didn't voice his concerns to Paul, though. Paul had stopped crying. He looked calm. Larkin didn't want to take that away from him, no matter what.

Larkin wondered sometimes if his Pa had guessed. If he'd read his son's guilt and puzzled out the reason for it. He had no real reason to think so. His Pa had certainly never indicated any such thing, and yet Larkin felt sure the experience had marked him in a way that all the world could see. He expected someone to expose him, to accuse him of sodomy or perversion or sinful behaviour.

Church was especially difficult, at first. The first Sunday after the incident he was certain that the Reverend would denounce him from the pulpit and expose him as a sinner of the most disgusting kind. When that didn't happen, he expected the Reverend to visit the farm and speak with his folks about his evil misdeeds. For months afterwards he shied away from the Reverend, hoping to shield his guilt from knowing eyes and thus avoid the inevitable revelation of his depravity.

But somehow the Reverend hadn't seen the signs of evil written upon him. He hadn't even taken notice of him. Larkin was left alone to guard his shameful secret.

Larkin shook his head at the memories as if trying to dislodge the impure feelings of a boy. He turned the wick down on his lamp and watched to make sure the flame was completely extinguished. Then, for good measure, he cupped his hands above the top of the glass chimney, leaned down, and blew a quick puff of air into it. Knowing the glass would now be too hot to carry and not particularly needing light, he left the lamp on the kitchen table and went upstairs in the dark. His feet knew the number of paces to the staircase, the number of steps to climb, the turn at the landing. The house was a mere extension of his body.

On the landing stood the apple basket with his Ma's dresses. Once his eyes had fully adjusted to the moonlight, he picked it up and carried it back down to the kitchen, placing it by the door so that he'd remember to drive it over to the Daleys. Despite being quite full, the basket wasn't at all heavy.

Imagine, thought Larkin. These clothes had once been a part of his Ma. She wore them to church and round the farm, and wore them when she was reading or cooking or working in her small garden. These dresses shared her life and knew things about her that Larkin didn't know. They hid letters in a pocket. They sat at her writing desk. They touched her. And now they were empty, just a bundle of scraps for a community quilt.

How did something so personal become reduced to being of such little value? It was like dying. When you're all done with your own body, how does it become such an empty thing so quick, so lacking in energy and life?

He reached down and picked up the dress at the top of the pile and held it to his face. The scent of her was long gone. If anything, the dress smelled musty and needed the dust shaken out. Mrs. Daley could deal with that, he reasoned, maybe give them a good wash before they were cut up and sewn into a patchwork. He knew it was foolish, but he pressed the dress to his lips before replacing it in the basket. Feeling like he was saying goodbye to a final piece of his Ma, Larkin stood beside the basket for a moment with his head bowed. Then he turned away and walked slowly back upstairs. His bad leg was aching; he gripped the railing as he shifted his weight to his good one.

Entering his room, Larkin moved to the window, pulled back the twill curtain, and sat down upon the bed. The moonlight created a brightening that left only part of the room in shadow. Slowly, almost meditatively, Larkin's hands reached up to unbutton his plaid shirt. His fingers felt each button as they performed their slow task. There was a rhythm to the unbuttoning. Grasp, tip, slip, pull. Grasp, tip, slip, pull. He slid off his leather suspenders and shimmied out of the thick cotton shirt, letting it fall backwards onto the bed. Next, he unbuttoned his trousers, the stiff canvas lined with soft flannel, and raised his bottom slightly so that he could ruck the pants down his legs, leaving them in a heap on the floor. Then he sat motionless in his woollen underwear and socks, listening to the wind as it whooshed on outside.

He hadn't intended for thoughts of Paul to follow him upstairs and into his room, but thoughts of Paul were there. Those pages from the letter, however little they contained, had brought everything to the fore. Larkin trembled slightly with agitation. The room was cool; he shivered. "Someone walking across my grave," he said to no one. He reached across to the iron bedstead and pulled the spare quilt that was folded at the foot end. Shaking it out, he draped himself in the patchwork and pulled it snug against his body. This quilt was an old postage-stamp pattern that his Ma had made with the church ladies at a quilting bee. Larkin liked it in particular because he could recognize pieces from an old shirt of his Pa's and a piece of dress material that had been his Ma's. In a couple of places, the shirt and the dress had been stitched together side by side, and Larkin had always thought as how perfect that was.

He stood up, carefully adjusting the quilt around his shoulders, and situated himself in front of the window. Moving the curtain more fully aside, he could see across the dormant fields to the woods. He knew that through those woods and across the creek, if you kept walking, you'd find the edge of the marsh.

There was good duck hunting down there in the fall. His Pa would often retrieve his gun from the barn, stride through the woods with Larkin till they reached the bog, then squat down in its tall grass to take his shot. But after the summer when he was eleven, Larkin began coming up with one excuse after another for not going. His Pa never pressed him on the matter, although Larkin was sure he'd figured something had put him off the marsh. He'd get a strange look on his face whenever Larkin said as how he'd forgotten a chore or needed to finish reading for school and wasn't for joining him.

Once, he saw his Ma and Pa exchange a private look between them—a tilted head and raised eyebrow on his Ma's side and that twisted, worried frown on his Pa's—but they never questioned him. Sometimes Larkin thought it would have been a relief if they had. Several times he found himself holding his breath, waiting for the question to come. Wishing they would ask. He knew his resolve would finally give way. So, he'd hesitate on his way out of the room, waiting for them to press him. But they never did.

If somehow his Pa *had* ever pried the story out of him, he thought his life might have turned out different. Been lighter maybe. But behind that thought was the memory of his cold fear: that even his Pa might turn from him in disgust. That the story would come out. That he'd be called "unnatural" or a "sodomite." And that Paul would be hanged, and maybe him, too. And so, the opportunity for absolution never came, and that afternoon, like the night of the fire, would beleaguer him like a haunting for all of his life.

Names had their own power, he knew. Larkin remembered a long-ago afternoon recess when the McCormick boys were chasing the Quinn girls, pulling their plaits and running after them with jeers and taunts. Not knowing what "dumb dogan" meant and too embarrassed to ask anyone at school, Larkin had asked at supper that night.

"Pa, do you know what a dogan is? The McCormicks said it today."

"Well, son, it's hurtful. It's what some people call Roman Catholics."

"But what does it *mean*?"

"I reckon it refers to the Irish, by folks who resent them taking work away. It's foul business the fighting between Roman Catholics and Protestants."

"But we're Methodists, right?"

"We are. But Methodists are also Protestants, dear," his Ma answered.

"Why we called two things at once?

"That's a big question, Larkin. Maybe we should save it for another time."

"I'm just trying to understand, is all. Jeb McCormick said his Pa was Grand Master of the Orange Lodge and that's why he knew the Quinns was dogans."

"The Quinns are a good, honest, hardworking family, Larkin Beattie, and I doan want you to ever forget that."

"What's a Grand Master?"

"The Orange Lodge is a men's organization. Jake McCormick is their elected leader. They meet together and discuss things they think are important for the community."

"Did you ever go to the meetings, Pa?"

"No, son. Your Ma and I doan hold much with that sort of thing."

His Ma had brought a warm apple pie to the table with fresh cream and a little piece of cheese on the side. Larkin forgot his questions as he and his Pa dug into the pie, savouring the sugary cinnamon syrup and tender apple slices. His Ma's pastry was light and flakey and had once won a ribbon at the fall fair. Information about the McCormicks, and dogans, and the Orange Lodge would wait.

They never did take up that conversation again. But over time Larkin was able to compile more information from Thom Granger, whose Pa also belonged to the Lodge. Thom told him there was a wooden box inside the Roman Catholic church in Collingwood, and you took turns climbing inside it. When you came out you were scrubbed clean, outside and inside. Leastways that's what Thom told him, and Thom had heard it from his Pa. And Abe McCormick told Larkin and a group of other boys that dogans drank blood at church. Larkin knew Abe was a storyteller, but he seemed dead earnest and swore on his Ma's grave that it was all true.

Larkin was so curious about the wooden box that he once went so far as to climb the front steps of the Roman Catholic church. He stood before its thick oak doors, deeply carved with curlicues, for what felt like long minutes. But then he chickened out. Sunday school had instilled in him a fear of the devil, and he couldn't risk trespassing in a place where blood was drunk and people climbed into wooden boxes. It didn't sound fitting.

Sergeant Cian Quinn didn't really seem like a dogan, thought Larkin. He was particular about how he dressed and how he carried himself, and his Missus always seemed sociable. Still, their girls had strange names. One was called Roisin but was called Raisin by everyone at school. Her sister was Brigid, and the children called her Bridge. Their teacher, Mr. Braithway, would always address them properly, though. Ro-sheen, he would pronounce it, and Bridge-it. He was emphatic about enunciating things precisely. He tried to correct the class's pronunciation when he heard Raisin or Bridge being used, but the girls didn't seem too bothered and he eventually abandoned his attempts.

Larkin, too, had been teased about his name. He came home from school in grade five with a black eye once, having fought Bill Dempsey who kept calling him a meadowlark, cheeping and chirping every time he walked by. Larkin waited until after school and ran after him, swinging his books by their leather strap and clobbering Bill hard on the back of his head. They'd tussled and rolled around in the dirt, punching and kicking until Mr. Braithway heard the commotion and came running. When Larkin got home his Ma was mightily unimpressed to hear what he'd done, no matter the reason.

"Your name, Larkin Beattie, means 'silent warrior.' I chose it special. It does *not* mean reckless fool. Only fools try to settle things with their fists. I thought a son of mine would know better." Larkin had been so chastened that he promised himself he'd never raise a fist again. And he'd kept that promise, with very few exceptions.

In truth, it took a lot to rile Larkin. It had been a long while since something had angered him. In more recent years there was the time he'd thought about smacking the Reverend Baxter, but the time before that—the time he actually *did* land a punch—was when Joe Currie and Pauley got into a tussle playing softball at school.

Pauley was pitching. Joe struck out, and when he did, he threw down the bat and rushed at Pauley, yelling, "You throw like a girl!"

Pauley erupted in fury. "I'll show you I'm no girl!" he shouted. And with a glowering face and fists flying in a blur of rage, Pauley attacked Joe. Larkin was astonished—it wasn't like anything he'd ever seen before. The suddenness of Pauley's outburst was frightening.

Now the two boys were slugging each other something fierce. Larkin stepped in and took a shot at Joe, but his fist was off angle and it glanced away from Joe's jaw with not much effect. Joe swung his own fist right back, punching Larkin square in the nose. Then everyone got involved. Abe and Jeb McCormick tried to peel Pauley off Joe but he shoved them away and turned on them instead. He was wound up in a frenzy and cussed and clawed and snarled at all of them. And he continued to hit and kick and punch Joe with a rush of violent blows, even after Joe was down.

The boys stopped fighting when they noticed the blood streaming from Larkin's nose. Pauley stood over to one side, breathing heavily. Joe had pulled himself up and was crouched on the ground near Larkin, looking badly hurt and a little dazed. Larkin was vaguely aware of Abe and Jeb trying to stop the blood flow by jamming a handkerchief up inside his nose. He screamed at them to stop but even as he did, he swallowed a mouthful of blood.

He started vomiting, and now the puke from his stomach and the blood from his nose were all over the front of him. He was ashamed and embarrassed and in pain. Abe and Jeb helped Joe up and then offered to walk Larkin home. Larkin looked around for Pauley but he'd disappeared.

It had been a pretty serious hit: Larkin's vision went blurry, and for hours after he had one nasty ache in his head. The bleeding stopped after a while, but his nose swelled up and he could only breathe out of his mouth.

Once the swelling went down his Pa took him to town. Doc Mather had his Pa support his head while the Doc pinched Larkin's nose and pulled it up and back into place. It hurt like the bejeezus.

"I'm sorry, Larkin" was all Pauley said later. Larkin accepted the simple apology, seeing how bad Paul felt about it. But the unleashed fury he'd witnessed *had* frightened him, and he had cause to remember it a few years later, during the time of the inquest. As did the McCormicks. They hadn't been called to testify but their Ma knew the story and made it her business to tell and retell it, vividly relaying Paul's sudden, violent rage and in the process underscoring community opinion that Paul was just like the rest of the Skinner men, with a blackened heart and a woeful lack of remorse.

When Larkin returned to school, he received the ten smacks of the yardstick the other boys had already received. Mr. Braithway grimaced each time the stick struck Larkin's upturned palms, and even through the sharp flashes of pain Larkin could tell they were being administered by a man who did not relish the task. According to accepted practice, both palms were hit at the same time while resting on a table, meaning they were pushed downwards onto the hard wood surface for additional impact. The punishment was meted out at the back of the schoolroom as the other students faced forward at their desks, listening intently to each forceful strike. The room was heavy with silence as every child counted soundlessly to ten.

It was the only time Larkin had ever been caned. The humiliation burned worse than his hands and he felt his face and ears turn bright red with the disgrace. When he got home from school that afternoon both palms were so swollen that he couldn't hold a fork or a spoon. His Ma fed him some supper like a small child, the embarrassment of it only adding to his misery.

His Pa was angry when he saw the state of Larkin's hands. "I doan understand what hitting a young boy is supposed to teach 'em 'bout fighting," he said, "excepting it's all right for adults to hit!" His logic impressed Larkin. And as he walked upstairs to his room, he heard his Pa say, "I'm vexed, Ellen! I doan hold with beating children no matter how wrong-headed they been." That struck Larkin as all the more remarkable—he'd never before heard his father expressing anger. He'd get irritated when something broke, often just as he was starting to use a piece of farm equipment, but Larkin had never once seen him lose control of his temper.

He wanted to linger on the landing to hear what else his Pa had to say, but he knew being caught listening would not go well. Larkin went to bed that night with his throbbing hands laid on top of the coverlet, his mouth open and panting slightly from his damaged nose, and his eyes leaking tears, feeling as miserable as he'd ever felt in his life. But at some point, he woke up from his troubled slumber to feel his Ma bathing his hands in water with Epsom salts. He sat upright and watched as she wordlessly swished his hands in the enamel bowl. The warm water felt soothing.

His father came in and stood against the door frame, watching quietly as she patted Larkin's hands dry on a piece of soft flannel. Then he stepped forward and took the white enamel bowl from her, acting for the moment as her assistant. Next she drew some cotton strips from her apron pocket and dabbed on some rosewater from her bottle of scent. The faint summer fragrance infused the room with a sweet gentleness that made Larkin almost delirious with unexpected pleasure. His Ma wrapped the cotton around his hands into soft white padded mittens. Finally, both his folks said "Good night, son, sleep well" and withdrew from the room.

The next morning when he went downstairs to breakfast his Pa looked at him and said, "Larkin, I been thinking about planting tobacco in that sandy silt-loam out by the south fence, next to Currie's. Old Currie told me the seeds have to get sowed in April and I reckon we might as well work up a small strip to try. He had luck on his side of the patch. How would you feel about missing school and going to the co-op for seeds? I figure you can learn as much with me for a couple of days as you can at that school."

Larkin was astonished. His folks never let him miss school. "It's not like you can do sums or writing," said his Ma, nodding her approval. "You can't even hold a pencil." Larkin looked from his Ma to his Pa, and back again to his Ma. His folks were always like that, he thought. They'd never say they thought the teacher was wrong, but they'd show up in his room at night to tend to his wounds and find a way to keep him home safe with them for a spell. Larkin knew he was lucky. Not everyone had parents so kind. They were what his Ma said *his* name meant— silent warriors. That was it all right. His folks were silent warriors.

And they certainly had their share of battles to fight. The weather being their foremost concern always. Before turning in at night his Pa would scan the sky and try to read the portents. "Red sky at night, shepherd's delight" was only one of a handful of sayings that predicted weather systems. "Red sky in the morning, sailors take warning" was another. But there were many more. "Clear moon, frost soon." "The higher the clouds, the finer the weather." "Rainbow in the morning gives you fair warning." His Pa knew about the winds, too, often stopping his work to lift his head and sense a change in its direction. These were the adages Larkin knew by heart—for although he never understood the point of poetry-learning from books, his Pa's rhymes were practical.

There were many other things his Pa taught him, too. When spiders spin webs, there's a dry spell coming. Frogs croaking in the marsh herald rain. If the geese are honking in a low tone, foul weather's on the way. Dew on the grass means fine conditions and no rain. When ash trees bud before the oaks, there's a dry summer ahead. Thunder in December forecasts snow in seven days. This was the only learning Larkin wanted to master. To be a man like his Pa, striding across the fields, seeing mare's tails in the sky and knowing that wet weather was coming.

Larkin would follow his Pa around, squinting upwards at the clouds and pointing eagerly at patterns. "Is that fish scales, Pa? Is it a mackerel sky?" And once when his Pa stopped and looked where Larkin was pointing and agreed that the sky was indeed mackerel, they rushed indoors and Larkin felt he would bust with pride.

~

The wind had gradually picked up again while Larkin was looking out the window. There wasn't enough light for him to see anything much, but the air close to the window was frigid and he felt the chill of it. Long, loud gusts were now whipping around the corners of the house, beginning to screech and howl as they sped past. Larkin listened to the wailing with a practised ear. He ran through a mental checklist, satisfying himself that the horses were stabled, the chickens in their coop, the milk cows in the barn. Everything was in its place and safely secured.

He remembered a night, windy like this, when the sound of pebbles thrown at his window had wakened him. By that time, it had been a couple months since he'd seen Pauley, not since the Agricultural Society Fair. But somehow, he'd known, without looking, that Pauley had returned. Larkin got dressed as quietly as possible and crept downstairs. On his way through the kitchen, he snatched a bowl of leftover potatoes. Moving softly, he opened the kitchen door and stepped outside. Paul was standing close by waiting for him, fifteen feet or so away. Larkin's stomach went queasy. He felt suddenly that it was wrong of him to be out here in the night, meeting Pauley in secret. He should a woken his Pa.

Paul came towards him at once, taking the bowl and stuffing potatoes in his mouth eagerly. He looked like one of those men who tramped the country trying to find work. He had a black eye and fresh scrapes on his face. Larkin moved closer, close enough to smell something feral. An unwashed, rancid scent. The odour was so strong that Larkin could taste it in his mouth and swallowed a couple of times with aversion. "Where you been, Pauley?"

"Here and there. Been following the lines, doing some work for the railroad."

"You all right?"

"Yeah, I'm all right."

"How long you here for?"

"Only a night. Need to keep moving."

"Where you stay'in?"

"In your barn, if you say. In the hay mow."

"My Pa might see you."

"I'll be off first light."

"You could talk to my Pa, Pauley. He could help."

"I doan want him involved, Larkin. I wanted to see you, is all."

"You seen your Ma?"

"My Ma and sisters are living with my Uncle Roy. Over Angus way."

"How was that?"

"He wouldn't let me in. Ordered me off his land."

"What happened to your face?"

"Uncle Roy. I been hit worse."

Larkin reached out and took the bowl from him. "Lemme get you sumpen else to eat."

"Sit with me in the barn, Larkin. We can talk a spell."

Larkin shook his head. "Wait here and I'll get more grub." He darted away from Paul and through the door and back into the kitchen. His heart was beating hard, his breathing was fast. He couldn't tell if he was scared or excited. He went to the larder for slices of bread and a hunk of cold pork, grabbing a piece of cake on his way out. He took only a few things, hoping his Ma wouldn't notice. Holding it all pressed against his chest, he went back outside. Paul was standing by the door. Larkin passed him the items awkwardly.

Paul nodded in thanks. "I guess this is so long," he said slowly.

"I guess."

"You take care of yourself, Larkin Beattie."

"And you, Pauley. You take care."

And Paul had loped off into the wind, headed in the direction of the barn. Larkin hesitated, wanting to follow him but frightened. The sense that he was doing something to be ashamed of won out, and he went back inside. He put the empty bowl near the sink. He'd tell his Ma that he'd needed a snack in the night. That part was true. He just wouldn't volunteer *why* he needed it.

He tiptoed upstairs and back into his room then, standing in front of his window looking out. He wondered if Pauley was still out there, looking up at him. Larkin squinted, trying to peer through the darkness. Part of him hoped Pauley was safely bedded down in the barn while the other part hoped Pauley was there, watching for him. He lifted his hand up in a stiff wave, just in case. The wind that night continued its uproar as Larkin eventually turned from the window and lay down upon his bed. He fell asleep listening to the clamouring din, the sounds outside corresponding to the pounding inside his chest.

He slept lightly that night, waiting for the familiar noises his folks made while beginning their morning. Finally, he heard the creaking of the floorboards as they walked past his room and went down the stairs. He recognized the screeching of the kitchen pump and the squawking of the Findlay stove door being opened. His father would be blowing on embers, delicately feeding it thin skivers of wood. His Ma would be setting the table, placing bowls for porridge and a little jug of maple syrup. Larkin twisted himself groggily out of his covers and rose from his bed, surprised that his pants and shirt were already on. The events of the night came back to him then. He flushed with a sense of his own wrongdoing and went downstairs.

His folks were taken aback to see their son before they'd called up to him as they did every morning. "You're up early, son," his Ma greeted him. "Did the wind keep you up? It was blowing a gale."

Larkin nodded guiltily. "High winds." And then, remembering the bowl, "And I was hungry."

"I saw that." She smiled. "Growing boy."

Larkin studied her then, and thought how she was mighty pretty. Her hair was pinned up tightly in a roll at the back of her head. She wore a patterned work dress, light blue with white stripes filled with pink rosebuds. Overtop was her baking apron, a cotton smock that hung down to her knees. And she had on her black lace-ups. His Ma was smiling brightly as she moved deftly around the kitchen, making a big pot of tea, stirring the porridge, lining up baking ingredients beside a big mixing bowl.

His Pa, meanwhile, had gone outside to check for damage. Larkin waited for his return with a heavy heart. If he found Paul, he'd usher him indoors and ask Larkin why he hadn't told them of their visitor. He'd be called upon to explain something he didn't rightly understand himself.

"All's well!" called his father, re-entering the house. "A few things tossed around but no harm done."

"That's good, dear," Ma said happily. She poured him a cup of strong tea and set it down at his place on the table.

Larkin joined his Pa there, picking up his spoon to toy with. "Nuthin' strange then?"

His Pa looked up sharply. "Should there be?"

Larkin coloured. "Just wonderin'." He felt his Pa's scrutiny for a moment but then his Ma dished up the oatmeal and together they all began to eat.

Even now, all these years later, Larkin felt horrible about his deceptions. "A lie is an intent to deceive" had been ground into him. That first visit wouldn't be the only one from Paul in the long months since the fire and inquest. But Larkin had kept them all secret. He knew opinion in the community had turned against Paul, and he wasn't for putting his folks in an awkward position. Still, he wondered sometimes if they'd noticed the missing food, or worried about his suspicious behaviour. If so, they never said. Once, after another clandestine visit from Paul, he heard his Pa say, "A boy is entitled to his secrets as long as they doan cause harm."

Several times Larkin felt so bad about breaking trust that he *almost* told his folks about Paul's visits. But then he'd feel afraid all over again that the events at the marsh might also come out. He couldn't unburden *all* his wrongdoing, he knew that. His Ma and Pa were good people. He wasn't sure how they'd manage knowing their son was a liar and a sodomite. And that's not all I am, thought Larkin with disgust. I'm also a coward.

Paul's visits always came in the night. He turned up again about a month later. A skiff of snow lay on the fields; winter would be coming on soon. The ground was frozen and the almanac was predicting a heavy snowfall. Pa said as how the hair on the cow's neck had got thick and he reckoned that meant a cold, harsh winter. There were other signs, too: the bees taking to their hives early, the number of acorns on the ground. And his Pa had seen a snowy owl coming back early, in November instead of its usual January. It was a beauty of a creature; he and his Pa spotted it perched on the top of a tall tree when they were hunting.

The owl was also a hunter. They'd watched it swoop down from its perch, white with tawny markings, skimming the ground for a field mouse or small rabbit. It would snatch its prey using its tiny stick legs and long claws. Sometimes they'd hear a short, rattling cackle as it pounced but more often it was entirely silent, its wings creating only a slight whooshing as it cut through the air. Its economy of motion struck Larkin as a kind of purity.

Paul had spent two nights in the hay mow that visit. The first night Larkin didn't even know he was there, but once he did know, he was afraid Paul would freeze in the cold. Paul told him he'd burrowed deep into the hay, snug and safe. Still though, Larkin's worrying made him think about telling his folks. But that might mean having to confess about Paul's earlier stays. Murder was a shocking thing, unheard of in those parts until the Skinner fire. His parents would be compromised if they knew about Paul's visits. It seemed so complicated that, in the end, Larkin didn't tell.

He'd saved out a thick flannel shirt from the rag bag, one with a bad rip in its tail that his Ma told him wasn't worth mending on account of the collar being so shabby. She'd turned the collar and cuffs once already and said there wasn't enough left to work with. Having thought Paul might come again, Larkin had stuffed the shirt under his mattress along with two dollars saved from helping the Curries with their haying. So, when the familiar scrabbling of pebbles woke him, he dressed, bundled the flannel shirt and the coins into his own shirt front, and went down to the kitchen. Looking around furtively, he seized upon a plate of tea biscuits under a cloth, taking six and rearranging the remaining ones so that the plate wouldn't look so empty. There was a pan of cornbread covered with a tea towel and he cut a small piece of that for good measure, wiping the knife and carefully putting it back in the drawer.

Paul was standing outside, shivering in the damp. Larkin walked with him to the barn and followed him inside where the heat from the cattle had created a warm fug.

"You been to Angus again?"

"I tried. Old bugger set his dog on me. I had to move quick. I'd teach him a lesson or two if I could." A look flashed across

Paul's face as though a deep black shadow had crossed over, hardening his features and the set of his jaw. It was a dark expression, filled with hatred and rage. "I just wanted to see them and talk awhile. The dog bit me good."

He pulled up his pant leg to show Larkin a nasty mess. The dog had torn at the flesh, leaving a thick flap of skin and tissue covering a deep lesion.

"We need to clean it," Larkin said. "There's iodine Pa uses on the cattle. I'll get it." He retrieved the bottle, found an almost clean rag that he soaked in the solution, and applied it to the leg. Paul winced at the pain but did not cry out. Larkin bandaged the leg as best he could, using another strip of rag to tie it snugly over the crude dressing. "You need a doctor, Paul."

Paul had taken the biscuits and cornbread from Larkin and was shoving them in his mouth ravenously. When he was done, he wiped his hands on his pants and said "Wish I had sumpen to drink. I'm dry as dust." Larkin looked over at their milk cow and Paul followed his glance. She'd been milked at six that evening and would be milked again at six in the morning. Maybe they could get something out of her, though. If they took too much milk she wouldn't produce in the morning and his Pa would know something was amiss. Reluctantly, Larkin stood up and looked for a container. The milk pail was in the house.

"Ain't no pail, Pauley."

"That's okay, I doan needs one." Pauley approached the side of the cow gently, being careful not to spook her. He picked up the milk stool and sat beside her, patting her side and talking softly. Then he blew on his hands and rubbed them together. The cow began to wave its tail. Larkin recognized the signs of threat.

"Pauley no—she's gonna kick!"

At that same moment Paul reached forward and grasped one of the teats. The cow skittered away and made some breathy sounds, kicking a hind leg up so forcefully that Paul fell backwards off his stool. It might have been funny had it not been so serious. A cow kick can smash a man's pelvis and leave him crippled. Paul and Larkin looked at each other gravely before Paul clambered to his feet.

Larkin pulled out the flannel shirt and coins and passed them wordlessly to Paul. "I best go. You take care now."

"I ain't never gonna forget you, Larkin. You can count on that."

Larkin hesitated, then turned to face his friend once more. He was alarmed when Paul moved towards him and pulled him into an embrace. Larkin stiffened and went to pull away but Paul held on to him firmly. Larkin fought against the intimacy, holding himself rigid. Then he felt a sudden surge of emotion and pushed apart forcefully.

Paul grabbed hold of his arm. "Stay with me awhile, Larkin."

"I can't, Pauley."

"I don't got nobody but you."

Paul hung onto Larkin's sleeve but Larkin twisted out of his grip, turned, and ran back to the house as quickly as he could. Safe inside the kitchen he stood still, breathing hard, waiting for his breath to level out before he went upstairs. He took a biscuit from the plate as an afterthought. He would eat it in bed. He wouldn't be completely lying if his Ma asked him about the missing biscuits.

To his utter mortification, his pecker had gone hard when Pauley had embraced him and it still hadn't subsided. He grabbed a towel from the washstand in his room and quietly rubbed himself.

At breakfast the next morning, his Pa was troubled. "Footsteps all over," he said, "leading right up to the house and barn. Must have been a tramp around in the night."

Larkin looked down at his oatmeal. His Ma spoke then. "You hear anything, Larkin?"

"Doan think it," he mumbled, taking the opportunity to gulp some tea. He thought his parents were both studying him but he didn't allow himself to look up.

"Larmer told me he saw a tramp moving around these parts two days ago," continued his Pa. "Ain't that much distance between here an Larmer's."

Larkin remained silent. He felt his ears burning red, giving him away, but he was trapped by his earlier mistruths and couldn't now confess. The scene in the barn filled him with shame. He wondered if his parents had puzzled something out. His Pa might manage somehow to forgive him, but he was unsure of his Ma's response. The idea that she'd be disgusted by him, and that he would read that in her face when she looked at him, was just too awful to contemplate.

He was not yet fourteen. His Ma still embraced him gently at bedtime, kissing him on the forehead and calling him "my man-child." With the farm requiring so much of their time and energy such tender displays were not overly frequent, and so they meant all the more to Larkin.

Larkin thought back to an evening just after the fire. He'd been upstairs in his bedroom and Pauley tucked in on the settle in the parlour, when Sergeant Quinn had come around to interview his Pa. Quinn had a sonorous voice that resonated in his barrel-shaped chest; he always seemed to be bellowing. As a result, a good deal of his questioning carried upstairs and Larkin could make out much of the conversation. Although his Pa's voice was strong and low, it was a softer timbre, so even when Larkin strained to hear he couldn't catch all of his Pa's answers.

"So, it was that you and your boy discovered your upset horses and decided te investigate?"

The response was partly muffled. "We woke up… and… flames… tried to do what we could…"

"And what time of day would that be, now?"

"After we been…"

"And so, you're after saying that you went outside te milk and weren't aware of te fire?"

"We were… horses… and… put in… supper… and bed."

"And how long was it you been abed when te fire woke you?"

"I said as… long…"

"So, you're saying now it was after ten when you dressed and ran to te fire, was it?"

"Yes."

"And your boy was already awake and dressed, you say?"

"My son... ready... together... we ran... saw..."

"So now, you and your boy went upstairs at nine, and woke again and got dressed at ten, is it?"

"Yes."

"It was eleven now, was it when you woke and ran te Skinners?"

"I already answered... why are you..."

"And the boy already dressed, would you say at eleven?"

"How do you dare... what on... you must... time to leave."

"Calm yourself, now. There's no reason at all, at all te suspect your son. I'm away after knowing where everyone was when te fire itself started. I'll not be after the boy, yea. Lessen there be cause."

Larkin was filled with dread and a terrible sense of foreboding. The shock of it all was still fresh; the acrid smell of smoke still lingered on his skin and hair. He lay in bed waiting for the inevitable. Despite his words, Sergeant Quinn would soon come upstairs and arrest him. He and Pauley would both be sent to jail. They'd be sentenced and hanged. All of their shameful secrets would come to light. He began to cry. Quietly at first but then deeper, gut-wrenching sobs that he did his best to stifle in his pillow. He curled into a ball and snivelled and blubbered, trying mightily to choke back his pent-up emotions and fear.

At some point, his Ma came into his room and sat on the bed beside him. When she pulled him onto her lap as if he were a small boy and not the lanky young man he was, he leaned against her, shaking with the trauma and awfulness of what he'd witnessed yet straining still to stop his tears. She kissed the side of his head repeatedly, patting his back and making shushing noises to comfort him.

His Pa came in after a time and sat in a chair by the desk. "It's all right, son," he intoned. "Everything will be sorted and put to rights." But this made Larkin cry afresh. He knew that some things could never be put to rights and that even his Pa couldn't undo what had been done.

And yet, as in the way of such things, in the weeks to come, the rhythms of the farming community resumed. People were drawn once more into the routines of their days. A farm in late summer, after all, is a greedy thing, demanding complete devotion. Those who lived their lives on its soil understood what was needed and bent to their labours. And so it was that, despite the shock and the upset of the Skinner fire, the community gradually shifted its focus to all that the earth required.

It had been a good growing season, and now many farmers were toiling steadily to take off last cut. Larkin loved haying even as he knew it would leave his arms and shoulders fiery with aches that wouldn't be soothed. The sweet smell of the cut was like a perfume to him, the back-breaking labour immensely satisfying. He'd stop a spell, look back across the field, and feel a sense of accomplishment. His Pa drove the horses while they pulled the mower with its revolving reel of sharp blades. Larkin followed along after with a scythe, swinging it expertly in a steady rhythm as he walked. Since the mower would often miss great swaths of hay, it was Larkin's job to cut down what remained. He and his Pa would welcome a breeze whenever it came.

On occasion, his Pa would hire day labourers to assist them. This was especially helpful when the weather was uncertain. Racing against the wet was always their biggest worry. If the rain knocked it down before it was cut, the hay would be ruined. Not only would the mower and scythe have difficulty cutting but wet hay was prone to moulds and would soon be spoiled for anything much. Larkin liked having extra men around the place, particularly when they were forking the cut hay into stooks. On those days his Pa would guide the horses pulling the wagon while Larkin and the men raked and shaped the stooks. The efficiency of the coordinated labour, the constant hurt in his arms and shoulders, the perspiration dampening his shirt—all of these things contributed to Larkin's sense of well-being. He made himself believe that the horror of the Skinner fire had somehow been a bad dream and that this scorching exertion was his only life.

But visions of Silas's dead body often appeared to Larkin unbidden. The sight of him lying still on the barn floor, a look of surprise and rage on his face, his eyes wide in anger. This was the picture that repeated itself and tormented him. Silas lying on his back, blood seeping from his wounds, making thick puddles on the floor. Paul holding the sheep shears, breathing heavily after his frenzied attack. Larkin staring at him dumbly, as though hypnotized. A drip of blood creeping down one of the blades, forming a perfect drop suspended on a sharpened steel point before finally falling in slow motion and landing in the dirt with the tiniest sound, a few tiny particles of dust bouncing upwards. Silas's trousers still unbuttoned and his pecker hanging out, a lifeless, vulgar reminder of his misdeeds. In his rage Paul had stabbed his father's groin and while the boys watched, the front of Silas's trousers had darkened with wet.

Larkin would squeeze his eyes shut, willing the picture to leave. He'd shake his head, trying to erase the scene from his memory.

The earlier picture—Paul, red-faced and furious, attacking Silas in a whirl of rapid thrusts—was just as horrific.

Larkin taught himself to focus on something pleasant, to call up a happy memory that would replace the horrible ones intruding upon his peace of mind. Sometimes he'd recite the twenty-third Psalm.

Larkin had long since figured the unfolding of events were an inevitable end to Silas's dissolute life, to his cruelty. But since the night of fire, he had never enjoyed a true heart's ease. Nightmares, spells of panic, and recurring flashes of memory plagued all sense of tranquility and well-being. He was always waiting to be exposed, shadowed as he was by the sinister events he bore as a private affliction.

As was his practice, Larkin now steered his mind back to a more pleasant time. One of the last big harvests. He went back to that. He remembered how on a mid-morning his Ma would walk out to the fields carrying a basket filled with mason jars of

cold water and thick slabs of bread heavily buttered. He and his
Pa, and any of the other men there to help would crowd around.
His Ma was a fine baker, but there was something about eating
fresh bread in the out-of-doors that made it taste even better.
She'd stay only as long as it took for the men to finish, and then
she'd go back inside carrying the empty basket. Later on, she'd
ring the triangle outside the door real loud and they'd know it
was time to go in for lunch.

Harvest meals were always hearty, with liberal portions. His
Ma said as how they "needed to keep their strength up to work
hard." Bowls of hot potatoes and a cooked ham or roast would
be waiting for them at the table. And there were always pies.
Apple mostly, but sometimes rhubarb or berry. Larkin's Pa was
proud of the spread she put on and would encourage the men to
"have another plate." Larkin liked that his folks were generous.
He'd relax into the familiar banter and goodwill, pushing aside
his flushes of anxiety. Then, when the men had their fill, they'd
tuck in their chairs and thank his Ma politely before returning to
the fields.

After the harvest was in, their church would organize a beef
supper attended by the whole community. Even the Roman
Catholic Quinns would come. There were thick slabs of beef,
scalloped and mashed potatoes, peppery brown gravy, and all
manner of preserves and pickles. Mrs. McCormick was famous
for her horseradish; large bowls of it were set out on the tables.
Once, when Larkin was very young, he mistook it for mashed
potatoes and helped himself to a big spoonful. He nearly coughed
out a lung, the heat of it taking him by surprise. For years afterwards he'd be teasingly offered horseradish at the suppers. "Have
yourself a helping of this, son, we know it's your favourite,"
they'd say, or "Larkin, have you tried the horseradish? It'll blow
out whatever ails you." For dessert there was a pie and cake table;
you could take your pick from a wide array. The women would
watch over their offerings carefully, discreetly competing to see
whose pies went first, and whose cakes.

That first harvest after the fire had been no different. On a
Saturday night he and his folks climbed into the wagon with his

Ma's pies, a pot filled with mashed potatoes wrapped in a quilt to keep in the heat, and a heaping platter of sliced roast beef. They drove to the supper, held that year in the upstairs level of the Dempseys' new barn. The location changed every time, each family taking their turn. Rough plank tables had been set up inside, where the women buzzed about setting out the food and organizing the buffet. Each family brought their own plates and cutlery and drinks. Most also brought blankets or chairs so they could find a place to sit down and eat. The men would take their plates outside and stand around together in a large group while they had a good chinwag.

This was Larkin's first time at the supper since leaving school. By rights he should have been with the men, but he felt awkward walking up to them in a silent declaration of his new status, intimidated as he was by the thought of their teasing. But neither was it fitting to stay inside with the women and little ones. So, Larkin took his plate off on his own, looking for a place to settle.

He found a lonely spot behind the barn, near the field where the wagons and horses and a few carriages were tied up—an out-of-the-way corner where he wouldn't be judged unsociable. He had no real desire to be sociable anyhow, so the solution suited him.

After a few minutes he heard voices and realized that three or four men had congregated around the corner of the barn, quite close by, sharing a flask away from the prying eyes of the women. Larkin heard their conversation and flushed deep red at their words. He couldn't get up and rejoin the others without either crossing in front of them or climbing a fence and walking through a largely fouled pasture. All he could do was stay still and hope they'd move away first.

"Quinn reckons the boy had help. Couldn't wrestle his Pa and his brother on his own."

"Maybe it happened to one first and then t'other."

"Doan think it."

"Who is Quinn thinking?"

"The Beattie boy. They been good friends an live close by."

"You doan say?"

"The Beatties are fine folk."

"Paul's too much a runt to manage on his own."

"Underfed."

"Silas never was over generous."

"God-damned bastard is what I heard."

"He was all right. A mean drunk is all."

"Who used a belt and fists on his own kin."

"My Ginny said the youngest was a quick lad. Good at book learnin'."

"The older one was a dullard. Couldn't read or make a mark for his name."

"Does Quinn have proof?"

"Naw. He says he knows it all right but canna prove it."

"You can know a thing without provin' it."

"Not when it comes to murder. Men hang for murder."

"Would they hang the lad, you think?"

"Yep. In Toronto."

"You think it's gonna come to that?"

"If'n Quinn finds the proof."

"I heard they keep the idiots in that Toronto jail."

"No. Separate building."

"Any chance Paul didn't do it?"

"Naw. No chance t'all. According to Quinn."

"An the Beattie lad?"

"Looks like."

Larkin had heard enough and more than he wanted. He picked up his plate, put the cutlery in his shirt pocket, and slowly crept away from the voices towards the paddock. He'd climb the fence and face Dempsey's bull rather than be caught in a compromising position or hear any more. His face was burning and he felt strange, sharp twinges in his chest. I'm too young for the angina, he thought. But his breathing was laboured, the pains continued, and he broke out in a sweat across his forehead and under his arms. His skin meanwhile had begun to prickle, as though a ribbon of ants had taken to walking up and down the length of his arms.

He'd heard of the Toronto jail. There was a picture of it in the paper once. A fortress-like building. "A building that people walked into and were carried out of." That's what his Pa said. Would Pauley be sent there if the truth came out? Would *he* be sent there too, alongside of him? Did they hang boys trying to defend themselves? These questions made Larkin feel worse. He picked his way around the cow pies and made his way back to the open side of the barn. His Ma saw him climbing the fence and waved at him merrily. His first thought was, How can she look so happy? Doan she know what people is sayin' about me? He wiped his boots as best he could on the dead grass and went to join her.

"Why, Larkin, you look feverish. You all right, son?"

"I doan feel too good."

His Ma reached out her hand and felt his damp brow. "I'll find your Pa and get my things. You wait in the wagon."

He was so relieved to hear the suggestion that he almost wept. He readied the horses and lay down in the back waiting for his folks. It wasn't hard to convince them that he was ill. He was sorry to have cut short his Ma's pleasure, but what he'd heard had so rattled him that he could barely maintain any sort of composure. He closed his eyes and feigned sleep as they set off for home.

"Did he eat sumpen gone bad?"

"I don't know." His Ma sounded worried. "He was in a real sweat."

"Dint see him at dinner. Where was he off to?"

"I didn't see. His friends I suppose." His Ma paused. "Was there any talk?"

"People reckon it took two killers."

"What do you think?"

"Can't really say. It makes some sense. But who?"

"What are folks saying?"

"That there's one logical choice."

"We gots to put an end to such talk."

"I can only do what a man can do. Cian Quinn is running things."

"Edgar, this is terrible. They can't really think it."

"Ellen, we've had a nice time. Let's not fret lessen we need to."

Larkin kept his eyes pressed tightly closed, but he still couldn't stop the tears from streaking down his face.

Larkin felt the pins and needles for weeks after. Jumpy every time someone or something startled him. Feelings of breathlessness and terror rising up and choking him at all times of day and night. He tried to keep what he believed were fits of angina to himself. He didn't want his folks dragging him off to see Doc Mather.

The Doc had been present the night of the fire. He'd seen Larkin when he came to treat Paul. And his was one of the voices Larkin had overheard talking outside with the men.

Doc Mather had penetrating blue-grey eyes. They were always intense. They'd look you up and down like you were missing your skin and they'd take in the measure of you deep inside. Larkin had known him all his life. The Doc had helped to deliver him, actually. Before the fire Larkin had never had misgivings about him, but since then he wasn't for letting anyone in close.

~

All this remembering was making Larkin restless. He didn't feel he could settle at anything much. No point trying to go to sleep, he thought. I'd just be laying there stewing. With a sigh, Larkin turned from the window, reached for his pants, and went back downstairs. He unhooked his jacket from its peg and lit the lantern again. Stepping outside, he walked smack into the still increasing wind and staggered a bit while finding his footing. Finally, more from habit than any sense of purpose, he headed to the stables. The horses nickered softly as he approached.

"Nuthin' fer ya right yet," Larkin whispered as he hung up the flickering light, "just some lovin'." He stood before Culloden, caressing his favourite's nose and scratching his ears. As the wind battered angrily against the wooden structure it creaked and shivered against the onslaught. Cold drafts whistled through the cracks and joinings. When Culloden inclined his head towards Larkin, he bowed his own head slightly so that he might rest alongside the horse. They stood together like that for some long minutes while Larkin calmed himself and Culloden waited patiently for further attentions. Then, patting him abruptly, Larkin broke the gentle spell and strode past the stalls to the little tack room at the end of the building.

Larkin looked around the panelled room with satisfaction. This was his special place, a source of some pride. Ribbons from multiple horses, spanning over twenty years of shows, were tacked up around the top of the walls. Flashes of red and blue and gold satin were briefly illuminated as he held up the lantern. Larkin circled the room thoughtfully. Waxed and polished saddles rested on thick pegs jutting out from the wall. There were three of them. Not much used but well made and well maintained. He ran his hand over the taut leather. The bridles, stirrups, reins, halters, and bits were all meticulously organized on other wall pegs. Horse blankets, fly masks, and grooming tools were stored neatly in the deep wooden chests lined up along one side of the room. Everything had its place. The room smelled of leather and wax and straw dust and horse sweat. Blended altogether, the aroma was pungent and rich and comforting. Larkin breathed it in deeply, relaxing his shoulders and sighing just a little.

Steadying the lamp, Larkin shoved the table to one side and knelt down awkwardly on the hard floor. His fingers, now thick and stiffened by age, prodded the edge of the planks. Brushing aside some grit, he felt along the edge of a short length until it reluctantly gave way and tilted upwards in his hand. Then he leaned forward, set the board aside, and reached into the exposed crevice, withdrawing a bundle carefully wrapped in oiled cloth.

Larkin stood up slowly, balancing himself against one end of the table. He turned to place the package on the table's rough surface. Untying the twine with a deliberate, almost reverent touch, he pulled the loosened piece gently through his fingers, letting it fall in a coil. Then, pinching the folds of fabric with care, he pulled them open until the cloth lay flattened before him. A dirty metal device lay exposed in its centre. Larkin stood back from his work and eyed it with distaste. The rusted piece of flat steel wasn't quite a foot long and was bent in half, each end shaped into a once-sharpened triangular blade. A thick, dark streak of blood had hardened along its sides.

From time-to-time Larkin tried to convince himself that the fire had never taken place, that it had all been one long, bad dream. The sheep shears were proof otherwise.

He'd brought them back from the Skinner place the night of the fire—had picked them up and run home with them in a panic while Paul was still shrieking. The sounds Paul had made didn't make words that Larkin understood. Everything seemed foggy and disconnected. Only later, would he remember some of the things Paul had screamed. The air outside had been welcome, he remembered. He'd taken deep gulps of it while he ran.

The horror of the events had terrified Larkin. It couldn't really have happened right there in front of him. Running felt like the only right response. And as he ran, he imagined he was watching himself race down the Skinner drive and across the road, cutting towards home. Home was what he needed to focus on. Getting home. But when he saw his house, he stopped running suddenly and looked around, feeling dazed and strangely exhausted. Instead of going indoors or seeking his Pa he stood there stupidly wondering what to do. His stomach and innards had begun to heave. Finally, he dashed to the privy. He'd barely seated himself when his bowels loosened and a strong stream of diarrhea passed. He sat there perspiring, breathing hard, panicking. He was afraid to get up. He was afraid to stay. Strange tingling sensations were running through his extremities.

When at last he stood up, he was shaky. His legs felt unsteady, as though they couldn't support him. He grasped at the board wall for balance while he wiped himself and then pulled up his trousers. As he did, he looked down and saw the shears. His first instinct was to pitch them down the hole. Then he hesitated. He was finding it hard to think straight. Maybe he needed them—maybe that was why he'd brought them along? Yes, he decided. He maybe needed to show them to his Pa. He sat back down in a quandary, feeling confused and sick.

A couple of loose floorboards lay by the door, away from where the deep hole had been dug. His Ma had mentioned they needed a nail. He stared at the boards. Then he bent down and pried up a strip of wood before slipping his hand underneath and feeling the solid ground an inch or two below. The shears would fit. Grabbing a couple of pieces of paper, he wrapped the shears loosely and slid them into the opening. They'd be safe there till later. Until he could show his Pa.

What he needed to do was find his Pa. But the awfulness of what he'd seen and done completely panicked him. Something so horrific had transpired that Larkin knew that even his Pa couldn't fix it. Paul's rage had staggered him. He felt dazed, and didn't quite believe what had just transpired. He tried to think but nothing seemed clear.

Then, when he did see his Pa, he struggled to find a way to begin the telling. There were the horses. The horses were upset. He said that much.

Later, when he and his Pa had been running towards the fire, Larkin's heart felt like it might burst right through his chest.

After that, everything happened so quick. Paul was burned and staying in the parlour. And when they were alone in the room for a moment Paul had locked his eyes on Larkin's and said, "You can't tell anyone or I'll hang." By then Larkin was so over-wrought that he was struck dumb. It wasn't a decision so much as not having the power of speech. The words simply refused to be spoken. So, the days passed and he kept silent. And while his folks saw that he continued to be mightily upset, they reasoned it was the trauma of the fire and didn't press him.

Every time Paul was alone with Larkin he reinforced his message. "My life is in your hands, Larkin." "You gotta promise you'll never say." And despite Paul's suffering his words felt menacing and further upset Larkin. He could only nod silently, overcome once more by the enormity of what they concealed.

Larkin took a couple of steps away from the table and studied the shears without picking them up or touching them. Finally, he stepped forward again and rewrapped them in their covering, being careful not to touch the surface. He grimaced in concentration as he completed each step: retying the string, bending once more to the floor, replacing the bundle in its hiding place, returning the board to its spot, sweeping grit and straw and dirt over it, shifting the table back into its place.

Sheep shears were common enough farm tools to have around, even though the Beatties did not keep sheep. Shearing events were held every spring and he, like the other local boys, had learned to wrestle sheep between their legs, pressing them against their own torsos while they took the shears and inserted them deep into the fleece, cutting quickly as they held the struggling animal. It was important to shear them before the hot days of summer came; otherwise, the sheep would sicken from the heat, or pests and maggots would lodge in their fleece, burrowing inwards. Lanolin would drip from Larkin's clothes and body afterwards. His legs and arms would ache from the bruising the struggling animals caused.

The sour smell of up-close sheep was rank; it would leave Larkin feeling nauseated until he could scrub the stench from his body. Traces of lanolin wouldn't be so easily washed away, however. He'd have to scour his softened hands with an old potato brush in an effort to dispel the last traces.

The annual Collingwood Agricultural Society Fair always had a timed sheep-shearing event, but Larkin had never entered. He knew he wasn't as quick as the other boys and had no wish to make a spectacle of himself. Besides which, he found the entire event unpleasant, particularly when the sheep were nicked by the sharp blades and bled profusely as a result.

Larkin stood still in his tack room, listening for the wind. All was soundless. He'd fitted the wooden boards snugly. Even the ceiling was double-panelled—he'd ordered the pine especially from the Hamilton Brothers over in Glen Huron. While most of the farm's outbuildings were made of rough-hewn hemlock, he'd paid extra for these fine finishing panels. Pine was soft and had knots aplenty, but it came in wide widths and was quick to install. He couldn't remember the extra it had cost but he was glad he'd spent the money.

Leaving his little sanctuary, Larkin stepped into the wide corridor bordered by stalls on one side and open pens that held bedding and feed for the horses on the other. The air felt several degrees chillier here, the tremoring of the wooden walls suddenly palpable. They groaned and whined as the wind outside continued its assault. Larkin loved the sense of enclosure the building provided. There was something rare about being safely sheltered while the gale raged. He thought of Pauley, sleeping in the barn in the cold of winter, nestling deep into the mounds of hay for warmth. And the baby Jesus who was born in a stable and who would also have experienced this singular feeling. It wouldn't be such a bad thing, really, to be born in a stable. Larkin debated curling up on the pile of straw and spending the night with his horses. At the last, though, he decided he was still too restless to settle. And so, shielding his lantern again, he made to return to the house.

He slipped out quickly, the door slamming hard behind him, banging open a little and then closing again with a loud crashing. He worried that it might splinter in the wind's attack and looked for a rock to keep it pressed shut. Bent into the wind, he stoop-walked and stumbled in the dark to the nearest fence bottom, feeling about for the largest boulder he could manage. His lantern blew out in the siege. Struggling under the weight of the rock, he tottered blindly back to the door and placed it into position. Then, as he fastened the latch, he listened for, rather than saw, the effect of his labour. The wind continued its battery but now the door didn't move as much in response, slamming softly against the frame. Although it grieved him, he would leave the lantern outside and look for it in the morning.

Still beset by the weather, Larkin felt his way back to the kitchen entrance. The door was pulled forcefully from his grip as he opened it. Grasping it again with both hands, Larkin stepped inside and then pulled it closed behind him. Gusts of cold air followed him indoors; he stood still for a moment, waiting for the warmth of the house to embrace him. Moving to the stove, he opened its door and shoved in a handful of kindling along with a couple pieces of cordwood. Then he reached up to the wall-mounted match safe and swiped a match on the striker plate. Cupping the flame, he extended his hand inside the maw of the opening, lit the kindling in two spots, then tossed the match towards the back of the stove. Finally, he shut the door, leaving it open just a crack for air intake while the fire caught. Then he sat down again.

How many times had he performed this task? How many times had he watched his Ma light the stove? How many times had he seen his Pa at it? A simple thing really, lighting a stove. The repetition as much a part of his life as it had been for his folks. In fact, much of his life was shaped by the very same routines and occupations. Feeding the chickens was the same now as it had been forty years ago. Weeding the tobacco was the same. Picking rocks the earth heaved up each spring was the same. Beating the weather at harvest was the same. His life was made up of sameness. He'd never done but a few things in his whole life that were different from his folks, and those things were the ones he regretted.

His mother would have liked another woman around the place and some little ones. She'd hinted so, lots of times. It was a disappointment to her that Larkin never married or had a family. She said once as how she didn't want him to be alone when she and his Pa passed on. Larkin had laughed and said, "I'll have the farm and this house to keep me so busy I won't hardly have time to notice." That stuck with him, though, her worrying about him.

His Ma was like that, always thinking about others. She'd been upstairs laying in her bed, shrivelling up like a wasted thing, and there she was, grabbing his hand and worrying about *him*. Larkin was almost twenty at the time. She worried about his Pa, too. Kept telling he and Larkin how to look after each other and how to turn out biscuits. She wrote down the baking instructions in a hand so shaky they couldn't make it out but Larkin treasured the paper anyway, knowing it were a final offering of love.

His father had moved himself to a spare room when she got sick. He stayed using it after, not wanting to go back to the room where she'd suffered. Theirs was a fine double-sized room at the front of the house, with two windows and an iron bed with brass finials. His Ma had loved that room. When she took sick, he and his Pa had carried up two pink chairs from the parlour and set them down beside her bed so that they could sit and visit. Later, his Pa carried up the tea table and it quickly became covered with powders, drops, and the tiny vials of medicine left by Doc Mather. They kept a jug of cold fresh water there, clean glasses, and an enamel bowl for when she needed to retch.

In only a matter of weeks the cheerful, sunlit room was transformed into a medical hall. The smell of liniment and stale bedding and bodily odours made for a choking, cloying combination. The windows were kept shut to prevent drafts, the draperies pulled tightly closed. Layers of blankets and quilts were piled on the bed because she was always cold. Women from all around took turns sitting with her, bringing with them pots of hot broth and bowls of pudding. When they arrived in the morning, clucking cheerfully with forced good spirits, Larkin and his Pa would cease spelling each other off and would return outside to engage in work that had its own rhythms. Work they understood, it was something they could control.

They seldom spoke of the disease as it took its course. There wasn't any point. They both knew what Doc Mather meant when he said "It's not good, Edgar. All we can do is keep her comfortable." His Pa had gone into their room that day and shut the door. After a minute, the Doc and Larkin heard a deep sob. It wasn't right to listen, so they both went outside. Larkin walked Doc to his buggy. Doc Mather put his hand on Larkin's shoulder and looked at him steadily. He wasn't foolish enough to say anything; he just nodded. Larkin nodded back and that was all.

Larkin had found the scrawled recipe tucked in the family Bible several years before; his Pa must have slipped it inside the front cover. Holding the precious scrap of paper in his hand had brought back a number of memories. He remembered sitting at the kitchen table with his Ma, a quart jug of maple syrup centred on the table. The syrup was their own, tapped from the bush lot. His Ma took a pan of biscuits out of the oven and poured a cereal bowl half full of the syrup. Then she passed Larkin a biscuit to dip into it. He ate three biscuits before finishing the syrup, then rubbed his forefinger along the bowl's inside rim to make sure he hadn't wasted any. His Ma had smiled indulgently.

He also recollected how light his Ma's biscuits were. He'd had boughten biscuits from the bakery and café since then but they were heavy and sat inside him like solid lumps. "Your biscuits could float in the air if you tossed them high enough." That's what his Pa had always told her. And she could whip up a batch faster than most folks could set the kettle to boil. Someone once said, "If Ellen saw a buggy on the road, there'd be a pan of biscuits in the oven before company made it to the door."

Larkin had once retrieved her instructions from the Bible and placed them on a cupboard shelf where he kept clippings from *The Murton County Chronicle* his Ma had saved out for one purpose or another. One was a column on "The Treatment of Choked Cattle"; this made Larkin smile. Another was a recipe for Sponge Cake. His Ma had drawn a small star at its top with stick lines: eight of them, intersecting in the middle of the star, making sixteen spokes. He wondered if this was significant. Would fourteen or twelve or ten spokes be less of an endorsement? There were so many things Larkin wanted to know but had no one left to ask.

He'd stared at the Biscuits recipe, trying to decipher what struck him as code.

Biscuits
Flour, 3 t-cups
Despn powder, 6
Hot stove/grease pan
Butter — 1
Cream — 1-2
Make dough, cut bake gold
Pinch salt

Larkin had reached into the cupboard and withdrawn the chipped teacup he'd seen his Ma use as a measure. After some long consideration, he decided that a Despn was a dessert spoon and not a soup spoon. The amounts of butter and cream were a mystery. He attempted a guess and used a pound of butter and two splashes of cream. The mess that ensued was nothing like the shiny dough he remembered her working with. Deciding to add more cream, he succeeded in flooding the mix until it was a soupy consistency that would not be moulded or cut or shaped into anything. When he scraped the bowl out for the chickens, they stepped around it disdainfully. It lay untouched on the ground until it gradually seeped away.

The failed biscuit experiment had left him feeling despondent. The promise of his Ma's biscuits had excited in him a craving for what had once been a household staple. He couldn't picture a time when there hadn't been biscuits in her kitchen. Thinking of those warm biscuits, hot from the oven, dripping in light golden syrup, made his mouth water. He closed his eyes to summon the look of his Ma smiling at him, flour on her apron front and sometimes a light dusting on her cheek or forehead, flushed from the heat of the stove.

Missing things was now the way of his being. Missing things and missing folks. He'd thought once or twice, when he was still young, about how he was missing out on marriage. Most of the men his age were settling down, building houses on the home farm, having children. Larkin had been in no hurry, assuming the time would come and everything would happen the way it was intended.

Before that, for no reason he could understand, there'd sometimes be a stirring inside and a longing for something he didn't have.

The stirrings weren't the sort of the thing he could ask his Pa about. And they were surely not something he'd go to Doc Mather for. The Doc might say as what was going on was unnatural, meant to happen only in wedlock. And then the Doc would figure out Larkin had done something dirty to unleash such things. Just thinking about it made him wonder about his time with Pauley, and that just made the stirring worse. He was certain he was bound for hellfire.

But instead of going away, the stirrings just got stronger. When they started to happen regularly, Larkin got worried that something unpleasant was swelling up on his insides and would cause certain damage to his waterworks. Then one Saturday, back when he'd just turned nineteen and was driving the buggy to Collingwood for supplies, he went by a row of boarding houses at the far end of the north side of town. There were women dressed in brightly coloured robes and cheap finery sitting on the front steps, calling out to passersby. They clearly weren't decent folk. He'd been in town enough times with his Pa over the years to deduce that these women were the town Jezebels. Larkin had never been to a house of ill repute, nor did he know anyone who had, but the idea took hold as a way of fixing things. He decided that the next time he came to town he might investigate their services. No different maybe than hiring out a bull or renting a ram, he figured.

His visit to #256 Cardigan Street was uncomfortable. He'd left the wagon and horses in town and proceeded north, sure that every passerby knew where he was going and judged him for it. He walked briskly with his head down, cheeks, ears, and throat flaming. There were a number of houses in the row. He sized them up critically, finally choosing the one at the farthest end of the short strip, and the only one with no women sitting outside on the wooden steps.

As Larkin passed the other houses he was beckoned inside with invitations to "come and visit." The words were innocuous enough perhaps, but when spoken by the rouged, scantily clad women they were almost enough to ruin his resolve. When he reached the last house he hesitated on its steps, wanting to turn and run but embarrassed to do so with the female onlookers casually observing him from next door.

He rang the bell—a large brass dial that spun easily at his touch—and was startled by the shrill *burringing* sound that repeated loudly. The door was opened by a dark-skinned man wearing a formal black suit, bow tie, and white gloves. Larkin stepped away from the door, sure now that he'd made a grave error.

"Welcome, sir. Please enter," said the man, moving aside as Larkin's feet mysteriously obeyed and carried him across the threshold. The finishings inside were fancy and lavish. A figured brown carpet was lush underfoot; dark green wallpaper adorned the walls. Oversized ferns on tall marble columns were stationed against the walls. Larkin followed his guide to a small parlour where he was asked to take a seat on a low padded bench.

"Two dollars for a song, a whisky, and a girl," intoned the solemn domestic.

"Is there a choice?" stammered Larkin.

"A choice of girls or whisky?"

"Girls," came Larkin's croaky answer.

"I bring four and you choose one."

Larkin nodded. He dared not speak again for fear that only further croaking would sound. The man disappeared and returned a few minutes later, followed by a selection of candidates. The first three were dressed flamboyantly in feathers and ruffles. They wore heavy makeup and sported elaborate hair arrangements. Larkin slumped in disappointment. Such foreign-looking creatures held no allure. He shook his head.

Then a fourth, a youngish woman nearer his own age, entered the room and stood silently for his inspection. Her hair hung down in soft brown curls, her face was clean-scrubbed and natural, her dress a simply cut blue gown. Larkin nodded and stood, withdrawing the money from his pocket and holding it out. The coloured man took it from him and left the room, shutting the door discreetly.

Larkin remained standing, waiting for an indication of what should happen next. The girl poured him a whisky and brought it to him before sitting down at the piano. Neither spoke. She began to tinkle the keys, only once glancing over her shoulder. Then she turned back to the keyboard and played a medley of tunes that Larkin had never heard. Some snatches were fast and happy, others slow and melodic. Her playing seemed accomplished to him; he watched her small, fine hands stroking the keys with gentle confidence. For the briefest of moments he imagined his mother's hands, thickened from years of hard work, playing a hymn in their parlour, her body bent towards the keys, coaxing out the spiritual notes.

The girl ended the performance and closed the lid, breaking Larkin's thoughts. She moved towards the door. Larkin followed her down a short hallway, up a narrow, carpeted set of stairs, then into a little room. He shut the door behind him. He felt a familiar stirring, and watched her eagerly.

Afterwards, as he lay facing her exposed back, he traced his finger along her spine, feeling the rising of its succession of knobs. Her curves were pronounced, her movements practised, the taste of her skin salty where she'd perspired a little. The experience was not entirely unlike his one previous encounter.

She dipped a large sponge into the wash stand that stood in a corner of the room. Then, while he lay still on the bed, she leaned over him to wash his privates. Her breasts with tiny reddish nipples swayed a little as she moved. He watched as she cleaned herself next. He wanted to take the sponge from her and gently touch it to her curves and private recesses. Just watching her unclothed while she patted herself dry stimulated him. She smiled when she saw his arousal but then turned away modestly and dressed behind a screen.

Later he would reflect that the entire interaction had been wordless. He hadn't even asked her name. Driving back to the farm, he wondered what she was called: Ruby or Sapphire or Emerald or some other fancy made-up name? Or maybe it was a

simpler one that suited her. Lila, or Beth? But would a Lila or a
Beth know how to clutch at him, he wondered, and make those
sounds while he moved inside her?

That was why, he thought, that was why you trusted some
things to professionals. He decided that he felt only relief. Larkin
took this as further proof of his moral failings. Still, he was so
grateful to know that all his parts worked as they should that he
whistled a tune, one from the piano playing, while he drove
home.

Larkin saw Doc Mather's buggy when he arrived back at the
farm. He left the horse and wagon in the yard and rushed into
the house, then followed the sound of voices upstairs. His parents' bedroom door was closed.

Larkin went back down to the kitchen and paced while he
waited for his Ma or Pa or the Doc to come down. One of them
must have been hurt, had an accident, burned maybe on the
stove, or fallen down. One of them had been in trouble while
he'd been in Collingwood, drinking whisky and investigating his
abilities. Shame washed over him in waves.

After some long period of waiting, with Larkin's nerves jan-
gling, the impatience and worry choking him, Doc Mather came
downstairs with his shirtsleeves still rolled up, carrying his black
case. His father followed shortly after. They both acknowledged
him with a cursory look.

"What's happened to Ma? Is she all right?"

"She had a spell, Larkin. One of her coughing spells. But she
lost her breath altogether and had trouble. I went for Doc Mather
when she recovered."

"What caused it? Is her cough worse?"

His Pa sat down on a chair. "We doan know, son. Doc needs
to do some tests when she's stronger."

Larkin looked at Doc Mather. He was rolling down his shirtsleeves and reaching for his coat, his movements unhurried and
methodical. Larkin watched him for a reassuring sign or signal, an
indication that things were not as serious as they seemed. Sure,

Ma had been coughing for some months now, off and on, but it came and went and didn't seem so bad.

"I'll take my leave now, Edgar. Larkin." The doctor nodded at each of them in turn.

"I'll walk you." Larkin's Pa stood up to escort the Doc to his buggy. Larkin watched them out the kitchen window. His Pa wouldn't have gone for Doc Mather unless he'd been genuinely worried. Ma wouldn't be upstairs in her room during the day unless she was quite ill. These weren't good signs. But Ma was strong. He couldn't remember a time when she'd lain in bed while he and his Pa were up and working.

His father came back into the kitchen. He was rubbing his right hand through his hair and scratching the back of his head—another sign that Larkin recognized. It was the same thing he did when the weather was changeable and the crops were at risk.

"Pa, what is it? What does Doc Mather reckon?"

"We won't know for sure, not till the testing's done."

"He must have an idea."

"Yep. He does. He reckons it's a tumour of the breast." His Pa coloured a little just saying the word.

"A tumour? How would that make her cough?"

"I doan rightly understand it, son. Apparently, there's a kind that grows and gets itself attached to other bits. She'll have to go to the hospital in Toronto to be sure. There's doctors there who know about these things."

Larkin nodded quietly. The news was a blow. The shock and the grief of it settled on him like a heavy coat. He felt his shoulders slumping under the weight. He looked down, avoiding his Pa's face. He couldn't bear to read what he might see reflected there.

The weeks and months that followed were taken up with her worsening condition. Larkin felt he'd somehow triggered his Ma's disease by his act of depravity in Collingwood. Although it hadn't seemed so at the time, he now felt fouled by the pleasuring. He tried to dislodge the thought of it, but a recurring sense of responsibility and guilt filled him along with the self-loathing he always carried. If he'd come straight home from doing his chores maybe he would have been the one to find her. Or maybe he could have gone for the doctor and Pa could have stayed home comforting her. Or maybe she'd still be fine and well and not paying the price for his sinfulness.

Doc Mather made the arrangements. His folks took the train to Toronto and stayed in a hotel; his Ma spent a day in the hospital being examined by a specialist in tumours. They came home three days later. When Larkin picked them up at the train station he saw at once that his Ma was exhausted. Pa lifted her down from the train and carried her to the buggy. Larkin followed with their carpet bag. He didn't ask any questions or attempt to make conversation. He saw that she'd fallen asleep against his Pa, who was cradling her securely.

The ride home was bleakly quiet. Larkin looked over at his Ma, still curled into Pa. His Pa was studying her, tears wet upon his face. Larkin had been without them for three days and had looked forward to their return without dwelling on what they might have learned. But now his throat tightened with emotion. He held the reins firmly and fixed his gaze on the road ahead, avoiding low spots and trying his very best to stay away from anything that might jar the buggy.

That night, Larkin finished the milking on his own and was setting things to rights when his Pa joined him. Larkin stood still and waited for the words.

"It's tumours. Doc Mather was right. More than one."

Larkin swallowed hard, then gathered some spit. "What can be done?"

"There's an electric treatment where they stick needles in the tumours and run a current through. It works for some, they say."

"We gonna have it?"

"I doan think so. It has risks. Bad burns, for one. And since your Ma has more than one, there'd be too many needles. The doctors weren't for recommending it."

"They must have sumpen."

"They could operate. She'd have to stay in the hospital a month or more. They'd cut her open and try to cut out the tumour. They could get the largest one but not the others. It's painful and risky and your Ma already said she dint want it."

"If there's a chance it will help, we should do it, Pa!"

"And there's a chance it won't. What's for sure is that the pain will be extreme. They cauterize everything as they go. And she could die from infection."

"So, we're not gonna do anything?"

"Your Ma wants to put it in the hands of God, Larkin. That's what she said and that's what she wants. And I ain't gonna cross her will in it."

"So, what do we do? What do we do, Pa?!"

At this his father just shook his head and walked away. Larkin stood there absorbing the cruel reality of his Ma's plight. An image came to him then of his Pa standing at the rain barrel, his hands clasped together, concealing the limp body of a small drowned bird.

It was shortly after that when they carried the pink chairs up from the parlour. Doc Mather stopped by the house twice and sometimes three times a week. And although he prided himself on keeping up with modern medicine, he told the Beatties that in cases like this he was not opposed to local cures.

The first thing they tried was dock root, widely used in country medicine as a cure-all; Larkin gathered handfuls of the stuff. Then, following the careful instructions they'd received from Mrs. Fee, they boiled it until it was soft and used the boiled water to bathe the sore places. Pa did this. Larkin meanwhile mashed up the boiled roots into a poultice that his Pa took and laid on his Ma's chest. After trying the dock root for a month and deciding there was no real improvement, they cast about for another cure.

Doc Mather proposed bloodletting, and Pa reluctantly agreed. The doctor arrived with a glass canister filled with leeches. These were placed on the lumps in Ma's armpit, on the side of her neck, and on her chest. Larkin's Pa explained the procedure to him. His Ma felt weakened by the sight of the creatures feeding on her. Doc left them in place for several minutes and then held a lit match to their bodies until they curled up and he could pick them off. Ma was repulsed by the treatment and would not agree to having it done again.

Wild sarsaparilla was another of the country cures they tried. Larkin was directed into the woods where he found some near the wetlands, close to the river; he filled a basket with the root, leaves, and dark berries. Upon returning to the house, he passed his small harvest to Mrs. Kay, who'd learned the Huron cure from her grandmother. Mrs. Kay shooed him out of the kitchen while she prepared the concoction. Larkin was grateful for her help but anxious about the plant's efficacy. Specifically, what if the sarsaparilla worked? Very little of it was left in the moist woods where he'd discovered it. He could search further afield, but that would require yet more time away from the farm and his responsibilities. First frost would soon be upon them; the plant would all but disappear. What would they do if the sarsaparilla gave his Ma relief but could no longer be found?

He needn't have worried. It didn't work. The disease progressed rapidly and his Ma remained upstairs abed. Neighbours, friends, and folks from church came each day to help take care of her. Larkin and his Pa were grateful for such care but grew weary of the intrusion. The house had women coming and going from early in the morning until supper was on the table at night. They brought meals and baking, they took away the laundry, they tended to the weakening patient. The only thing they didn't do was allow the family any privacy.

Sometimes unmarried daughters were sent in to do light housework. The girls would flutter about importantly, showcasing their skills and attractions, but while Larkin was not immune to their charms he, like his Pa, was so despondent that he couldn't even acknowledge their efforts. His Ma would sometimes tease him when he visited her in the evening. "Did you see

Nora today, Larkin? She is a pleasant girl. She'd make a good farm wife, I reckon." But Larkin just smiled sadly, knowing in his heart that the only farm wife he could imagine was his Ma, hale and healthy again, at work in her kitchen or tending her patch of garden. The sight of all other women in the house only made him uncomfortable, as though his mother had already been dispatched.

His Ma was the one who ultimately resolved their situation. When it became clear that she wouldn't be leaving the earthly world immediately, she called the men to her side one night. "You remember the Barker girl, Annie? She used to help me sometimes with the butter and other chores. I like her. She's sensible and easy to be with. She's finished her schooling now. I want you to ask her family if we can pay to have her keep house and help with nursing. My friends have been good but they can't be spending so much time away from their own families. Edgar, you should drive over to Barkers and make the arrangements."

And that's how it was that Annie came to work at the Beatties. She would arrive at first light and leave when the supper was ready. She didn't need any direction, and would slip quietly around the sick room and the kitchen. One evening early on Larkin found his bed made with fresh sheets, clean ironed shirts hanging on hooks, and a basket of laundered personals set on the floor. It felt a treat to slip between the covers at night, the smell of fresh air lingering on the bedding. Food just appeared at mealtimes, and his Ma was well tended by Annie's clear broths and mashed-up pap. Now, with their new routines, his Ma seemed happier and calmer.

There was still the sense that his Ma had become communal property, with visitors pulling up at all times during the day. It was hard not to resent the moments of intimacy these women shared with his Ma. Larkin felt as though they were stealing away precious bursts of her energy and time. But they spelled off Annie, and Larkin found he could force himself to ignore the steady parade of daytime visitors as long as he didn't have to exert himself to be hospitable. Annie took care of ushering them in, monitoring how many visitors Ma received, and sending folks away when her patient needed rest. A semblance of equanimity was restored to the household. Larkin and his Pa once again adjusted to their new circumstances.

Larkin's Pa didn't like Annie walking the mile home at the end of the day and so had taken to driving her back in the buggy before he and Larkin sat down to the evening meal she'd prepared. While his Pa was gone Larkin would visit with his Ma, passing the time by filling her in on the day's labours. "You know, Larkin," his Ma said once, "it would be good for you to take a turn driving Annie home."

Larkin had been wounded, pierced through the heart, to think his Ma preferred his Pa's company over his. But the next night he said to his Pa, "You stay with Ma awhile and I'll take Annie." His Pa accepted the suggestion, going upstairs eagerly to sit with his wife.

After that Larkin drove Annie home every night—it became just one more of his chores. She was a quiet companion at least, and didn't prattle foolishly. Sometimes she'd make a small comment: "Your Ma took in a bowl of soup today," or "I thought your Ma had some colour tonight." Nothing to excite a real conversation. When she'd climb down from the buggy she'd look down at the ground and say "Thankee Larkin, for your trouble." Larkin would nod and drive quickly away home.

From time-to-time unsigned get-well postcards would arrive in the mail. "Imagine," wondered his Ma, "imagine who it could be, sending me such a pretty card and not signing it." His Pa would look at the cancelled stamp and try to identify from whence it came. Larkin coloured slightly to hear them speak of it. He was sure the cards were from Pauley.

They hadn't seen each other for two years by then. Not since their last encounter, when they were seventeen. Larkin shrank from the memory. But Paul must have forgiven him. He must have heard of Mrs. Beattie's illness and wanted to convey to Larkin that he was thinking of them. Having his Ma so unwell and his Pa so upended had left Larkin feeling alone with all his worries—and so the notion that Pauley was out there, somewhere close maybe, and knowing what was going on, was a comfort. In this way the unsigned postcards worked like a kind of magic for Larkin even as they were a mystery to the rest of the household.

Annie worked six days a week, with Saturday afternoons and Sundays off. She was paid five dollars every Saturday morning and the Barkers were to be given a side of beef in October. For the most part, Larkin and his Pa just abandoned care of all things domestic to Annie. Saturday afternoons and Sundays they'd spell each other off between their regular chores, scraping together meals and looking after Ellen. Annie always left prepared food for them, so it wasn't hard to manage. Pa in particular thought Annie was a blessing and would often extol her merits. To Larkin, though, she was merely a necessary fixture who did no more and no less than the situation required. He didn't have it within him to appreciate the ways in which she'd quietly stepped in and taken over those things that had been his Ma's.

It was only now, in these last years, that he'd come to fully appreciate Annie. It would have been convenient, he realized, if something had sparked between them. But Annie was reserved. She saw to her work. She never sought him out or drew his attention. Thinking back, he supposed she would have been a natural choice for a wife. The idea just hadn't occurred to him when they were young. And by the time his Pa died, eight years later, the two of them were so set in their ways that they carried on as if nothing much had changed.

Not for long, though. He was astounded when Annie told him one day that she was moving to Stayner to marry a widower with small children. "I always wanted little 'uns," she offered apologetically. Larkin had assumed that their arrangement would simply continue. He'd never thought she might want something more.

At George Larmer's wife's suggestion, Larkin hired a "widow lady" to replace Annie. Mrs. Harris set about reorganizing the kitchen to suit her needs. Larkin was distraught at this, but kept silent. Mrs. Harris attended to the basics of running the house with efficiency and determination, offering her views on such things in a way that intimidated him. After several weeks of her command-ing presence, she suggested that Larkin call her by her given name of Elsie and that she, in turn, would begin to call him Larkin. This final suggestion seemed overly familiar. Larkin panicked and ran from the room.

The string of housekeepers he found to replace Mrs. Harris were unsuitable to the point of being astonishing. He was certain that the younger, more foolish girls among them spread rumours around the country. Calling him eccentric, perhaps, or difficult, or hard to please. Word carried: the shrine-like conditions in which he left the parlours and his mother's bedroom; how he wouldn't let them dust her ornaments or discard any of her per-sonal effects. It choked him knowing the tales would be repeated, and repeated again, until everyone thought him a little queer in the head.

Larkin took comfort and solace in his horses. His beautiful stallions.

The beef herd had become too much work. When his Pa was alive, they'd gradually reduced the number of cattle they ran. His father needed to feel useful, and so continued to labour as he'd always done on the jobs that needed doing. But as time passed, he did so more and more carefully, his back stiff and his knees often locked. He started taking what he called his "after-noon reflections." A rest upstairs on top of the bed for an hour after his midday meal. The lengthening time of his naps seemed to correspond with the onset of weakened arms and an inability to pitch heaping forks of hay or straw for hours at a time.

Larkin had steadily taken on more and more of the heavy farm labour, leaving the lighter chores to his Pa. These changes crept up on both men until Larkin became the guide: setting tasks for the day, making the decisions, organizing the intimacies of their lives. Their livestock had always done well. The farm had a good reputation; they easily sold their cattle for top dollar. And so, Larkin and his father continued to make large, if infrequent, deposits in the farm account. Meanwhile the house had long since been paid for. And their expenses were modest.

Saving for a rainy day had always been taken seriously in the Beattie household. One never knew when the rains might come and ruin a harvest, when disease might blight the crops or spread through the cattle. All Larkin's life his father had held that it was biblical to be prudent about saving, insisting that the expression came from Proverbs. Larkin's Ma had smiled and refrained from correcting him. And so while bank deposits were made from time to time, withdrawals were frowned upon. They could always "make do" or "wait a spell." When a piece of equipment broke and needed replacing, a couple of animals would be sold off instead of dipping into their savings. Unlike many other families, they did not keep a tab at Mathison's Mercantile or at Harkin's Feed Supply.

Larkin's parents' way of conducting business was one of the many practices he continued. He paid cash for everything and set aside as much money as he could.

But one Saturday morning all that changed. Larkin had sold the last of the beef herd not long after his Pa had passed. He'd been living alone for nearly a year. The pair of drays were getting old; he had in mind to replace them with younger animals, and so he'd gone to Prenticeville for one of their regular horse auctions. Larkin was walking round the fenced enclosures when he noticed a beautiful colt. The animal was a sight to behold: shiny coat, flanks contoured beautifully, pleasing conformation, proudly held head and neck, prancing with a spirit and energy that seemed barely contained in his muscles and legs. Larkin had always liked horses, and had stopped to watch him. Somehow the power and life force in the creature made up for a small portion of the losses Larkin had sustained: Pauley, his Ma, and then his Pa. It was a lot to take in, so many leavings. And the colt... well, the colt just seemed like he needed space to run.

One colt became a steady succession of horses. And their care involved a series of pleasant endeavours that Larkin happily took on. Unlike the gruelling tasks associated with running a large herd of cattle, Larkin felt that the work he did for his horses was a type of privilege.

The cattle had been something else altogether. Larkin remembered his introduction to calving; he wouldn't have been more than five. It was a heifer, he learned, and her first time birthing. His Pa had laid down lots of clean, sweet-smelling straw for bedding. She'd been lying on her side and had struggled to get to her feet but then appeared to tire and lay back down on her side again. His Pa got excited when two feet emerged, but they were sucked back in directly.

Larkin stood on a wooden stool behind the enclosure, watching for the feet. They poked out, and went back in. The heifer grunted meekly while Larkin's Pa attempted to catch the forelegs with a rope. He'd just succeeded in looping the rope around the legs when, in a tremendous shuddering, it was drawn inside along with the forelegs. His Pa bent over the heifer, wrapped the length of rope around his waist, and walked backwards slowly. Shortly the legs reappeared along with the nose of a calf.

Now Larkin's Pa wrapped the rope more tightly, and heaved. The calf slid out, finally, with a loud bawling from the heifer. The calf was a dark, slippery-looking package, all slick and shiny. It began to unfold its bent back legs but then stopped and lay still. Larkin's Pa took a handful of straw and rubbed at the calf vigorously. Meanwhile the heifer bellowed deeply, lifting its head as if to eye the newborn. His Pa continued to rub at the calf and tried to help it stand. Despite his Pa's efforts, the calf collapsed beside him and made no further effort. The heifer likewise showed no signs of standing and continued to make distressing sounds.

"The calf needs colostrum," his Pa grunted. "I need it to feed." He picked up the calf and guided it towards a teat. The heifer grunted, and yet still made no attempt to stand. Pa held the calf in place, but it too seemed unresponsive. Finally, his Pa looked at Larkin and said, "You best go inside. Tell your Ma I'll be a while."

Larkin had walked back to the house all by himself, wondering at what he'd seen. The cow was hurting, he knew this. But the calf was the real disappointment. He'd expected to see a bouncy baby cow emerge. His Pa had said as how he could name it. The slime and gore and deep sounds had not been nice. He was glad to see his Ma in the kitchen and tell her about it.

"Sometimes it goes that way," she said, comforting him. "We can't always know how these things will turn out."

"Why?" he had asked in his innocence.

"That's just the way of it, Larkin. There's no real way of saying otherwise."

And Larkin had learned, over the years, that there really wasn't a better explanation. Sometimes a heifer was too heavy and sometimes she was too thin. Sometimes her pelvis was angled wrong. Sometimes when birthing she just up and died. It was a huge loss financially, of course, and the loss of the calf besides meant a double burden. But sometimes there was just no avoiding it.

Larkin had also learned over the years that things weren't always so different for womenfolk. Mrs. Duncan Stringer, for instance, never could bring a living child into the world. She carried them right through, but each time when the baby was born it refused to take a breath. Four, maybe five times it happened that Larkin knew of. His Ma probably remembered more details, but to him it just reinforced the truth of her prognosis. There was no real explanation for it. Just a lot of suffering and then afterwards a big disappointment.

Birthing wasn't the worst of cattle husbandry, either. To Larkin, dehorning was downright sickening. Every year, in late summer, the two-year-old steers were separated out and kept together in the front pasture, nearest the small barn. And that's when Doc Chester would come over with a couple of men. Larkin's job was to chase a steer through the chute that led into a wooden enclosure. "Har he comes!" one of the men would yell while the others, waiting at the end of the chute, readied themselves for the ensuing struggle. They'd pull the steer down to the ground as it writhed and kicked until they finally managed to tie its hock joints firmly together with a stout rope.

One year, back when Larkin was fourteen, Hank Burgess got himself trapped under a steer and was smashed up pretty bad. He broke his collarbone, dislocated his shoulder, and crushed his arm, all on the one side.

Hank's terrible screams of pain put Larkin in mind of a time he'd been in the woods hunting deer with his Pa. They'd been following multiple sets of tracks, and had seen among them the diagonal trail of a fox before coming upon its scat. When they bent down to look at it they could make out hair and tiny bones in the dark droppings. Then they heard the intermittent cries. They ran towards the sound: the fox, struggling in a trap, squealing pitifully. When they drew closer, they saw that the animal had been gnawing on its own leg, trying to get free of the metal clamp. His Pa shot it out of kindness. And that was exactly how Hank's screams sounded while the men worked to heave the steer off him, finally pulling Hank to safety.

While Doc Chester and one of the men looked after Hank, old Levi Davidson signalled to Larkin to come help. Larkin, not knowing what he was in for, walked around to where the steer was laying on the ground. Levi showed him how to hold its head down in the dirt while he picked up a small cross-cut saw and began sawing at its left horn. He set the saw blade close to the base of the horn, cutting close to the skull and carving the skin down a half inch or so at the base. But as he sawed with firm, rapid strokes, the blade got stuck a time or two. The partially removed horn spurted blood, shooting past Levi and covering Larkin in a fine spray. The steer was trembling violently, but it seemed to know not to struggle against the restraints.

Levi swore loudly as he worked to free a jammed blade, taking a few seconds only to wipe the blood spray from his face with the sleeve of his shirt. Finally the horn fell to the ground; Larkin saw that the thick shell was mostly hollow inside. Now Levi motioned to Larkin and together they heaved at the steer, rolling him onto his other side so that Levi could remove the second horn. It was a gory business. The feel of Larkin's blood-soaked shirt clammy against his chest was particularly disgusting to him. So when Levi was finished with the second horn, Larkin removed his shirt and used it to wipe the blood from his skin as best he could. The ghastly procedure was repeated again and again until all the steers were dehorned.

By the time he and Levi completed their work Larkin had developed a slight metallic tang on his tongue. He was certain that some of the spray had entered his mouth and that he was tasting blood. The smell of the bodily fluids—gore and urine and sweat and blood—had permeated the air and now the stink hung over them in a foul fog. The sight of so much blood traumatized Larkin in a way that no one would understand. It hadn't been two years since the fire. He had to steel himself not to vomit or panic. He could not afford to lose control with so many men around.

Doc Chester returned after some long while and informed the men that Hank had been taken home and Doc Mather sent for. Larkin eyed his Pa and saw that he looked troubled, both of them knowing that Hank would be no good for the fall harvest and that they'd need to work the Burgess farm as well as their own. That was simply the way of things.

Larkin watched as Doc Chester circulated among the steer, checking their heads and daubing the bleeding wounds with antiseptic. The animals were surprisingly docile after their dehorning. His Pa told him later it was on account of the trauma. He assured Larkin that they'd recover in a matter of days, that they were sparing the animals from a goring or a worse accident.

But the stench of so much blood pooling on the ground had set off the worst of memories for Larkin. The scent of a scared animal shitting itself, along with the smell of its fresh warm blood on top of that, is not unlike the reek of a man dying in his own shit with blood leaking out of deep wounds, all of it mixing with straw and manure and the stench of fear.

That night, alone in his bed, Larkin woke from yet another of his nightmares. He was trapped in a dark building, its floor slick with fluid. Trying to find a route out, not knowing what had happened, he tried to find his way in the blackness. In his hands was something warm and heavy, leaking thick blood down his torso and legs. But he couldn't find his way; there was no light and no sound and only the knowledge that what he was holding was now squirming and fighting him.

He woke up then, crying out. And his Ma was right there, stroking his forehead, murmuring comforting words, calming him down—just as she'd done the other times he'd awakened screaming in the night.

That first dehorning stayed with Larkin over the following days. He kept thinking with revulsion of the pink water in his washbowl when he'd cleaned up before bed. His face and chest and arms streaked with smeared blood. The shirt he'd been wearing: he'd silently passed it to his Ma that night. She'd taken it from him just as silently and put it to soak with some lye.

Goddamn steers, thought Larkin. Goddamn steers and their goddamn horns. "As long as I live," he said to the glass while he was soaping up, "I ain't never gonna do that again."

But he did. He had to. Every year when it was time, his Pa would make the arrangements and Larkin would work the chute.

A little later that same fading summer, long before she became ill and started her coughing, Larkin's Ma asked him to drive her in the buggy to a revival meeting. Normally this was something his Pa did. Couldn't *he* take her? Larkin tried to keep the desperation out of his voice.

But she wouldn't hear of it. She wanted *him*. His Pa had smiled—neither of them wanted to go but neither wanted to disappoint her, either. Pa didn't hold with the shouting and carry-on and Larkin didn't have the patience for the lengthy hymn singing. So Larkin had gone, just to please her.

On that evening, at the appointed time, his Ma came downstairs wearing a good Sunday dress and hat. The hat was a source of some amusement to his Pa. When she put it on you knew she'd shifted herself from being a farm wife to an upright woman seeking after righteousness—the very picture of serious, high-minded piety. Shoes tightly laced, striped dress neatly pressed, white gloves on, and that tiny saucer of a straw hat perched precariously on her head made for an intimidating presentation. Larkin knew he was in for a long night of it. He threw his Pa a quick pleading look before leading his Ma to the buggy. His Pa helped her up into her seat and then patted Larkin heartily on the back, grinning at him broadly.

The revival was at Larmer's place, just outside of Murton. The meeting was organized in the sheep pasture, the sheep having been corralled somewhere else for the duration of the three-day event. Buggies and horses had been tied up along the fence and crowds of people were walking towards an enormous tent erected on the far side of the field. Wooden benches and chairs had been set up in tight rows inside, and many attendees were carrying their own stools and chairs. Larkin remembered with a sudden twinge of concern, realizing that he hadn't brought something for his Ma to sit upon.

They entered the tent amid a throng of other people. The weather all week had been hot and humid; the ground itself seemed to be steaming. His Ma led him to the front of the tent where there were still empty places on the benches.

Sighing to himself, Larkin sat down beside her and tried not to peer around. His Ma was sitting perfectly still, her gloved hands holding her little handbag primly on her lap, her ankles crossed in a demure, ladylike manner. Larkin shifted uncomfortably on the hard bench. He felt cramped and claustrophobic. A rotund gentleman sat down beside him, his generously sized buttocks pushing against Larkin with a warm and heavy sensation. Larkin shifted slightly, attempting to rein in his legs and elbows in order to make room, but ended up crushing his Ma's skirt instead. She pulled it from under his leg and fluffed it out, mildly indignant. Larkin apologized.

The gentleman beside him was perspiring copiously, dabbing at his face and head and neck with a massive handkerchief. He waved this around rather indiscriminately, even brushing it against Larkin's face a time or two. Larkin recoiled in distaste, careful not to do further damage to his Ma's frock.

Suddenly his neighbour turned to him, his hand stuck out for a handshake. "Henry Hansen," he said. "Pleased to make your acquaintance."

"Larkin Beattie, sir. Same."

Henry's hand was moist with perspiration and left traces of wet on Larkin. Larkin tried to discreetly wipe his hand on his pant leg.

"Ever been to one a these afore?"

"Only once. A couple of years ago."

"Can't get enough of 'em. Been to one in Barrie last month. Heard tell Owen Sound was planning a big one. They fill me up, they do." Henry smiled happily at Larkin.

"I'm… uh… glad you enjoy 'em."

"I do, son, I do. Makes me feel so close to Jesus I could just shout, Hallelujah!"

And then of course, he did just that. Apropos of nothing, he stood up and shouted, "Hallelujah!!"

"I hear you, brother!" replied the preacher who had just entered the tent, wearing a shiny black suit.

Larkin looked at the preacher and looked at the suit and tried to puzzle out where such clothes might have come from. He'd never seen a man wear such a thing. Meanwhile Henry had stood up on the bench, teetering only slightly, and with his hands raised in the air had continued to shout, "Hallelujah, Jesus' name be praised!"

And the preacher had continued to shout back in response, "I hear you, brother. Hallelujah!"

Once more Larkin shifted uncomfortably on his haunches. He was being careful not to injure his Ma's dress but was holding himself so stiff and rigid that he wasn't sure he'd manage the whole meeting just sitting in one place. Henry had climbed down from his perch and thunked himself back on the bench, perspiring profusely, his chest heaving violently. He started using his handkerchief to fan the air around his face, brushing it across Larkin's nose from time to time.

The proceedings began with the preacher shouting "Praise the Lord!," a rallying cry he continued to repeat until the crowd thundered it back loudly enough to satisfy him—and apparently loud enough to spook the sheep in a neighbouring field: Larkin could hear faint *mehs* coming from outside the tent. A young girl in a ruffled violet dress was called up; she stood by the preacher and began to sing a rousing hymn. The audience sat quietly through the first verse but then, with great zeal, joined in when she repeated it. The hymn had only four verses but in this way each one was sung twice. When the final verse was finished the girl nodded at the preacher and sang it right through again.

She had a lovely light voice, although as the hymn continued into its third round Larkin thought he could hear her becoming a bit hoarse and faltering. The preacher, however, looked positively elated as she sang on. He stood beside her clutching an oversized Bible to his chest, his eyes closed, his face tilted heavenwards, rocking back and forth. Larkin assumed him to be deep in prayerful meditation but he rather looked as though he was rocking himself into some sort of private rapture.

Henry Hansen did not possess a melodious voice, or indeed one that could carry a tune, but his enthusiasm was unrivalled. He belted out the words, his arms straight up in the air, his hands opening and closing in a sort of spasmodic rhythm. Larkin kept himself stiffly apart, concerned lest the hysteria spread. When the hymn was finally over and the girl in the violet dress thanked for "sending joyous song and acclamation to our Father in heaven," the preacher himself began to give witness. He testified as to how the Lord God had worked miracles in his life, calling on him to travel the continent "preaching the word of God and claiming sinners for God's holy purpose."

Henry Hansen was now weeping loudly, using the self-same handkerchief to swipe away the tears streaking down his reddened face. Larkin tried hard not to stare. Instead, he searched the crowd for familiar faces, craning his neck to see who he might recognize sitting nearby, until his Ma reached over and gripped his leg with a white-gloved claw.

It seemed to Larkin that the testimony had ended, the preacher now outlining the ways in which he supported ministries all across the continent. Monies raised from today's offerings, for instance, were to be donated to a Widows & Orphans ministry. The location of the ministry wasn't specified, nor were any of the particulars. The thrust of the message was "God loves a generous giver." The widow's mite was mentioned, as was the good Samaritan, all of it rounded out with the rather menacing verse from Proverbs 21:13:

> *Whoso stoppeth his ears at the cry of the poor, he also shall cry hisself, but shall not be heard.*

Larkin listened politely, trying not to disappoint his Ma with another transgression. He couldn't quite help himself, however, and finally whispered, "It sounds like a threat the way he's putting things."

"Shush, Larkin," responded his Ma impatiently. "Don't be disrespectful. It's the word of God."

Fortunately, a break in the proceedings had been arranged, and Mrs. McCormick was introduced. She was sporting a new hat for the occasion, its profusion of silk flowers bouncing merrily on the straw brim as she stepped forward. Mrs. McCormick, a soloist in their church, had a distinctive, somewhat strained warble. As she launched into "Holy, Holy, Holy" the men began passing huge collection baskets up and down the rows.

> *Holy, holy, holy! Lord God Almighty!*
> *Early in the morning our song shall rise to Thee;*
> *Holy, holy, holy, merciful an mighty!*
> *God in three Persons, blessed Trinity!*
> *Holy, holy, holy! All the saints adore Thee,*
> *Casting down their golden crowns around the glassy sea,*
> *Cherubim an seraphim falling down before Thee,*
> *Who wert an art, an evermore shalt be.*

Holy, holy, holy! Though the darkness hide Thee,
Though the eye of sinful man Thy glory may not see;
Only Thou art holy; there is none beside Thee,
Perfect in power, love, an purity.
Holy, holy, holy! Lord God Almighty!
All Thy works shall praise Thy name in earth an sky an sea;
Holy, holy, holy, merciful an mighty!
God in three Persons, blessed Trinity!

Some in the crowd sang along softly but most listened respectfully as Mrs. McCormick executed her signature repertoire, after which she curtseyed awkwardly and returned to her seat. Larkin looked down at his feet throughout. He'd been privy to her singing often enough to know exactly what was coming: every time she sang the word "holy" she shook her head back and forth, creating a warbling effect and making her somewhat fleshy jowls flap. He didn't dare look up for fear of laughing outright.

The men carried the baskets forward to show the preacher— who began to remonstrate with the crowd, urging them to give more generously and to do without, all in the service of the Lord. The men proceeded to walk through the tent once more. Larkin watched askance as his Ma dipped into her handbag and deposited a further two dollars in the basket.

Finally, the preacher seemed satisfied, and commenced a protracted prayer of thanksgiving. "My brothers and sisters in Christ," he began, "had heard the need and responded to God's leading with open hearts filled with a generosity of spirit." There was much more about how earthly treasures were but dross in the eyes of God, but by that point Larkin had truly lost all interest. If earthly gifts were but dross, he couldn't help wondering why the preacher had insisted upon two pass-throughs. His Ma had donated at least four dollars, a not insignificant sum. Larkin wondered how his Pa would feel about that.

Raised voices and shouts of "Praise the Lord!," "The Lord's name be praised!," and Hallelujah!" began echoing around the tent. Larkin looked up in surprise. He must have dozed off for a moment. The girl in the violet dress was once more standing beside the preacher and had begun to sing "Just As I Am." Over top of her singing, people were crying and praising God.

Larkin watched as people rose from their seats and walked up the aisles to the preacher. After greeting them with open arms he placed his hand upon their heads, repeating loudly over the singing, "I claim you in the name of Jesus Christ our Lord and Saviour." Thus inducted, they returned to their seats with tear-streaked faces, shaking hands joyfully with those seated in the aisle as they walked past.

The white-gloved claw was once more on Larkin's leg. "You could go up too if you wanted," his Ma offered. Her imploring look took him aback. This, Larkin suddenly realized, was what she'd intended all along—why she'd chosen him to accompany her. Out of care and concern for his nightmares, she wanted him to go forward and to somehow be transformed.

He recoiled instantly and shook his head. She withdrew her hand. Had she guessed at his secrets? How much had she put together? Did she see he was in need of redemption and was trying to set to rights those things that should never have happened? Or had she come to believe that his frightening dreams were the devil's work?

Larkin was aware that his face and neck and ears had turned bright red. He could feel them burning. Suddenly the nightmare tight chest happened and he began to have trouble breathing. A large incursion of red ants began to crawl across his skin, but when he looked down there was nothing there—the feelings were inside of him, struggling to get out, clawing their way through his skin, trying to destroy him. He got up abruptly. "I need air. I'll see you at the buggy."

He navigated through the crush of people, shaking his arms and hands as though they were wet. Then, with giant strides and stopping for no pleasantries, Larkin pushed his way out of the tent and kept going till he reached the horse and buggy. There he threw his arms around the horse's neck and stood catching his breath, regulating his breathing with that of the animal's.

He was still standing there some time later when he heard a chorus of voices singing "Abide with Me." Straightening himself, he patted the horse and tried to focus on the words of the hymn.

> *Abide with me; fast falls the eventide;*
> *The darkness deepens; Lord, with me abide;*
> *When other helpers fail an comforts flee,*
> *Help of the helpless, oh, abide with me.*
>
> *Swift to its close ebbs out life's little day;*
> *Earth's joys grow dim, its glories pass away;*
> *Change an decay in all around I see—*
> *O Thou who changest not, abide with me.*
>
> *I need Thy presence every passing hour;*
> *What but Thy grace can foil the tempter's pow'r?*
> *Who, like Thyself, my guide an stay can be?*
> *Through cloud an sunshine, Lord, abide with me.*
>
> *I fear no foe, with Thee at hand to bless;*
> *Ills have no weight, an tears no bitterness;*
> *Where is death's sting? Where, grave, thy victory?*
> *I triumph still, if Thou abide with me.*
>
> *Hold Thou Thy cross before my closing eyes;*
> *Shine through the gloom an point me to the skies;*
> *Heav'n's morning breaks, an earth's vain shadows flee;*
> *In life, in death, O Lord, abide with me.*

To his great relief, his Ma was among the first to leave the tent three-quarters of an hour later. She came rushing across the field to stand beside him. "You all right, son? It was close in there."

"I'm fine, Ma. It were close."

They scrutinized each other uneasily before climbing aboard the buggy. The two of them silent all the way home.

That fall he and his Pa nearly killed themselves harvesting Hank Burgess's fields as well as their own. Hank did his best but his bashed arm never did heal right; he couldn't do much lifting or anything requiring a bit of strength. The damaged arm hung limp while he tried to do with one arm what he mostly needed two for. Larkin and his Pa felt responsible, and did what they could to make things right.

Larkin's body had ached, night after night, never resting long enough in his bed to recover by morning. Often his Pa would leave him alone at the farm while he rode off before dawn to the Burgess place. When Larkin had done what he could do on his own he'd ride over to join his Pa and the two would work side by side until dusk. They'd drive home together and discover that his Ma had fed the stock and milked the cows. For although she had a fear of all livestock, she knew, in the resigned, matter-of-fact way of all farm folk, that without her helping out, her men couldn't possibly get everything done. Larkin tried to do the heaviest jobs before he left for the day, but even though he rose earlier each morning and pushed himself harder, he didn't always have enough time.

Afterwards, the three of them would walk inside and eat a cold supper of scraps or a quick fry-up. That fall his Ma had no time for baking or putting meals together. They made do, knowing their debt to Hank must be repaid.

Still, it wasn't a grim time for all that. One evening Larkin sat at the kitchen table forking cold boiled potatoes and laughing at his Ma's story of how the chickens had been mean to her and chased her around the yard. His Pa was laughing so hard that tears trickled down his burnt face and he bent over, trying to stop the loud guffaws while attempting to look sympathetic.

Ma smiled and tossed a tea towel at his face, saying, "Edgar Beattie, you best stop making light of me. I was right terrified. They pecked at my leg and made it bleed... I was *very* brave!"

His Pa tried to compose himself but ended up biting the tea towel instead and hanging his head in mock shame, which made Larkin laugh even harder. The three of them were so exhausted and so sore that their laughter felt close to crying before they abruptly stopped and went upstairs to bed. Larkin heard his folks talking as they readied themselves. "I *was* brave, you know…" his Ma was saying, followed by something soothing from his Pa spoken in soft, low tones.

Third cut had been a worry. Although it was never as good a crop as first or second, no farmer would turn down the chance at a third if the season had been good and the weather permitted. And that year the sky had been mostly clear with ample rain the temperature hot. Still, Larkin's Pa said as how third needed to come off at Burgess's before they cut theirs.

His Pa used Hank's team of oxen and had most of it down by the time Larkin arrived. Hank was raking with one arm, attempting to make piles. Larkin, who'd driven the hay wagon and team over, began to follow Hank's progress, pitching great messy forkfuls into the wagon. They worked without stopping in the hot sun until Hank's wife came out with mason jars of cold spring water and hearty sandwiches with thick slabs of boiled pork. After that they worked past dark till finally the wagon was backed up the ramp and inside the barn. Hank said as he would take care of the rest.

Larkin and his Pa were grateful. It was near midnight before they made it home. They were just inside the house when a loud crack of thunder sounded. Larkin looked at his Pa, who just shrugged his shoulders. "If it's ruined and we doan get another cut, we'll be alright yet. The second was fine."

They climbed upstairs that night without even eating the meal Ma had left for them covered under fresh towelling. Larkin lay in bed listening to the thunder cracking like gunfire. As lightning illuminated his room with bright blue flashes, he counted the seconds between the light and the sounds, trying to estimate how far away the hits were. But he struggled to keep track and fell asleep without knowing the answer.

The next morning he overslept, and went downstairs to find that his folks had already finished breakfast. Larkin rushed outside and saw at once that the storm had done its worst. The crop lay flattened and ruined. His parents were walking down the drive towards the road where a couple of massive tree limbs were down, blocking the way. They were headed towards the damage, holding hands.

His memories of those days were scenes that Larkin could easily summon when he wanted to remember his Ma and Pa. Such intimate glimpses left him feeling deeply bereft.

The cattle they kept were Shorthorns. The breed came over from England and were dual purpose—good for both beef and dairy. They weren't the most attractive-looking of breeds, but they were even-tempered and that was something.

The first Thursday after Thanksgiving always marked the start of the cattle drive. Pa had dealt with the same agent, a man from Chicago, for close on twenty years, and Larkin felt that, despite his peculiar method of expressing himself, he was a man to be trusted. Mr. Wilkins had a way of speaking that, in Larkin's mind, was on the amusing side. He pronounced his sentences with extreme clarity and would use ten words for one, often choosing flowery, fancy words when plain ones would have done just as well.

Mr. Wilkins would arrive at the farm in late September and take a cursory look at the livestock. He wasn't one for walking across the field and actually putting his hand on a steer for close examination, however. He'd stand safely back on a dry patch of dirt and admire the animals from a distance. Larkin and his Pa both found the ritual ridiculous.

"Why, yes, sir, Mr. Beattie, those are some mighty fine bovine specimens. They are stupendous-looking beasts and have obviously benefited from your expert ministrations."

He was entirely serious in his manner, yet his appearance was not, as he must have intended it to be, quite as solemn. His striped trousers and waistcoat failed in their attempt to maintain upright lines as stripes ought to do. Instead, the strained fabric waved the stripes around a rather corpulent body, trying valiantly to cover the not inconsequential figure without splitting apart at the seams. Larkin would watch him breathing heavily in the warmth of the sun, the fabric heaving rhythmically.

After the cattle "inspection," they would all go inside to the kitchen where Mrs. Beattie would serve tepid tea with milk and sugar and huge slabs of pound cake. Mr. Wilkins appeared to relish this part of their transaction with the greatest of pleasure. He took his time. Finally, after some long period of eating and drinking, and with his Pa growing fidgety at the waiting, Mr. Wilkins would propose that they "commence with the proceedings and get down to the order of their business."

Larkin and his Ma would take this as their cue to leave the men to their negotiations. The number of head was decided upon, as was the price per head. Finally, the date for delivery to the train in Collingwood was established. These deliberations were fairly prolonged and, to Mr. Wilkins's great enjoyment, often carried until the next meal was served. With very little protestation, Mr. Wilkins declared that he "could surely delay his further business in the area to take in some much-needed sustenance, for, after all, the travel had been quite exhausting."

Larkin and his Ma would wait to hear the familiar phrase, and would stifle their laughter before re-entering the kitchen to prepare the meal. Then, when at length they had finally waved Mr. Wilkins away, the three of them would have a good-natured laugh at the agent's expense. And for days afterwards, whenever Ma called them to the table Pa would remark as to how "I could surely take in some much-needed sustenance," and they'd laugh all over again at their family joke.

With the date having been established for delivery to the train, Pa would set about hiring drovers to drive the cattle for him. Moving that much livestock over the course of several days was no simple undertaking, and his Pa believed in hiring experienced men with trained horses and dogs to do the work.

But when Larkin turned seventeen, he'd pleaded with his Pa to join the drive. It would mean sleeping in the open for several nights and living rough with the men, but Larkin was keen for the adventure and was finally given permission to go.

He enjoyed the first day out, riding in the crisp air while remaining at the back of the herd, watching how expertly it was being guided. They stopped late in the afternoon and found a place to set up camp for the night—a good-sized creek ran nearby and there was plenty of long grass for grazing. Once the cattle had been herded tightly together next to the creek bank, the drovers began organizing a fire to cook a meal. Larkin scurried around collecting deadfall and trying to make himself useful, feeling suddenly timid in the company of these seasoned men.

A couple of hours later, as they were finishing their supper of boiled potatoes, fried bacon, and bread, the cattle and horses shifted amongst themselves, signalling an interloper. A dark silhouette appeared in the gloaming, walking towards the group. "Sure smells good," said a voice approaching nearer. "Don't suppose there's any left?"

It had been three years since Larkin had seen him—three years since the coroner's inquest. But Larkin recognized the voice at once. He glanced up at the figure to confirm his instinct and then looked right down again, shrugging himself deeper into his coat, hoping not to be noticed. The men had been passing a flask of whisky between them and now it came his way; Larkin declined a drink, feeling suddenly uneasy in his own skin. Paul's presence made him feel vulnerable and exposed.

One of the men handed Paul a heel of bread and the nearly empty fry pan. "We're done eating, lad, but there's bread and drippings if you want." Pauley looked around the group for permission, seized the pan and bread, then sat down on the other side of the fire to devour what had been proffered. Then, when the flask went round the circle again, he took a long slug, wiping his mouth with the back of his hand when he was done.

Larkin finally allowed himself to look over. But when he saw recognition light up Paul's face, he looked down again immediately, signalling his wish to remain unacknowledged. For reasons he didn't understand, it seemed wrong to be sleeping rough with a group of drovers and Paul. Without knowing why, it suddenly seemed that their friendship should be kept secret.

When he woke in the morning, Pauley was gone.

"Thought as that one would have stayed for some grub afore he left," one of the men remarked.

"He was asleep by the fire last I saw."

"Must have had somewhere else to be."

"Did he say where he was travellin'?"

Larkin listened to the chatter but stayed silent. Out of nowhere a Bible story came to him, about one of the disciples denying he knew Jesus. He couldn't recall which disciple—was it Andrew, Thomas, or Peter? The details suddenly seemed important. He concentrated on trying to remember the whole of the story while they packed up their camp and prepared for the day's ride. Finally, Larkin mounted his horse and followed the others, the question of which disciple had betrayed his friend still niggling at him.

It was a cold morning, the dew thick on the ground but not yet icy. The men were shouting good-natured comments back and forth at each other, and Larkin, bringing up the end of the herd, smiled despite himself at some of the remarks.

"Get along you old doggy!"

"Over here, mother!"

"Move your precious arse this way!"

Still, Larkin continued to brood over his treatment of Paul. It occurred to him that this might well have been the last time they would see each other. Paul wouldn't risk returning to Cemetery Hill if he thought his oldest friend had turned his back on him. He hadn't come back for some time, as far as Larkin knew—Paul's dramatic collapse at the end of his testimony seemed to mark his finale, of sorts—but Larkin had never stopped wondering if he'd hear the sound of pebbles at his window. He felt sick now to think Paul might have felt rejected by him. As he rode along behind the herd he worried an old wound in the back of his hand, scratching the scab off and wiping away the minute drops of blood that slowly rose to the surface. If he *had* acknowledged Paul, Larkin reasoned to himself, the men might soon have recognized him as "the Skinner boy." That would not have been good for either him or Paul. And yet, chewing on the open sore, Larkin couldn't help feeling he'd done something cruel.

The anxious animal sounds, mooing and bellowing, snorting and grunting, along with the dull thundering noise of hooves hitting the ground created a punishing cadence that filled Larkin's head. He tried to concentrate on the animals, on the other riders, on the dogs. Instead, he found himself remembering other moments with Paul. Those private, innocent times before everything changed.

They left the cattle in a pen just outside of town. Mr. Wilkins met them there, expressing "his extreme delight and pleasure." Larkin had been given express instructions from his Pa to count all the animals carefully as they entered the feed lot, making sure no strays had been left behind and that the payment from Mr. Wilkins was for an accurate head count.

The drovers, once they were satisfied that the cattle had been safely accounted for and having been paid by Larkin, left for Collingwood, presumably in search of a drink and a comfortable bed. Larkin, anxious to ride home, managed to politely take his leave of the still long-winded Mr. Wilkins.

The ride back to Cemetery Hill was far faster than the three-day cattle drive. Larkin found himself looking around as he rode, searching hopefully for a further glimpse of Paul, rehearsing conversations in his head in which he explained why he hadn't acknowledged him.

None of these imagined conversations satisfied Larkin. Deep inside he felt certain he'd committed a grave betrayal. If that disciple, whoever he was, had stood up to the Romans and defended Jesus, maybe Jesus would have escaped with the others and stayed safely hidden. Maybe the brave disciple would have become a hero. And maybe if he'd introduced Pauley to the drovers they would have taken him in stride and not been bothered at all. Or maybe they would have put things together and known he and Paul were hiding deep secrets. Still though, Larkin reflected, most people are so caught up in their own stories that they only ever give passing thought to those they come up against.

It was to be the first of many drives Larkin undertook for the farm. As his Pa aged he grew less inclined to sleep out of doors and expressed himself grateful for Larkin's "young bones." And although Larkin became more comfortable with the drovers and familiar with the three-day sojourn, he was never fond of the trip, forever shadowed as it was by his shameful act of disloyalty.

Larkin remembered coming home after that first drive and asking his Ma, "Which one a the disciples pretended he didn't know Jesus?"

"I'm glad your Bible learning is taking hold, son," she replied. "It was Peter."

"Why do you think he did it?"

His Ma had stopped kneading the bread dough and wiped her hands on her apron. She turned to look at him curiously. "What a strange question."

"Just wondered, is all. Trying to make sense of it."

She nodded thoughtfully and watched her son while she replied. "Peter loved Jesus something fierce. He was a good friend and a faithful follower. His first name was really Simon. Jesus renamed him Peter. It means rock. We're told Peter was the rock upon which the early church was founded."

"But he said he dint know Jesus when the soldiers came?"

"He did. And I reckon he was sorry after."

"So, why did he?"

"Some say it was in fulfillment of the Old Testament. What I think is, he was afraid."

"Of the soldiers?"

"Maybe. He was probably frightened or afraid of admitting love for his friend. Sometimes people are."

"Oh."

"What's important, Larkin, is not how Peter failed but how he made up for it. He became an important preacher. And he was martyred for it."

"Martyred?"

"It's what we say when someone is kilt doing God's work." Her hands paused their work for a moment, her voice softened a little. "I had a cousin Matthew once. A long time back. He went to India as a missionary. We heard later that he died of leprosy. People called him a martyr."

"Did I ever meet him?"

"No. He died before you were born and before I met your Pa. Matthew was my first sweetheart. I was going to join him on the mission field once he was established, and we were going to get married."

"Does Pa know?"

"Of course he does, Larkin. Your Pa knows everything about me. Matthew died and *then* I met your Pa. And he was so kind and strong that I fell in love all over again."

"I dint know you was ever in love with somebody else."

"Well, it was a long time ago. The heart expands to let you love more than one person. Matthew is part of my past but he's still part of who I am."

Larkin took a minute to take this in and swallow it down. "Ma, do you think Jesus forgave Peter?"

"I think Jesus forgives everyone, Larkin. You worried about something?"

"Nah, just wondering, is all. Sometimes those stories get stuck in my head an I wonder how they turned out."

"Well, that's good, son. It means you're paying attention to God's word. You can't never go wrong following that."

His Ma turned back to the bread dough with a happy smile. She folded and punched down the rising mass, sprinkling pinches of flour on the sticky surface, the fine powder falling softly from her fingers and settling in a light dust on the oak table. Larkin drew his finger through it, leaving a clean streak before slipping out of the kitchen.

A couple of weeks after that he was working with his Pa on the fences when he asked him casually, "Hey Pa, you think we ever gonna see Paul Skinner again?"

His Pa had kept at his work, fastening wire to the post they'd just set. "Why I doan rightly know, Larkin. What I do hold to is that we done as much for him as we saw to do when we had the chance. Past that, all I can do is hope he's all right and found his way somewhere good."

"But do you think he might come back and visit?"

"Life gets busy. People get connected and then they move on and connect with other folk. It's the way of things. You can't go through life being a collector of people."

A collector of people: the phrase had stuck with Larkin. In the years since the inquest Larkin often thought about Paul. Must be that he was a collector in his mind.

Yet on the day Paul testified there hadn't been a single occasion for the two to actually speak. Curious onlookers, reporters, neighbours, and other witnesses had all crowded into the courtroom; the Beatties were able to find seats near the back. And although the windows had been opened there was no breeze and the room was stifling, even first thing in the morning.

Larkin's chest felt tight with worry. A couple of people had stopped to congratulate him on his clear testimony from the week before, but he hadn't known how to respond and so had just stood there, looking at them blankly.

He hadn't wanted to return to the inquest at all, but his folks insisted. They said it wouldn't look right if they weren't there. He'd dressed for the day reluctantly, once more putting on his Sunday best outfit. When he went downstairs, he saw that his Pa had laid a sheet of newspaper on the kitchen table and was polishing both Larkin's boots and his own. He whisked the shoe brush back and forth in a firm, steady series of strokes, coaxing the worn leather into a grudging shine.

Larkin hated being centred out, which was part of the problem. The stiff, official setting contributed to his unease. But mostly he felt frightened for Paul and ashamed for himself. He *hadn't* told the whole truth the week before, and he was worried that people would discover this. That they'd look at him accusingly, with hatred and distrust, knowing he was a liar. That they'd see him as a murderer, or at the very least an accomplice to one. And his parents would be shamed. He'd have to leave the farm and find somewhere else to work and live far away from home, or worse. The unfolding seemed inevitable.

Restful sleep had eluded him for months. He'd often wakened in the night with his covers twisted around, his body covered in sweat. Images of a shadowy barn and a sense of dark foreboding haunted him. Some nights there was also a fire, other nights simply large pools of blood.

He had felt certain that all of his misdeeds and lies and pretense would be exposed by the end of Paul's testimony. There could be no more secrets. Paul would take his oath and answer the questions honestly. He'd have to in order to avoid the hangman. Only by implicating someone else could he save his own life. And Larkin *had* been there. It was right that Pauley should name him. It was time for every awful thing to be revealed.

Larkin trembled when the session was called to order and the room quietened down. Already perspiring, he kept rubbing his hands against his trousers, along his thighs and then down over the knees, trying to dry them and to disguise their shaking. Finally his Ma reached over and placed one of her hands on top of his.

"He'll be fine, Larkin," she whispered. "You don't need to worry."

She kept her hand in place, attempting to reassure and steady him. Larkin felt beads of perspiration dripping into his eyes, mildly stinging. He squeezed them shut, willing to block out everything that was about to happen. But when Paul was brought in he opened them. Paul was looking down and didn't see him. But did he feel his presence? Did he know Larkin was silently pleading with him?

The questioning was intense and forceful. The prosecutor was angry. He'd pieced it together and was pushing Paul, trying to get him to admit to the sequence of things. Larkin held his breath until he felt sharp pains in his chest and had to force himself to exhale and breathe. He began to chew the ragged cuticle on his thumb, tearing it with his teeth until it bled.

Paul was standing behind a wooden pulpit, the same one Larkin had stood behind the week before. Larkin had clenched

the sides of its top to ground himself. To draw some strength
from the solid lumber. It had been a tree once. A strong tree.
Maple, thought Larkin. It looked like maple. The grain was
smooth, the base colour a light cream. Whoever made the pulpit
had used thick slabs of wood, nicely sanded. He liked thinking
about the wood while he stood there, waiting for the questions.
Wood was easy to think about. Wood was easy to talk about.
And now Paul was standing there too. Holding onto the sides of
the pulpit just as Larkin had done.

The prosecutor hammered away at Pauley—*Your Pa and
Elgin... already dead before the fire started!... Another person there with
a knife, perhaps?... You grabbed at the knife and fatally stabbed him!*—
until he reached his last terrible demand, *Tell the court, Mr.
Skinner!*

And then Paul started to sob and all of a sudden it was as
though someone had pulled a string or something. He just fell
down in a heap and didn't get up. Women screamed as a rush of
folks went forward to help. People tried to revive Paul with
water but they finally just carried him out and that was the end
of the inquest that day.

Larkin remembered the feel of his own chest heaving as the
room throbbed with activity. He'd had to hold himself back from
joining the rush to help Paul; it pained him to see his friend so
overcome. And yet, it was done. Larkin couldn't help thinking
he'd been given a reprieve. The secrets were safe.

After the crowd began to disperse his Pa took his arm and
guided him and his Ma through the crowd and out to their
buggy. Larkin moved in numb obedience to his father's directions. He felt that people were staring. Strangers pointed at him
when he passed. He imagined that he heard his name spoken:
"Larkin Beattie, the boy from last week," and "Wasn't that his
friend?" His parents were tight-lipped, neither one acknowledg-
ing the surge of interest in their family.

And his Ma and Pa kept that silence as they drove away from
the courthouse—right up until they were safely on the road
home.

Finally, his Pa spoke. "It dint sound very good for Paul."

"No," said his Ma after a moment. "It did not. But things are not always what they seem."

"Cian thinks two people were involved."

"It's not up to us to be guessing at such things." There was something in Ma's voice that Larkin couldn't identify.

"Well, whoever is to blame will have to answer to their Maker," his Pa said. "They sure as hell doan have to answer to me."

"Edgar! Your language!"

Larkin only half listened to his folks. He didn't dare speak, and wasn't sure he could even if he did know what to say. He still felt shocked by the narrow escape. The turn of events made him feel dazed. It was more than he could have hoped for.

Then he began replaying the scene in his head. He thought about Paul's dramatic collapse. And he began to wonder.

The next day was an earlier than usual start: a couple of men were coming to help with the branding.

Branding was another part of cattle breeding that Larkin loathed. They branded only those cows going to market, but that still meant up to a hundred and forty head in a day. Years before his Ma had apparently cried to see the men branding the calves, so his Pa now only ever did the mature animals.

The branding that year, however, was a welcome distraction. Larkin was up before five, feeding both horses and saddling them before his Pa joined him outdoors.

"You're early this morning!" his Pa said with a smile and an approving nod.

"Lots to do."

"Good weather for it."

"Looks like."

"You should see your Ma and have a bite to eat. It's a long day."

"Yes, sir. You comin'?"

"I ate already."

"Back soon."

Larkin took his time walking from the yard to the kitchen door. It was late summer; the colours had faded all around him, the greens taking on a dulled look. It wouldn't be long till there was frost, and that would be followed by a harder frost, and the leaves would change colour completely while the heavy summer air turned fresh and cool. Soon, Larkin knew, he'd be able to see his breath when he walked, and that the smells too would be different as the cycle of all things continued. And while Larkin wasn't particularly given to waxing poetic, he couldn't help but say something about it all when he entered the kitchen.

"Sure is a beauty of a day."

"Yes, it looks it."

"Can tell we're at the end of summer though. Greens starting to deepen."

"It's time."

"Still humid though."

"It will be a warm day's work."

"I was glad to get an early start."

"The men here?"

"Not yet."

"Eat up. There's more for later."

As Larkin wolfed down the hearty breakfast his Ma had prepared, he watched her stepping back and forth around the kitchen, fixing to bake pies for dinner. She had six pie plates set out and was busy laying pastry in each one. Bowls of peeled and chopped apples were set beside her, thickly coated in sugar. Larkin considered the fact that he'd never seen her bake fewer than six pies at one time. It just seemed to be the way she figured things out.

He smiled at her industry and pinched a couple of apple chunks before going back outside. She swatted him with a tea towel when she saw what he was doing.

Larkin began to feel that all was right in the world. He had avoided trouble. He could try to pretend it had never happened, that he'd had nothing to do with any of it. Fresh apple pie was in the making and here he was, home on the farm, about to set to work with the men. No one hated him. Everything seemed possible. The weather was dry and not rainy, which would make herding the cattle more pleasant. Besides which, you couldn't brand wet hides—it fried them and caused more suffering than was needful.

His Pa was talking to the men when Larkin joined them. As they divided up jobs for the morning shift his Pa held two branding irons, full-sized four-inch ones, half an inch thick.

The farm brand was an entwined "e" and "b" for Edgar and Ellen Beattie. ℮ℬ was simple enough to be clear from some distance when you read it on the side of an animal. Larkin thought it looked well and was proud to see their animals in the feedlot, the clarity of their brand standing out among the more complicated ones other people were using. Most brands didn't make any kind of sense. But ℮ℬ was straightforward; you could explain it if someone asked.

The first job was to sort the cattle. The ones going to market were kept in a crowding pen to be guided into the chute and branded. The young bull calves were led to a paddock where they'd be castrated—it was important to do this while they were still young, as their aggressive natures began to show when they were about six months old. The rest of the herd were sent out to pasture.

The cattle chute was the same enclosure they used for dehorning: a tunnel of sorts, open and wide at one end, then narrowing till it reached a sliding head gate at the other. The animals were guided in until they were firmly positioned within the narrow end. There they were held while the brand was applied high on their right hip.

When he was a youngster Larkin had helped in the rounding up and guiding of the livestock. As he got older, though, he was expected to take on a more active part in the proceedings. The first time he'd done the actual branding he'd been inundated with multiple, often contradictory instructions, mostly shouted at him by the men who'd come to assist. The organized chaos of so many frightened animals meant he didn't have time to ask for clarification. Still, he was aware that the pandemonium was for his family's benefit, and that he and his Pa would need to return the favour by helping out at the other men's farms in turn—and that the scenes he found so unsavoury here would be repeated three or four more times that season, with all their horrible smells and sounds.

Branding, as he'd discovered, was far more complicated than most people understood. The first time he applied the iron it was red hot and the cow reacted badly, kicking and bawling and trying to move as far away as it could in the small space. The smell of burning hair and burnt skin was acrid; it got up Larkin's nose and wouldn't leave. At the sound of the commotion his Pa had come running over. He patiently showed Larkin how to first let the brand heat bright red and then let it cool to ash grey before applying. Afterwards Larkin had run his fingers over the cow's hide apologetically before signalling that it was time to free him from the chute. It charged off in a fury. Larkin had studied the ground for a few seconds, squinting hard to blink away his unexpected tears.

But the misery of the task sickened him. And as he thought about the marks he was applying he remembered a different kind of brand—the quilting of scars incised on Paul's back. A clear picture had come to him of the deeply bruised skin, a mass of yellow and purple and black shadows marking the pale surface. And overtop those colours were fresh wounds, angry red welts from a beating so fierce they had bled. Paul's entire back was ridged with such scars, a lattice of cruelty.

Eventually, Larkin had gotten into a rhythm. He learned when to lift the brand, letting the skin turn a light buckskin colour, counting twenty-five seconds, rocking the iron slightly to keep the mark clean but relieving some of the pressure on the animal. The first few cows he did he held the brand on too long—one of the men had shouted that he was "blistering 'em" and to "leave off sooner." Such was the explicitness of his tutorials.

At night, when he and his Pa were finally finished for the day and Larkin had scrubbed the irons with a steel brush, he'd go to the outside pump and run water through his hair, trying to scrub out the stench of the smoke. He'd peel off his clothes outside the house and leave them in a pile by the kitchen door, running upstairs to pull on something clean.

Then he'd stand in his room, holding a newly laundered shirt to his face. It smelled of fresh wind and soap and he'd rub his nose in it, breathing in deeply. Pulling on clean clothes helped with the smells, too. But the suffering he'd inflicted on the unsuspecting herd still upset him.

It usually took a couple of days for Larkin to get past the branding. One of the things he'd do to clear his head was saddle up and go for a ride. He had to check with his Pa to make sure he could spare the time and that they wouldn't be using the team for anything, as he didn't want to tire them before their workday started. He'd get up early and ride for an hour before breakfast. In those days they had a pair of Canadians, mostly for driving the buggy and for light draft work. His Pa had bought them six years before from a farmer out Prenticeville way.

The horses were well matched. Dark black, sixteen hands, with short, high heads, broad foreheads, and thick, heavy manes and tails. Their necks were arched gracefully and their chests, backs, and loins strongly muscled. Both were mature and strong, yet still young and spirited enough to make a ride exhilarating. They'd been named by a schoolteacher boarding with the family in Prenticeville. She called them Austen and Dickens after her favourite writers, and the Beatties had seen no reason to rename them.

Larkin's favourite of the two was Dickens, who seemed slightly more friendly; he'd respond to carrots or apples with a nuzzle before chomping them down. Austen, though, would snap up any offering and only then patiently endure an ear rub or patting. He seemed much more self-sufficient and independent, even a little haughty. Dickens was definitely the more sociable. Larkin was insecure enough in those days to take Austen's indifference as a personal slight, and although he tried to treat both horses without favour, Dickens was his preferred companion on those morning rides.

The morning after the branding Larkin rose and dressed before five o'clock, taking two apples from the cold cellar before going to the barn. Sliding open the heavy doors, he relaxed immediately in the space, warmed and scented as it was by the animals, their feed, their fresh hay bedding. Familiar, simple smells. As he walked towards their stalls Larkin held out the apples and called to the horses.

"Good morning, gents, I've brought you a special breakfast. How would you like an apple apiece, eh?"

Dickens whinnied but Austen looked disdainful. Larkin waved the apple in front of Dickens's velvet nose and the horse responded by lowering his head and butting softly against Larkin's face. Larkin fed him the apple while patting his neck and speaking soft nonsense words to him. "How ya' doin', fellow, miss me? I missed you. Wish I could tell you 'bout it. Sure have been busy, ya' know. You been up to much?"

Austen, meanwhile, had looked off into the distance. Larkin walked over to him with the second apple. "Well Austen," he said as the horse crunched away, "I warn't ignorin' ya'. I got that sweet treat for you as well. Now are you feeling like a ride this mornin' or should I invite Dickens? What do you think?" Austen had nothing to say to that, condescending only to have his ears rubbed.

"Well all right then, Dickens it is. You hear that, Dickens? I'm just gonna get you saddled and then we can go for some air."

Larkin opened Dickens's stall, laid a blanket across his back, then heaved up the saddle and centred it carefully. Pulling down the straps, he fastened them snugly and checked to make sure the horse looked comfortable. Before leading Dickens out of the stall, Larkin lengthened the stirrup so that he could mount easily. It was still dark when they walked out of the barn. Swinging up and into the saddle, Larkin adjusted the stirrup leather and gave Dickens a gentle prod.

Larkin didn't have a destination or a route in mind, particularly. He just felt the need of some space around him. He loved the farm, but sometimes its routines felt confining, and after the savagery of the day before he was eager for some open views. He let Dickens choose their direction; the horse indicated north, towards the mountain. It wasn't much of a mountain, really, but that's what it was called.

As they rode, light began to break in a line and seep gradually into the sky until the orange ball of sun finally made its appearance and the black faded into its light. The mountain peak was masked by a thick ring of fog and cloud, while to the east, near the Pretty River, Larkin saw mist rising from the water like thin wispy curls of cigar smoke. The elements, he reflected, were out of balance. Larkin read in this a sign that frost would soon come.

He nudged Dickens and followed the banks of the river for a couple of miles before turning round. It was late in the season, but Larkin knew the salmon were still there and made for good eating at this time of year. He'd have to come back with his rod before winter set in hard. Thinking about the fish, making plans to come back, maybe even with his Pa, renewed Larkin's feeling that all was once more right with the world. He was free. No one but he and Paul knew what had transpired at Skinner's that night, and maybe now no one else would ever need to know. Was it too much to hope that Cian Quinn would leave well enough alone?

But certain questions continued to niggle at him. Why had Mrs. Skinner ignored Paul after the fire? Did she blame him? And if she blamed him, it stood to reason that the girls did too. One word to Cian, and Paul could be hanged. And if Paul wasn't safe, then Larkin wasn't either.

His shoulders tensed at the thought. Dickens, sensing the change, stopped cantering and waited. Now Larkin sat still atop him, disoriented. Why had Dickens stopped? What time was it? How long had he been away? Panicked now, a rush of adrenaline surged through him—and he kicked Dickens gently but harder than usual and rode swiftly back to the farm.

Larkin dismounted outside the barn. He unbuckled and hauled down the saddle, dashed inside for a brush, then came back out and gave Dickens a fast currying. This was a treatment the horse enjoyed, and Larkin would often linger at it, but not this morning. The sun was quite high by now; he must have been overlong at his ride.

"Good ride, son?"

"Sorry to be so long."

"We're in no hurry this morning. There's always work to be done and it always waits."

"I'll be quick."

His Pa came close and stood beside him, placing his large calloused hand on Larkin's shoulder. "There's no fire, son. We can take time to enjoy ourselves every now and then."

At the word "fire," Larkin tensed again. His Pa could surely sense it. Wound up tighter than a clock is what his Pa would have thought. Larkin felt this. He felt both his folks watching and waiting.

"Go inside and get some breakfast. Your Ma fried sausages and eggs this morning. She's keeping some hot."

And just like that, Larkin was dropped back into the comforting routines of domestic order. But why had his Pa mentioned fire? And what would his folks *really* think, wondered Larkin, if they knew what I done?

The fear of discovery and the worry of disappointing them welled up once more, seizing his insides and lodging like a lump in his throat. The privy still hid the evidence. The shears remained there, wrapped in paper, under the floor. Larkin worried someone might find the bundle but he couldn't think what else to do with it. Some days he expected his father to approach him, holding it out and asking what it was doing there. Would he lie then, or own up to things? Maybe that would be a relief. Maybe his Pa would turn him in. He didn't know.

The burden of secrets followed Larkin like a dark shadow, always there, a black, menacing shape. Every now and then the darkness would startle him; he'd have to brace his legs firmly and hold his ground lest he disappear into the blackness. It was nothing that others could see or hear or feel, but it was attached to him; it would rise up and appear at will. Sometimes he'd feel a prickling at the back of his neck and he'd stand still, waiting for the tingling to run up and down his arms. Then his chest would tighten and he'd have trouble breathing. The panic would choke him as he flapped his arms, pacing back and forth till he wore himself out. Then eventually, at last, it would subside.

His Ma referred to these events as "his spells." She was sure Doc Mather would have a powder or a cure. But Larkin steadfastly refused to even see him.

The fleeting horror of the attacks marked Larkin. He was afraid of them. He tried to fight them off when they began but didn't always succeed.

His Pa had once found him in the barn in the middle of one. He'd stood back and watched Larkin flapping his arms and pacing furiously. Then his Pa just walked over, pulled him in against his chest, and held him tightly. He held him without saying a word for maybe twenty minutes. Larkin felt surprisingly calmed by that closeness, by his Pa's touch.

Larkin always liked to remember the feel of his Pa then, the stubble on his face scratching against his own, the smell of pipe smoke lingering on his jacket and shirt. The gloved hands gripping his forearms tightly while pulling him into an embrace and then the feel of them strong and comforting on his back, making patterns of small circles. It was the embrace of a man who could fix almost anything.

~

Larkin sat motionless. It had been a long time since he'd been touched like that. He thought hard, memories thundering around inside him, trying to recollect. But it was his Pa's touch that he last remembered. That silent, lingering embrace that had so steadied him. What did it say about a man, wondered Larkin, when it's been over thirty years since anyone had come that close?

The stove had gone cold. Suddenly aware of the chill, Larkin went upstairs to fetch a warm sweater. But when he reached the landing something overtook him; he walked towards his parents' room and stood at the door, trying to conjure an image of them back before his Ma took sick—a happier version of them both.

At the foot of their bed stood a cedar chest where his Ma used to keep things that were special. It had been her hope chest once. Do girls do such things anymore, he wondered vaguely, all that fancy work before they marry?

The chest. Larkin stopped. He kept his mason jars of money there, but had he ever really examined what else it held? He thought of those pages of the letter to his Ma, the ones she'd secreted so mysteriously away, and he wondered.

He bent over the chest and slowly lifted its heavy lid. The strong fragrance of cedar wafted out and prickled the inside of his nose. A quilt was the top item; he removed it carefully, keeping it neatly folded, and placed it on the bed. Below that were the four mason jars stuffed with the cash he was saving for the motor car. He set these gently on the floor. The next layer contained some lacy personals, which he pushed aside rather than lifting them out. At the very bottom of the chest were tissue-wrapped baby clothes—knitted booties and caps and sweaters in pale colours—and several soft blankets. They must have been his, and his Ma must have intended to use them again. Larkin marvelled at how delicate they were—his entire thumb filled one of the tiny mittens. It didn't seem possible that he was once small enough for those things. He picked them up carefully, laying them on the quilt and patting them smooth.

That was all the cedar chest contained. Disappointed, Larkin replaced the mason jars and then the knitted infant clothes, setting them down on top of the personals. Finally, he lifted the quilt in both hands and laid it carefully over everything else.

He was about to close the lid when he reconsidered the quilt and took it out again. Standing up straight, he held on to one edge and let the rest of it waterfall against his legs and spill onto the floor. Even in the rippling half-dark he could see it was a beauty. Although he knew nothing about quilting, he appreciated the tiny stitching and the careful piecework that must have gone into such a pattern. Larkin didn't recognize this quilt as one they'd ever used, so he held it up to the lamp for a minute to see whether he remembered any of the fabrics. He couldn't say with certainty that any of them looked familiar. And although some of the pieces looked soft and worn, the binding and the back of the quilt were stiff, with a new-material feel. He wondered what his mother had been saving it for.

Larkin tried inexpertly to refold it into a smallish parcel so that he could fit it back inside the chest. It took a few tries and a number of punches to get the fabric pushed down flat enough, but finally he was able to close the cedar lid.

As Larkin went to leave the room, his socked foot slipped a little and he heard a slight crinkling. Looking down through the gloom, he saw a folded piece of paper. It must have fallen from inside the quilt. He picked it up and stared at it, incredulous at his good fortune.

And nervous, too. If this was indeed a missing page from the letter, he might discover something he wasn't entirely ready to know. Words held power for Larkin, and he wasn't sure, now that he'd found it, whether he was prepared to read it. But Larkin was both alone and lonely. His memories and recollections of events from long ago were his truest companions. If there was any part of this page that could speak to him, he wanted to know it. While he deliberated, he held it tremulously in his hand.

Then he made his decision. Larkin went back downstairs to retrieve the first two pages from his scrapbook. He laid them out before him on the kitchen table, next to the lamp, then unfolded the third. He saw at once that the handwriting was the same. He began at the left, with the first two pages.

23rd November, 1871

Dear Mrs. Beattie,

You maybe no that my sister and me and Ma are living with Uncle Roy over in Angus way. We been here since after the fire. My Ma's been taken down sick with stomach troubles and we're aiming to restore her. She's been fratching about our brother and wants us to find him. Uncle Roy told us

*that he ain't welcome here and that he sent him away the couple
times he already come. So we thought as how you live close by,
you might of seen him on the old place or round about. We no
that him and your boy were friendly and wondered if any of you
had news of how to get word to him. Ma is right poorly and we
think she needs to see him. We no too that when Ma went*

*to see you how kind you were in understandin all that she
told you and why she couldn't see her Pauley lyin there so
poorly in the parlour. We thanks ye for that and for takin
good care a him. Ma says as how she be sorry to have tole
you what the boys done and all her own worries on account
a you havin your own troubles. Do not be frettin on our
account. We knows your Larkin is a good lad.*

God bless, Ethel Skinner

Larkin stared. *Understandin all that she told you.* What had
Paul's mother said? Larkin thought back to that day. *How long
Mrs. Skinner had talked with his Ma in the kitchen? Just the two of
them?* And then this letter, kept safe all these years yet carefully
hidden away. His mind reeled as he tried to take in the letter's
import.

But now that struggle was overtaken by an overwhelming,
searing feeling of remorse. He'd caused his Ma such distress.
She'd suffered more than he knew. And it had fallen to Ethel,
a girl he could barely remember, to console her. *Do not be
frettin.*

That undid him. Larkin moaned and doubled over, shuddering while he rocked, tears wrenched from deep within,
more tears it seemed than he'd ever before allowed himself to
shed.

Dawn was approaching and Larkin was utterly spent. Finally,
summoning the last of his reserves, he stood up, gathered the

three pages, and opened the door to the Findlay Oval and jammed in the entire letter.

It was time to tend to his horses. Soon it would be fully light; they would be expecting him. Just as he'd done the morning before, Larkin crept cautiously down the steps into the cold cellar, where he chose a handful of carrots. Outside, the air was fresh after the violent storm. He felt exposed and chill in the open, the lack of sleep heightening his senses. He took hold of the pump handle, pressing it down and then up to work the piston. When the water came, he filled a bucket.

A thin line of bright orange was widening on the horizon as the sun began its steady rise. He found the overturned lantern he'd left out the night before; miraculously, it had escaped damage. Then, carefully putting down the pail, he moved aside the boulder he'd set against the barn door. With both arms he slowly pushed the door, finding that it only reluctantly agreed to slide on its rusted rail. Larkin eyed the steel critically, making a note to himself to run some steel wool along its length and coat it with oil.

There were always these invisible jobs to be done, done once and then repeated, and repeated again, year after year. It was the way of preventing nature from reclaiming all that had been ordered and subdued.

Culloden whinnied at Larkin's approach. But Larkin stopped first at Guinevere's and Merlyn's stalls with his offering, Culloden stomping impatiently. This brought a smile to Larkin's face as he approached him with carrot extended. Then, as Culloden chomped away, Larkin tended to Pirate and Thunder, giving these two sturdy dobbins their own due attention. After that he filled all the feed bags with oats and splashed fresh water from his pail into the troughs. Finally, he leaned against a stall to watch his horses at their breakfast, enjoying the intimacy of the morning feed in the barn's warm, musty air.

Everything about it felt good to him: the familiar smells and sounds, the look of the shiny, well-brushed animals, their muscles tightly defined. More than that, though, was the sense that he was part of something good, something he'd helped to create. The beauty of the horses was so powerful that pride gave way to emotion and Larkin knew that if he ruminated too long tears would not be far. The horses were all the family he had left.

Wellington, in particular, had been spectacular. He'd won best in show at the Toronto Industrial Exhibition in 1888—the wide, extravagant bow and the ribbon extending from it still hung in the tack room. And even now, more than twenty years later, it was an accomplishment that made Larkin swell with happiness.

He, George Larmer, and Bill Dempsey had all agreed to travel to Toronto together. It had been George's and Bill's idea, of course. Larkin hadn't planned on it at all.

The whole thing had started a month before, when the two had ridden over one night and asked whether he'd be showing stock there. George was planning to take his ram and a couple of ewes. Bill would be taking a very ornery sow.

"Pity that," George said when Larkin shook his head. "Heard there was a big prize for the best-in-show horse. Picture in the paper even. Thought as how you'd want folks to see your stallion now he's two years."

George and Bill, it transpired, had already been to the train station to inquire about arrangements. George was good at organizing and undertook to take care of the registrations. The trip from Collingwood station to the city, they told him, would be a mere four hours.

And so, without knowing exactly how, Larkin found that he'd agreed to take his horse to Toronto.

On the morning of their departure George had some difficulty managing his small suitcase as he climbed aboard the train; Larkin grabbed it to save him from losing his balance on the steep steps. After his efforts with the church bell, George's shoulder had never properly healed.

And that little mishap preceded Wellington's own difficulty: he'd balked at boarding, and so stubbornly that once George and Bill had their own animals crated and loaded they'd come over to hold open the door of the stall. By that time Larkin was walking backwards onto the ramp and into the car, leading Wellington. It was dangerous, he knew, to be pinned in the tiny stall with such a large animal, so he manoeuvred his body in such a way that he could stand along the side wall. It was a very tight squeeze and Wellington was unhappy about the close quarters. Still, reaching past his favourite's nose, Larkin fastened the tether to the ring in the end wall and then pulled it short and tight.

Finally, Larkin slipped out through the stall's open door and together with George and Bill fastened it tightly, drawing the bar across and hoping it would remain secure. Wellington was shifting uncomfortably, raising and twisting his head, fighting against the tight tether. Larkin knew he was frightened. So, while his friends went to find seats he stayed with his horse, talking to him calmly from outside the enclosure.

In truth, Larkin was not unsympathetic. This was his own first trip to Toronto, his own first time on a train. By choice, his world had remained centred in Cemetery Hill.

And so, when the train began to move, he was as startled as Wellington by the sounds and jerking motion. The shrill whistles and the screeching and grinding of the wheels echoed loudly in the car as Wellington, truly panicked now, tried to rear up, pulling at the short tether with his neck and raising his front legs, all to little effect. As the train picked up speed, rocketing forward in a series of jerks and bumpy thrusts of power, Larkin soothed his animal as best he could until finally Wellington stopped thrashing and seemed to settle. Only then did Larkin go to find his companions.

When he opened the heavy door at the end of the car he was treated to a gust of acrid-smelling smoke. Coughing, he stood in place, holding the door open, swaying with the movement of the car. He ventured a look down, saw the earth passing rapidly beneath the linkage, and was struck by the notion that, for the first time since childhood, he was moving far from all he knew towards a city of unknown marvels.

The passing ground was hypnotic; Larkin felt drawn to the blurring images and strobing ties as they sped by. It would be easy to take a step forward and miss his footing, to slip down between the cars, to be crushed as the speeding train moved above him. There he would lie, feeling the heat of the engine as it passed overhead, the whooshing of the carriages as they shot forward. Not an unpleasant ending, he thought, and quickly over.

Each of the three men took turns checking on the animals. Larkin remained uneasy about Wellington, but his companions jollied him along, encouraging him to look out the window and enjoy the passing scenery. Still, Larkin couldn't help himself—and continued to make additional forays to the livestock carriages to make sure Wellington wasn't unduly uncomfortable. After all, Doc Chester had cautioned Larkin. Train travel, he'd said, would be hard on such a large, powerful stallion. The tight stalls meant short tethers, and not much room to secure his footing amidst the constant shifting and jostling of the journey. Besides that, of course, were the unfamiliar noises. They might spook him. He might even rear up enough to pull free of his restraints.

To help matters and according to Doc's suggestions, Larkin had had a leather worker custom-make leg wraps using thick padding, a leather cover, and simple straps. Before the trip Larkin had left them in place for hours at a time just to acclimatize Wellington to the feel of them, and he hadn't seemed to mind overmuch.

Larkin had also engaged one of the local women to fasten several horse blankets into a thickly padded cover that would hang down low on both sides. Wellington wasn't as enamoured with this, rearing up to free himself from the weight of it. Larkin was obliged, after a time, to pierce the blanket in order to thread through long leather straps that would hold it securely on the animal's back. Wellington snorted and pawed the ground, swishing his tail indignantly, his ears pinned back against his head. There was an established bond of affection between them, however, and Wellington finally and reluctantly submitted to Larkin's ministrations.

The final piece of gear—a padded helmet—was the most difficult both to manufacture and to apply. The hat, with its two ear holes, its thick padding, and its smart leather top, was attached to a bridle whose straps had been tightly wrapped with padding and a thin leather casing, the whole tied neatly in place with strips of fine rawhide. Yet Wellington was singularly unimpressed: each time Larkin approached him with it he'd shy away, snorting and grimacing. In the end it took a combination of gentle cooing and crisp apples to subdue him. As Larkin pulled Wellington's smooth ears through the openings and felt their softness, he wondered if there was ever anything more alive or more beautiful than one of his horses.

Over the duration of the trip, Larkin made sure to check the protective coverings each time he visited Wellington. His poor horse remained frightened, and so he continued to soothe him as best he could. It was fortunate that the trip itself would take only four hours, give or take a little extra. The difficulty was in knowing how long each of the stops would take. Depending upon what was being loaded or unloaded and how many passengers embarked or disembarked, some of the stops seemed interminable.

The train—a "special"—took them to a new stop created especially on the edge of the exhibition grounds. It began to slow and then made a sharp turn; now, gazing out the window, the men were able to view the lake. All three were accustomed to seeing Georgian Bay, but the sheer breadth of Lake Ontario, so close to the train and to the sprawl of buildings on its shore, was a curiosity. As the train approached its destination, jerking and shuddering before screeching to a sudden stop, Larkin made his way to Wellington once more. The train's final lurching was so rough that he lost his balance and had to grab hold of a seat to maintain his footing. He swayed unsteadily as he kept moving towards his horse, cursing the endeavour and the prospect of a prize that had so tantalized him.

Mercifully, porters appeared to help unload the animals and convey them to a crudely constructed temporary building. Larkin had no difficulty in freeing Wellington and lengthening his tether. Then he backed him up carefully. Wellington, smelling something different in the air, pawed the ground before allowing himself to be led to his new temporary stable. That's when he tried to bite Larkin—and not a gentle nibble, either: he quite intended to communicate his displeasure. But Larkin moved fast, grasping Wellington's jaw and holding it firmly, speaking gently to him all the while. When he saw the lips curl downward and the nostrils relax and soften, he loosened his grip. Wellington's temperament, for a stallion, was docile. He only ever tried to bite when he was under extreme stress.

One of the porters told Larkin that all the showings and judgings were held outdoors. And indeed, the scale of the grounds, and of the building that housed the animals, was enormous. Larkin, who'd anticipated something only a little larger than Collingwood's Agricultural Society Fair, was unprepared for the magnitude of what he could only now glimpse.

A vastness within a vastness, that is. From the windows of the train Larkin had for the first time seen Toronto, with its clusters of factories and industrial buildings all along the lakefront. Smokestacks were belching plumes of dirty smoke, and despite the pristine blue of the lake, a grimy layer of dust seemed to coat the sprawling landscape.

Once Larkin had secured Wellington in his stall, he went in search of fresh water and feed. Vendors, he discovered, were placed throughout the building, and with very little difficulty he was able to purchase what he needed.

He'd planned to meet George and Bill at the hotel, whose name and address he'd written out and placed in his jacket pocket, but he couldn't bear to leave his horse, even for their one-night stay. Larkin felt sorry for Wellington—a feeling that was gradually replaced by a keen sense of proprietary caution. Anyone could walk into the building, open the stall door, and lead away his prize stallion. No one seemed to be watching over the animals. And so, Larkin prepared to rest there, directly outside Wellington's stall, until morning.

The ground was hard-packed dirt with a layer of straw on top. Manure and urine from the many animals housed in the building had been left where it landed, the muck since trampled into the straw. Larkin used the side of his boot to clear an area; then he arranged the horse blankets there. As he lay down, his nearness to the waste mixed with the fetid straw made for a rank, pervasive smell. Not that it bothered his horse. Wellington turned himself around in the stall a time or two and nickered softly in response to Larkin's quiet conversational banter.

Talking to his horse was far easier than talking to anyone else. And so Larkin, lying on the pile of blanketing, fell asleep whispering to Wellington.

George Larmer woke him in the morning. If he wondered at Larkin's choice of ground over bed, he didn't say. He simply offered to remain with the horse while Larkin went to the hotel to clean himself up and have some breakfast. Larkin accepted gratefully, for the ground had proven hard on his joints. He was more than ready for a warm wash and something nourishing.

Despite George's very specific directions, Larkin was overwhelmed by the sense of the encroaching city once he began to walk across the exhibition grounds. Packs of people were milling around, seemingly waiting for the day's events to begin. Others were scurrying across the grounds, looking purposeful and busy. Larkin ambled through the crowd, heading towards the large gate that George had described. Families with small children were walking together, looking pleased and happy with their outing. A couple of little girls in party dresses were holding handing hands with their father, skipping and laughing as they tried to keep up with his steady stride.

Larkin envied them their ease, their delighted groupings. He longed for that kind of closeness. It had been years now since his Ma had passed. She would have loved the finery on display today. Larkin noticed a couple of the hats the women were wearing, brightly coloured confections with wide ribbons and cloth flowers piled on broad brims. He thought of the modest straw ones his Ma had worn. These hats actually looked top-heavy, as if the women might topple over. He chuckled to himself at the ludicrous sight.

When he reached the gates, Larkin turned first to gaze upon the lake and then turned east, as George had directed. Their hotel, he'd been told, was a five-minute tram ride away. Larkin needed to cross a very wide street and join a group of people waiting for the horse-pulled tram. On any other occasion he might have enjoyed the novelty of the ride, but he'd already experienced too many new things in too short an interval. He elected to walk instead.

Crossing the road was its own adventure. Of the many buggies, wagons, and single riders on horses, most kept to one side of the road only. But some riders seem to weave indiscriminately around the vehicles, darting in and out impatiently. Larkin was unsure whether it was safe to cross, and worried that he might be breaking the law. He watched for a few minutes before deciding to take his chance. Then he made a mad dash for it, narrowly escaping injury from the back of a buggy wheel.

The hotel was a slightly further walk than he'd understood. But despite the unfamiliar surroundings, he was happy for the exercise. It had been a hard day and night, without much activity, and he was glad to be moving around. In the end, the hotel wasn't hard to locate. Larkin entered the lobby and was directed to their room.

He'd agreed to split the hotel room three ways with his companions. The cost seemed excessive—he suspected it might have been a contributing factor underlying his invitation—but Larkin didn't feel particularly hurt by this; it was simply one of the realities of his situation. Bill and George had left him a printed schedule of events propped up on a tiny writing desk in the corner of their modest room. Larkin saw that Wellington needed to be ready for a one o'clock judging, and that a six o'clock special would take them back to Collingwood.

It would be a busy day. Larkin hurried back downstairs to the hotel's little dining room for breakfast.

The judging happened so quickly that it didn't seem entirely real. Wellington heeded Larkin's commands and stayed at his shoulder the whole time. Larkin concentrated on ignoring the crowds and the judges alike, devoting his full attention to his stallion. Together they walked and jog-trotted through the routine. Wellington moved straight and true without looking around or pulling away. Then, when it came time for the judges to review his stance and conformation, he stood entirely still, allowing them to run their hands over his neck and shoulders and lightly touch his legs. Only once, when one of the judges stood directly behind him to check his buttocks, did he raise his hoof slightly as if in warning. Larkin whispered in his ear and the hoof went back softly on the ground.

Wellington was the fourth entry of four, and so, right after his showing, the judges conferred with an official. Then, after only scant minutes, they returned—bearing a massive silver cup and a vivid blue ribbon and striding directly over to Wellington. Larkin was dumbfounded. He knew his horse was special. He'd hoped for a ribbon, of course he had. But first prize: that was astonishing. He thanked the solemn gentlemen who shook his hand firmly by turns, stood still for a photo, and led his horse back to the stall.

It was after that, when he was organizing Wellington's protective gear, that he saw, out of the corner of his eye, someone watching him. A man about his age, with a heavy beard and moustache, his clothes shabby and overlarge. And he was staring at the horse. Larkin turned to look at the man full on. He didn't recognize him, and nothing about him seemed familiar. And yet Larkin felt uneasy and frightened. The man doffed his cap and bowed deeply at Larkin before turning away and walking straight out of the building.

Larkin determined not to leave Wellington alone for a minute. He was certain that the stranger had wicked intentions, that he could well be watching for an opportunity to steal his horse. Feeling fiercely protective, Larkin led the now well-padded Wellington from the stall and out into the open field. Well-wishers shouted out congratulatory messages and stepped aside, creating an open path; he found he could head directly to the loading area.

As he made his way through the crowd Larkin turned his head from side to side and kept looking over his shoulder. The man might reappear. He may have meant no harm at all—Larkin knew that. Yet he still felt anxious.

Bill was the first to join him at the loading dock, unencumbered now, having sold his sow. George arrived not long after, also having successfully sold his livestock. Bill kindly went in search of water and brought back a pail for Wellington.

Both were full of congratulations and compliments at the news of Wellington's showing, possibly no less pleased with themselves for having suggested the excursion in the first place and having made all the arrangements. After taking in some of the other exhibits and shows, they were also full of stories about what they'd seen. Larkin in turn told them about the shady-looking character who he felt sure had designs on his horse. When George and Bill assured him that such a thing was unlikely, Larkin felt instantly ridiculous. And yet he couldn't shake the feeling of foreboding.

They were not long home, only a few days, when Larkin bought a dog. Fearfulness had taken hold: someone, now aware of Wellington's status as Best-in-Show, might creep undetected into the stables and steal him away in the quiet of night.

The dog was a two-year-old Australian shepherd, one of several owned by the Larmers. Larkin hadn't wanted a puppy; feeling the need for a watch dog right away, he'd asked for one of their older ones. George referred to all his dogs as "Laddie," and had trained them to respond only to whistles. And although he used them to help with herding, he assured Larkin that the shepherds could be trained to be good guard dogs.

Larkin made a bed for the shepherd in the stables and watched him carefully to make sure he didn't get underfoot with the horses or tease or nip them. But the dog seemed intuitive around horses, and wasn't overly excitable. It may have been his early training with the sheep.

Larkin hadn't the facility or the gift of whistling, and so he set about training Laddie to respond to a new name—Spike—hoping by this to instill in him a sense of menace and purpose. Plus, he liked the sound of it when he called him. "Spike, food," was the first command he successfully taught him. Buoyed by his achievement, he then taught him to respond to "Spike, here," "Spike, sit," and "Spike, stay."

He also trained Spike to sleep on a soft bed of hay across from Wellington's stall—and for the first weeks after his triumphant return, Larkin himself slept on a cot in the tack room, with the door open. It wasn't just the man watching his horse that had prompted this, either. It was the amount of attention Wellington had received since coming home.

A prominent notice had been printed in *The Murton County Chronicle* alongside a picture of Wellington, the ribbon pinned to his halter, and Larkin, standing beside him, gripping the cup as he squinted at the photographer's repeated flashes of light. After that a steady stream of neighbours and friends had come to visit, all of them wanting to see the cup and the ribbon and the horse. Larkin, sometimes begrudgingly but always with a secret pride, would escort them into the barn so that they could admire Wellington and the prizes he'd won.

One night Spike began to bark excitedly, running back and forth between Larkin and the barn door and rousing Larkin from a deep sleep. He lit a lantern and made his way nervously to the door. "Who's there?" he shouted. "My gun's loaded!"

"It's me, Larkin. Paul. Don't shoot."

Larkin's eyes widened in the lamplight. He hadn't seen Paul since he was seventeen—not since the cattle drive. Years ago now. Still, he'd know his voice anywhere. As he stood, suspended in time, Spike remained at his knee, growling in a threatening manner.

"Just a minute, Paul. I got a dog here."

. "I hear him, all right."

"Spike, sit!" commanded Larkin, pointing at the floor. Once Spike had sunk down obediently Larkin held up the lantern and opened the door. Then, to the sound of Spike's low, rumbling warning, Paul walked in.

"When you get a dog?"

"Got 'im from Larmer."

Larkin moved forward to grasp his friend's hand. "You hungry?"

"I can always eat."

The two men left the barn and made their way towards the house. Spike began to follow, but Larkin sent him back.

"Friendly dog," Paul remarked wryly.

"He ain't supposed to be. Too many people interested in my horses."

"So, you done all right at the show…"

"Grand Champion." Despite himself, Larkin smiled proudly. "Come away in."

They walked into the dark kitchen, Larkin busying himself lighting more lamps and tending to the stove. Paul stood inside the door and looked around. "I ain't been in here since I dunno when."

Larkin paused in his work, straightened himself up, and looked at Paul steadily. "You ain't been inside since the fire." The statement hung there between them. Both of them unsure how to proceed. "Sit ye down," Larkin said finally. "I'll get us sumpen."

Paul pulled out one of the pink chairs and sat, close to the door. He looked uncomfortable, as if he might bolt. He left his jacket on. Larkin uncovered a loaf of bread and placed it on the table with a big knife and the butter dish. Then he opened the little icebox and pulled out a block of cheese that he also put on the table, along with a jar of strawberry jam.

Handing Paul a plate, he said, "We can make sandwiches."

Paul cut into the loaf and passed Larkin a couple of thick slices. Larkin in turn was shaving the cheese and passing the first several shavings to Paul.

"I can make tea after," offered Larkin.

"Anything stronger?"

"Some whisky, maybe. I doan take to it much."

Once they'd finished the loaf of bread between them, not a word spoken as they did, Larkin got up to fetch the whisky, wiping the bottle with his sleeve before passing it to Paul. The glass was greasy with a thick film of grime.

Paul poured himself a generous amount and sat back in his chair. "I was sorry to hear about your Pa. He was good to me."

"He would a been happy to do more."

Paul held up his glass. "The Queen!" He took a long slug. "It ain't so easy taking help, Larkin. And I needed to go."

"What about your Ma and your sisters?"

Paul shook his head. "They was glad I was gone."

"The farm is sittin' with nuthin' on it."

"It's cursed."

"All these years I been tryin' to puzzle things through…"

"Be best to forget that night."

"I can't forget… can you?"

"Here's the thing I remember. I remember you're the best friend a fella could have. And you stuck by me when no else did."

"That ain't true, Pauley. Lots a people…"

"My Uncle Roy wouldn't let me near. Folks here look at me and still see a murderer."

"That ain't so. You were the smartest boy in school. You read books and showed me Polaris. That ain't all people see."

"Larkin, if you was honest, it's what you see."

"I was *there*, Pauley. It warn't all your fault."

Paul stood up, tucking his chair in under the table. "I gotta go, Larkin. I ain't coming back. I wanted to say a proper goodbye, is all." He paused for a moment, and then continued.

"I'm to marry. I wanted to tell you. We're headed to Manitoba—we heard there's plenty work there. She's real special. I'm gonna change my name and start a new life."

Larkin stood. Paul stuck out his hand and they shook solemnly. Larkin saw that Paul had tears glistening in his eyes.

And yet he didn't linger. He slipped out the kitchen door without another word and disappeared into the breaking of dawn. Larkin remained in the kitchen, standing stock-still.

Although it had been so long since they'd last seen each other, it had always seemed to Larkin that they'd meet again— that they'd somehow keep meeting. There was still so much that Paul hadn't told him about that terrible night.

After what seem like a long time, Larkin sank back down into one of the pink chairs and rested his head in his hands.

It wasn't long after that when Doc Chester showed up and suggested to Larkin that breeding Wellington might become a profitable enterprise. Larkin dismissed the idea at first. But Doc persisted, pointing out that it would do no harm to Wellington and would provide an easy source of revenue. He offered his services as an unpaid assistant for the first of these encounters. Finally, he mentioned that he knew two or three men with mares who would welcome the opportunity.

Larkin's affection for the animal had been of a private nature— he'd had no mind to exploit him, to have him turned into a money-grabbing scheme. But when he tried to say as much, even to his own ears it sounded confused and downright nonsensical.

"It ain't fittin' to use an animal in that way," he began. "It ain't natural-like."

"I assure you," laughed the Doc, "there ain't much that *is* more natural. If you'd ever been married, my friend, you'd understand that there's pleasure to be had for all parties."

Larkin blushed deeply at this, but continued his protests—to no avail. He found himself once more agreeing to something he hadn't ever thought to do.

And the prospect only reinforced the notion that Wellington might be a target for thieves. The idea had taken hold. Not until Spike was fully trained would he go back to sleeping in the house.

That night, long after Doc had left, Larkin turned on the cot uncomfortably. *This* particular sense of worry was new, he reflected. It wasn't just the fear of Wellington being spirited away in the night. His last meeting with Paul had stayed with him, bringing with it a heightened desperation to hang on to what was his.

~

Larkin now looked over to the place where Spike had slept. He'd been his companion for fifteen years. He was gone, near on ten years now.

Spike and Larkin had been walking down by the creek one spring when they came upon a bear cub. Knowing its Ma would be close by, Larkin started backing up. But Spike's instincts took over and he tried herding the cub closer to the retreating Larkin. Frantic, Larkin had hissed, "Spike! Spike, here!" But the mother bear loomed out of the bush then and moved rapidly towards them. Larkin had no choice but to flee, leaving his dog to a certain fate. The memory still grieved him.

Wellington, too, had long since died. The sores had come on quick. Larkin had noticed a small, hard lump on the back leg some time before. Over the course of some weeks more of the little lumps appeared, although they didn't seem to bother the horse. But then Larkin noticed a swelling—and when he probed it gently, the skin ruptured and a mass of puss drained out. He'd wrapped it with clean strips and brought in the vet.

Doc Chester said it must have been festering a long while: the infection had got to the bone. It was only a matter of time, he said, till the leg snapped. Doc looked at Larkin kindly when he told him that it would be cruel not to end things.

Larkin didn't like to remember it.

Culloden was the last stallion he'd bought, and was all the more cherished for it. Larkin also kept Guinevere and Merlyn, his two mares of good stock, intending to breed them with

Culloden. This was one of the things he still hoped to accomplish.

His folks were buried in a family plot on the hill. He tried to go most Sundays. In the warm months he'd remember to pick fresh flowers and leave them in a mason jar with water. He knew his Ma would like that. Larkin would sit a spell with his folks, telling them what was what and how things were going on the farm.

He'd stay till dusk some afternoons, unless other folks came by to pay their respects at other plots, and then Larkin would feel self-conscious and scurry away.

The Skinners didn't have a family plot. Instead, Silas and Elgin were buried, one on top of the other, at the end of a row, on the other side of cemetery. Larkin walked by it from time to time, searching for evidence of visitors, flowers perhaps, or weeds pulled away, but he never saw any signs of care. It was a dismal patch, with a plain slab laid flat in the ground. Silas Skinner 1834–1871 and Elgin Skinner 1853–1871. No poetry or scripture verses or anything else. "But what could you say?" mused Larkin aloud. "*Here rests a poor excuse of a man.*"

The Beattie plot was much grander, far more elaborate and lovingly tended. It contained, within its black iron fence, a tall, four-sided red granite obelisk on a plinth. On one side it read:

GONE HOME
Ellen Marie Beattie (Ferguson)
1837–1877
Beloved
Wife to Edgar G.J. Beattie
Loving Mother to Larkin
In his favour is life:
weeping may endure for a night,
but joy cometh in the morning.

And his Pa's side read:

LAMENTED
Edgar Gilbert James Beattie
1833–1885
Though lost to sight, in memory dear.
Husband to Ellen Marie
Father to Larkin
Together in their Father's house,
With joyful hearts they go,
That dwell forever with the Lord
Beyond the reach of woe.

In the end, Larkin had been mightily pleased with the stone. After his Ma passed, he and his Pa had driven to Barrie to choose it—the tallest and second most impressive stone in the workroom. Larkin had thought the process would be upsetting, but the shop was so novel that he actually found it interesting. Initially, at least.

Mr. James, the proprietor and stonemason, greeted them sombrely when they entered. He was wearing a large canvas apron and was covered from his hair to his feet in fine greyish powder. His hands, when he extended them in a handshake, were dry, heavily calloused, and had a very strong grip.

"How de do," he said. "I am sorry for your loss," he added, bowing his head in a gentle, respectful nod.

"Good day," replied his Pa. "We need a stone for my wife." He spoke the words tersely. Larkin knew how much they pained him.

Mr. James nodded again in a show of kind reverence. "Do you have something in particular in mind? An angel, perhaps? I have a marble one in the back room that might suit."

His Pa shook his head. "No. Something for the whole family."

Larkin turned to look at his father, surprised. This was news.

"We need a stone for a family plot."

"Of course," agreed the obliging proprietor. "Would you like to look in my workroom or would you prefer to describe it?"

"Tall," said his Pa.

"And nice," added Larkin hopefully. "Ma deserves some-thing special."

"Walk this way, if you please." Mr. James preceded them through a heavily curtained doorway. When Larkin grasped the cloth, his hands left an imprint on the dusty fabric. The air was thick with it. Larkin licked his lips, tasting the fine grit that had settled lightly on every surface.

The workshop was a large, unheated space lined with cut stones and sizable chunks of rock. Tables strewn with chisels, mallets, and other tools stood at one end. Mr. James walked to the farthest side of the room, where the biggest pieces of stone were standing, and pulled a draped sheet off a tall, shapeless lump to reveal the angel.

Larkin thought she was beautiful. He walked up close and studied her wings. The feathers were etched in stone with remarkable detail and care. Each shaft and vane had been deeply lined, making the wings look as though they might move in the wind. The angel's face was looking downwards and smiling, her eyes either blank or closed, he couldn't tell. The eyes were a bit disappointing. His fingers reached up of their own accord to stroke a cold, lifeless wing.

His Pa shook his head definitively. "No, not for us." He walked towards a red column-like stone and ran his hand up and down the smooth surface. It stood two feet taller than his Pa and was entirely plain.

"Ah," said Mr. James, drawing closer, "an obelisk. A very fine one. Red polished granite. Four sides on the base, as you can see. Very appropriate for a family plot."

"This is the one," his Pa agreed. He looked over at Larkin, who nodded dutifully. It would not do to aggravate his Pa by asking for the angel. Pa had decided. In any case, the carving that had created the angel would have made her costly—and his Ma was never in favour of making a show of things. He was sure she'd be embarrassed by an expensive carving. Still, he couldn't help looking at it longingly, drawn by its graceful lines and form.

"Come with me," prompted Mr. James, "so that I can record the details and make further arrangements."

"Of course," answered his Pa, following him meekly into his office. There, in its crowded space, he sat down awkwardly across the desk from Mr. James on an ornate gilt chair. With no second chair available, Larkin stood by uncomfortably while his Pa filled out the forms.

Mr. James waited patiently. Larkin looked up from time to time and cast his eyes over the kindly man. Nothing in his manner or appearance had been off-putting or upsetting. He had somehow developed the ability of quietly putting people at ease while conducting the business of death. It was a rare quality, Larkin supposed, knowing how to help folks with broken hearts.

When his Pa finished with the papers he passed them across to Mr. James, who read through the responses quickly. "Would you mind," he asked, "if I went over some of the spelling with you? I would not wish to make an error."

When Pa nodded, Mr. James read back everything his Pa had written, being careful to spell out each word after he read it. "Now," he proposed, "there is the matter of a verse. I find that many families choose to include a favourite line from scripture, or a hymn, or a poem, after the particulars."

His Pa had hesitated. "I don't go in much for poetry, myself."

"I have a book," offered Mr. James, "with samples of things other families have found useful. Shall I bring it to you?"

His Pa looked at Larkin. Larkin nodded. Mr. James stood up from his desk and retrieved the book, placing it before them. Larkin peered over his father's shoulder while he turned the pages. Written in beautiful script were a series of verses and sayings and poems. Larkin spied "Gone Home."

"Pa, look at that one. Ma had said she was 'going home.'"

"She did."

"I think she'd like it, Pa."

His father nodded at Mr. James, who wrote it down on the form. His Pa continued to turn the pages. "What about this one, Larkin?" His father had rested his finger on lines from Psalm 30.5:

In His favour is life: weeping may endure for a night,
but joy cometh in the morning.

Both of them were silent as they read and reread the words. It was fitting.

Unexpectedly, and to his great embarrassment, Larkin began to cry. Not little tears that were soundless when they leaked out, but the loud kind, the ones that came from deep down inside and made your guts heave while you bawled. His Pa stood up and clasped him tightly as Larkin tried to control his grief.

When he had composed himself, Larkin realized that Mr. James had slipped out of the room and left them alone. He was grateful for the small courtesy. He wiped his face on his sleeve and tried to apologize.

"Never apologize for crying, son. It means you know how to feel things… Why doan you wait outside? Some air be good."

Larkin was glad to leave. He was ashamed of crying. It made him feel diminished and younger than his nineteen years.

Years later, when Larkin returned to Barrie to order the carving for his Pa's side of the stone, Mr. James was still there, although much older now, and with an assistant. Larkin wondered if the man remembered his childish outburst. If he did, he gave no sign of it. He was as kindly and gentle as ever.

When his Pa's name was added, Larkin paid extra to have all the lettering edged in black paint. And every time he visited he took a soft rag and polished the lettering till it shone in the sunlight. He knew that in time the paint would fade, or chip off, but he wanted to keep it in good repair while he still could.

Sometimes when Larkin was visiting there, having a conversation with his folks, a faint sense of sorrow would well up for all the ways he must have disappointed them. He knew they'd expected him to marry and fill the house with children. That would have made them both happy. Especially his Ma. Larkin suspected they'd been troubled by his solitary ways. He knew now that they'd guessed at some of his closely guarded secrets. He wished he'd trusted them more.

Not for the first time, he wondered whether his life would have unfolded differently if he'd shared those things with them.

So Larkin would stand still in all kinds of weather, with the sun kissing his face or the bitter winds slicing his body, and unburden himself quietly, telling them those things he couldn't when they were alive. Then, when he'd return to the farm afterwards, he'd feel lighter, calmer. Closer to his folks. It was a comfort to him to make these confessions, to believe that his words mattered.

Just as Larkin had learned to read the sky for an impending storm or scrutinize the trees for signs of change, he knew in himself that a more profound change was coming. He'd been having pains down his left arm, sometimes gripping him with a burning sensation, followed by a tightened chest that was different from what he'd known in his younger years. It left him breathless. But these too had become familiar to him, just like his other afflictions of old, so that when they came again he was ready.

He sat still, now, and waited to let it pass. These would be among the last of his days, and there was much he needed yet to do. When it left him, finally, he wiped the sweat from his face and steadied himself for the walk back to the kitchen.

Larkin gulped down a glass of water and then tended the stove. When its fire burned brightly, he began to rip out pages, one by one, from the scrapbook, rereading each "Murton Murder" newspaper story before committing it to the fire. The first few pages contained short clippings on the progress of the initial investigation. He did not hesitate in consigning these to the flames. Then, pushing back his chair, he paused.

Nobody, excepting his folks, had ever much bothered about Pauley after the fire. Consensus was that he must have done it and he must of had help. It was only on account of Silas being so poorly thought of that they didn't push any harder and squeeze the truth out of him.

Not a single person in the county had one nice thing to say about Silas Skinner. People didn't like to repeat the bad stories, but there were enough of them going around, for sure. They talked about his cheating and stealing and foul temper and all manner of things, going back for years and years. "The wonder of it," people would say, "was that nothing happened to him before." A lot of folks had a grievance and a grudge. And nobody much even pretended to be sorry he was gone.

Folks were like that. And Pauley was tainted by association. Even though some spoke about how smart he was at book learning, when his name came up, most folks went quiet.

No one ever asked *why* Pauley might have done it, or why things happened the way they did. Instead, they just figured Pauley was provoked and that Silas got what was coming.

Pa was a king among men in that way. A real Christian example. Not like that damn fool preacher who was so heavenly minded that he was no earthly good. He could have done something for Pauley. Him and his damn bell. And dressing up every Sunday in his collar and frock coat like he was in some fine cathedral instead of just knowing that folks came to church because they needed something to hang on to. Ask me, said Larkin to himself, if you want to preach on Sunday, you ought to have to work alongside folks during the week.

Larkin reflected that while he might not know much, he remembered his Bible stories well enough to know that Jesus didn't dress up and swan around preaching. Instead, he worked damn hard fishing, visiting with folks from all around, and even feeding them, too. Jesus never asked for a fancy bell. He gave what he had to the people. There's something wrong when some do without while the preacher never gets his hands dirty. If that preacher had been worth anything, he would have got hold of Paul and taken good care of him. He would have taken him in and seen that he was looked after.

Larkin ripped out the next few pages and fed them to the flames. Then he kept turning the stiff pages till he came to his questioning at the inquest. He grimaced, bit his bottom lip, then pulled the lamp closer so that he could make out the type.

DAY ONE OF MURTON CORONER'S INQUEST!
A large and sombre crowd gathered outside the Pine
Street School in Collingwood early this morning.

*I was surprised by the number of people crowded round. Some were
familiar but most I dint know. They stared at us while we went up the
steps and into the building. I remember stumbling against Ma at one
point and grabbing at her arm while she steadied me.*

Despite the weather, neighbours, well-wishers, and
the curious waited in the rain for hours before being
allowed to enter.

An expectant hush fell when fourteen-year-old
Larkin Beattie was sworn in. The honourable Judge
Harold Campbell, recently retired from the bench,
presided. Seated to one side, eight gentlemen from the
surrounding counties were assembled as a jury of peers.

Well-known prosecutor Finlay Taylor, acting as the
Coroner's Counsel, led the questioning with vigour,
striding backwards and forwards in front of the bench,
bellowing his questions in a voice that resonated richly
within the room.

*That man unnerved me for sure. He knew I warn't speaking every-
thing I knew. If we'd ever met outside that room, I was certain he would
of grabbed me by the throat until I spilled out the whole of it. Maybe he
would a done it anyway if the judge had allowed it.*

The onlookers were spellbound by the testimony of
young Beattie, who described in detail the events of
August 7th as he knew them.

*The details of the events as far as I was gonna say. And only those
things that wouldna done more harm.*

No charges have been laid in the fire that claimed
the lives of Silas and Elgin Skinner.

What follows is a partial transcript of young Beattie's statements to the Court.

"*May it please your Lordship, the Court will require the first witness to stand. Thank you. Please state your full name and address at the time of the events in question.*"

"My name be Larkin Ryan Beattie. I live on Cemetery Hill and that's where it took place."

But the killings and the other things that took place weren't sumpen I was gonna talk about. Ever.

"*Thank you. Mr. Beattie, what is your relationship to Mr. Skinner and his family?*"

"Silas Skinner was my Pa's age and we was neighbours. My Pa said as Silas dint have a decent bone in 'is body. He was a real mean sonofabitch."

That's the gospel truth. I got it from my Ma after for using that language in front a them, but Pa said as she should leave it be, as I was nervous and did just fine. "He did us proud" is what my Pa said. Only Pa dint know all of it. If he had've done, I doan think he would a said it.

"*Mr. Beattie, the Court takes a dim view of that type of language and I must ask you to refrain from using it again.*"

"Sorry, sir. I'm aimin' to speak plain."

That's what I said, anyways. They dint catch on. Sergeant Quinn and that lawyer was the only ones who suspected I had more I warn't sayin'.

"*Please continue.*"

"Only a certain type of man kicks a dog, and they say Silas was born kickin' and he just never stopped. Kicked dogs and kicked his kin. And Silas, he dint need liquor to be mean; that's just the way he was."

He was an evil sick bastard.

"*Please confine your remarks to the questions as I ask them, Mr. Beattie. Do you understand?*"

"Understood, sir."

"*Thank you. Now will you please describe your relationship with Paul Skinner.*"

Well, how can you stand up in a room and say in front of all these folks what your relationship was? Do you start by telling 'em about the hunting cabin and what it's like to have a place of your own that you only share with one person? And how you supposed to explain carin' for a friend so much that it ached inside when you saw how his Pa had taken the belt to him or knocked him about. Them's hard things to talk on. No wonder I choked and had to take a breath before answerin'. But the honest truth was so much more than that. Layin' out what we did that afternoon would be like strippin' down in front of that whole room and lettin' people see right through my skin.

Larkin shook his head and skimmed past the next several exchanges. Then he narrowed his eyes again and continued reading.

"*And tell us what, if anything, did Paul Skinner say to you about the fire.*"

"When my Ma left the room, I sat with Paul and I told 'im we was goin' to take real good care of 'im. And he turns 'is head to look at me, and he closes 'is eyes, and he says, 'I started it, you hear? *I* killed 'im.' And I takes a minute and asks him, 'Was everyone else in bed?' And he says, 'Ma and the girls were away visitin'. They been gone a week. Just me and Elgin and Pa home.' And I thinks what a good thing the others warn't there. And then I think how strange it was the fire burnin' the barn and the house on account there bein' a piece of distance between 'em."

And I already know Silas is dead and so I can't figure out who he means he kilt. And I think maybe the shock has 'im confused and he doan know who he's talkin' to. But later on, I realize he means Elgin. He kilt Elgin. And that surprised me when I figured it out. Why Elgin got kilt, I doan know. And sumpen 'bout that worries me. I wonder did Pauley go after 'im like he did 'is Pa? I know what Silas did was demeanin' and humiliatin'. But I doan know what Elgin did. I just gotta believe that if Pauley had a hand in it, then Elgin done sumpen as bad as Silas. Or worse maybe.

"And what do you think he meant by saying, 'I started it. I killed him'?"

"I doan rightly know. I thought as he was sayin' he had an accident and started the fire."

I thought I knew all about everythin' there was to know, but as things were piecin' together, I saw as how there were secrets in that house I dint know about. An I think Pauley was sayin' that he knew he'd kilt Silas, but that I warn't to say I was there when it happened. I think Pauley was tryin' to protect me. An maybe someone else too. Whoever it was that helped 'im move the bodies.

"The bodies of both Elgin and Silas were recovered from the fire. The coroner says they died from multiple knife wounds. Do you know, or think you may know, what happened before the fire?"

"I doan know 'bout no *knife* wounds."

But I do know 'bout sheep shears. And I know when you hold 'em with the blades together they pierce flesh and sink down deep. And I remember what that feels like, grabbing a pair and pushin' 'em in a man's back so as he gasps a long screechy whine.

And I can still see 'im on top a Pauley, and Pauley underneath with his face in the dirt while Silas is poundin' into him. I know cause I went round to meet Pauley for some fishin' and heard strange grunts comin' from the shed. And I snuck round and looked through the cracks in the wood and I saw Silas's bony ass heavin' and Pauley bein' hurt. And there weren't no time for gettin' help, so I ran inside and jumped on Silas's back and started poundin' 'im tryin' to get 'im off Pauley. And he let go a Pauley and twisted round, hitchin' up his trousers and then punchin' at me, and I saw that Pauley had crawled away and was tryin' to stand up but he was cryin' and he looked an awful sight.

And Silas was screamin' "I'm gonna kill both you little fuckers!" and I believed him. There was a murderin' look to him and a meanness like no one decent ain't never meant to see. And I was rollin' on the ground, tryin' to avoid his kickin' and my hand touched sumpen and I picked it up and was flailin' around and that's when it happened. I stabbed Silas. And he tried to get up and he was some mad and I was so scared that I dropped the shears. And Pauley rushed over and grabbed them and he stabbed Silas again and again and kept at it until Silas fell down and laid there just makin' watery sounds till he stopped. And I just watched. Paul was yellin' and cryin' and kept on at it with the shears.

It dint seem real. And I wanted to run for my Pa but Pauley said "No!" And he yelled at me, and he said "You ruined everythin', you shouldna' come! You shouldna' come!"

And I just gawped at 'im, I was so shocked by it all, and I tried to say sumpen but no words came out. And he yelled again, "Get outta here! Get out now!!" And I dint understand what he meant but then he pushed me hard with both hands. And so I ran. I ran scared and got home and kept busy tryin' to stay away from my folks so they couldn't see how I was troubled. And it all seemed like a terrible mistake. And it dint seem like it really happened. And later on I saw the fire and I guessed what he done.

And I think if maybe I'd run straight home and told my Pa maybe Elgin wouldn't of died, or maybe Silas neither, and Pauley wouldn't of have set the fires. And so what happened was my fault too. And after it all happened I couldn't tell my Pa what I saw, it would shame Pauley awful. And after, Pauley made me promise not to ever tell a soul and I kept my promise.

"Maybe you could tell us what happened next, after the night of the fire."

What I remember most is the stink of warm blood as it spurts out and mixes with the shit and straw and dirt, and the smell of fear.

"The Doc came and he checked on Paul. I heard him tell my Ma that she done a good job. The Doc had linseed oil and lime-water liniment for the pain. He said it looked like Paul tried to grab a knife by the blade and the cut went deep in his thumb. He was covered all over in bruises. I seen 'em when Pa and I lifted him inna the tub."

I seen 'em before. My folks must a seen 'em and figured out where they came from. I guess that's why my Pa was worried about him. He knew Pauley needed someone to look out for him.

"Every time anyone touched 'im, like when my Ma went to comb 'is hair, he whimpered some."

"And did you encounter any other members of the Skinner family after the fire?"

"Mrs. Skinner and the girls come back after the fire and first they stayed in town but then they moved to the Plowrights. I heard the girls went right back to school like nuthin' happened. Mrs. Skinner came one time to visit but she stayed in the kitchen with my Ma and never did check on Pauley. Like she forgot he was there or sumpen. It seemed queer. I know Paul heard her talkin' 'cause he got all quiet. He got stoppered up after."

The thing he said then that never made no sense was about her. He spoke real quiet. He said, "I just did what she wanted so he wouldn't spoil the girls."

"I tried to get 'im to come outside with me a spell but he wouldn't and finally I just had to leave 'im. Pauley stayed with us about a week and then one day Doc Mather says as there was a doctor in Collingwood who was good with burns. And me and my Pa drove him there an left him be in a big hotel close to the shipyards."

"Go on. What happened next?"
"Nuthin' happened."
"Is there anything else you can add?"
"Doan think it."

Larkin sighed, pulled more pages free from the scrapbook, and ripped them into four smaller pieces. Then he stood up thoughtfully from his chair and fed them into the stove.

His left arm pained him but there was more yet to do. When he was done, he'd lie down and have a rest. It had been a long night; the sun was high now, and he hadn't really slept at all.

DAY TWO OF MURTON MURDER INQUIRY

All those present as the coroner's inquest resumed were deathly silent when the name "Paul Skinner" was called aloud. Heads turned to watch as a thin young man in an ill-fitting suit entered the courtroom. With his eyes on the floor, Mr. Skinner navigated the short aisle towards the judge's bench and stopped still, waiting for direction. A clerk of the court led him to the wooden enclosure where he was quietly sworn in and seated.

And I was looking down the whole time but I sneaked a look and I saw him lookin' pitiful.

Lead prosecutor Finlay Taylor began the proceedings in earnest by bellowing, "Good of you to join us, Mr. Skinner! We understand that you have only recently returned from town!"

What follows is a partial transcript of the interview on the second day of this much-anticipated coroner's inquest.

"Mr. Skinner, would you be so good as to describe to the Court the events of August 7th as you know them?"
"I can't say that I know much… I can't remember."

Was that ever true or was that what he decided to say? Was that how he figured his way round without havin' to tell so many lies? I thought as how he might try to say he knocked over a lamp or sumpen. But I reckon that wouldn't explain why the house and the barn caught afire. Maybe he knew better. He likely thought the whole thing through.

"You do remember the fire, Mr. Skinner, do you not?!"

"I heard 'bout it and 'bout my Pa and Elgin. But I don't remember it."

"You sustained injuries in that fire, did you not?!"

"Yes, sir, so I been told."

"But you claim not to remember how you sustained those injuries to your person?"

"I do not remember, sir."

"So tell me, Mr. Skinner, how do you explain the injuries you received?!"

"I been told I escaped the house when it was alight and that Pa and Elgin didn't get out in time."

"In time for what, exactly, Mr. Skinner?!"

"In time to escape from the fire."

"And how do you propose that your Pa and Elgin could have escaped the fire when they were already dead before the fire started?!"

"I... don't know."

"Mr. Skinner you appear not to know very much. I wonder if you can tell me who else was at the farm on the day of the fire. Was there another person there with a knife, perhaps? A very large knife, I'm told. A knife that was used repeatedly to stab both your father and your brother?"

"I don't know."

This was a strange thing. It must of been a knife kilt Elgin. I took the shears when I ran. He must of got a knife somewhere and got it into Elgin. It doan make no sense to me why Elgin was kilt.

I dint puzzle it out until much later. Elgin must of been as cruel as Silas. He likely had a go at Pauley, or maybe the girls. And Mrs. Skinner, she maybe planned it with Paul. He said once that he only did what she wanted him to do. How much of that godawful night was planned ahead? Pauley was real smart, and I figure he got his head from somewheres, and it weren't Silas. I reckon his Ma was the one with a head for figurin', and that Pauley got his ways from her. If I'm right, then it was her that helped Pauley and maybe her as planned it.

"Will you tell the Court anything about that day, Mr. Skinner, or are you deliberately obfuscating? Is this a ploy to avoid your personal responsibility? Are you the man with the knife, Mr. Skinner? Did your father fly into one of his drunken tempers and attack you, and did you grab a knife to defend yourself? Did Elgin intervene in the fight and try to take the knife from you? Or was it the other way around? Did Elgin stab your father and you grabbed at the knife and fatally stabbed him in a struggle? Tell the Court, Mr. Skinner! Tell me!"

"I... don't... know..."

The lawyer sure got some riled with Pauley. His face went all red and he was huffin' to beat the band. He was the kind of fella used to havin' his way 'bout most things, I figure. But he warn't smart enough for Paul. Paul had him figured out all right.

Even though it took a while, I finally puzzled it all through. I was goin' by the train station one day and was thinkin' about that time my Ma came back from Toronto when she was so sick. And I was thinkin' on that, and thinkin' about how I only ever been to Toronto the one time myself. And so I went and had a look at the train schedule. I was interested in where they was goin' and comin' from.

We all knew Mrs. Skinner and the girls were away at the time of the fire and dint come back until the mornin' after, which was a Tuesday. But here's the thing I pieced out. The milk-run train back from Angus doan run on a Tuesday, which means they had to of come back on a Monday or a Thursday. I seen the train schedule. Sumpen struck me at the time but I couldn't piece together what it was. And then I looked at the paper calendar when I got back home, and the truth of it was right there. They must of come home Monday after we done the deed on Silas and before the fire, 'cause they were already back on Tuesday, for sure and there warn't no other train.

And they wouldn't be cut up 'bout Silas neither 'cause I figure what I seen him doin' to Pauley, well he might of been doin' it to the girls or worse. I dunno. And I think that after I left the farm runnin' his Ma and the girls came home, and there was a scene with Elgin and maybe Elgin was as mean a fucker as Silas, and Pauley had to fight him. And Pauley or his Ma took a knife to Elgin and together they laid him and Silas out in their beds before startin' the fires. And his Ma took the girls away in the buggy and they hid out somewhere once the fires got goin'.

An Pauley never told, 'cause he knew the shame of it would keep 'em from gettin' married to anyone decent. An that's why his Ma never would see him at the farm, 'cause she dint want to give anything away. Silas was a big man and so was Elgin and there warn't no way Pauley could of moved 'em without help.

I couldn't figure where exactly they must of hid, not for a long while. They couldn't be seen ridin' up and down the road. But then one day when I was at the cemetery, I saw it. There was a big old sugar shack in the bush beside the graveyard, right across the road from Skinners. It belonged to the Bakers but they stopped usin' it years back after they built a new one on the other side of the bush. The old shack was large enough to hold a buggy and horses, for sure. And Mrs. Skinner, she was sharp enough to take the girls there and hide until the early mornin'. And in the confusion of the fire, they could reappear and pretend like they was just comin' back from the train and be all shocked an upset.

Even Cian hadn't puzzled out what I had. Leastways not that he ever said.

And there's somethin' else. That letter Ethel sent my Ma. I know why Ma hid it now, and why Paul's Ma and sisters were so grateful. Ma woulda made a fuss when Mrs. Skinner came to the farm after the fire but wouldn't see poor Pauley lyin' there right in the next room. Mrs. Skinner woulda had to explain to my Ma. How much she told her—I'll never know that.

"Thank you for understandin," Ethel wrote. And my Ma, who'd always insisted on telling the truth and who went to church every Sunday, she kept that terrible secret, or leastways what she'd learned of it.

She was a mother. She protected Pauley, just like she protected me.

In a dramatic end to the questioning, Mr. Skinner appeared to collapse and was carried from the room by two clerks of the court.

Pauley always was good at play-actin'.

DAY THREE OF MURTON MURDER INQUIRY
Expert witnesses including the fire inspector, the medical examiner, and the homicide sergeant testified today. Here follows excerpts from their testimonies.

Larkin skimmed Chief Hardy's testimony, remembering how tedious it had been. "The large bedroom in the southwest corner of the house would indicate that sumpen similar to a kerosene lamp may have been the starting point for the fire," Hardy told the court in a slow, laborious fashion. Then, after a series of lengthy responses—"Three distinct areas in the barn that indicated the presence of a fire starter... Again, I propose that kerosene was the likely agent"—he finally wound up. "There is no doubt in my mind," Hardy said, carefully adjusting his spectacles, "that this was a case of arson."

No shit. Dint take no fire inspector to reason that out.

The medical examiner, Dr. Graeme Gillanders, was the next official to be called forward and sworn in to provide testimony.

"Dr. Gillanders, I understand that you have examined the remains of Silas and Elgin Skinner. I wonder if you would, for the benefit of this jury, share with us your findings."

"Upon examination of both decedents, I discovered multiple knife scores in the bones that had not yet begun to heal. Given a similarity in the number of injuries and the pattern of wounds to the hands and chests of both victims, it was clear that a violent attack had taken place and claimed their lives prior to their partial incineration."

"*Thank you, Doctor. Would you conclude definitively that these men were deceased prior to the blazing fire which consumed them in their surroundings?*"

"There was no indication of a struggle for life. Both bodies were posed at rest with their arms crossed over the chest area."

That was a mistake. It might a been better if Pauley had left 'im in the barn an just burned the one buildin'. Course I dunno where Elgin was.

A break in the proceedings followed this interview. After a recess, the homicide sergeant, Sergeant Cian Quinn, was the next official to be called forward and sworn in to provide testimony.

"*Sergeant Quinn, would you be so good as to describe to the Court the scene that greeted you when you attended the Skinner establishment on the morning of August 8th?*"

"It were a sorry thing to see, it were. The house in blackened ruin and the barn a pile of charred timber. It's not a thing you would wish for."

"*Would you describe for the Court how the bodies of Silas and Elgin Skinner were found?*"

"Having a kip, as it were. Asleep on their beds."

"*Were there any signs of a struggle? Any indication of intruders, perhaps?*"

"Aw, sure look it."

"*Would you clarify, please, Sergeant Quinn?*"

"Yes. Grand. Lying stretched out as easy as you please on their beds. Arms crossed in prayer. It were quare strange."

"*Are you of the opinion, Sergeant Quinn, that these unfortunate souls died of natural causes?*"

"An eejit may say so but no man sets his own grange alight and lays down for a kip. It's murder, it is, as sure as the Shannon."

Larkin got himself another glass of water and sat down heavily in the kitchen chair. The room had grown hot; he was perspiring now. Only a few pages remained in the scrapbook. Using his right hand, he massaged his left arm.

CORONER'S INQUEST CONCLUDES!

Judge Harold Campbell has filed his final report into the gruesome murders of Silas and Elgin Skinner. After five days of questioning and the submission of several forensic reports, the judge concludes that the two deceased men were stabbed to death prior to the devastating fire which destroyed their home and farm operation, including all livestock. The crimes were deliberately committed by a person or persons unknown. It is believed that the assailant set fire to the farm to destroy evidence of evil misdeeds. It must be assumed that a vendetta of some form was at the root of this tragedy.

Paul Skinner, a survivor of the blaze who is currently recuperating from his own injuries, is not considered to be a person of interest in the case. Coroner's Counsel Finlay Taylor and the eight members of the jury who have served throughout this inquiry were thanked by Judge Campbell.

Sergeant Quinn has confirmed to this reporter that the file will remain open on his desk until the mystery is solved and residents of Murton are safe.

All that time and they were no closer to solvin' it.

I wish I knew where Pauley got to. I doan even know what he's called now. I would of liked to see him one more time. I hope he and his girl made a life together and that he found a place where folks is decent and kind. There's things I should of said.

He was a good friend once. I suppose I been learnin' that things doan always line up in black and white. There's a whole lot of grey.

I spent so much time thinkin' I warn't worth much; always feelin' like my outside dint match up with my insides. But I think Pauley saw me for who I was deep down. People can't always choose who or what matters to 'em. Pauley mattered to me.

Larkin opened the stove door and placed the remaining pages inside. He was thirsty again and his left arm was aching something fierce. He left the stove door open while he pumped another glass of water. His chest felt heavy, like something was binding too tight. The flames darted around quickly and flared up when they touched the papers. Tiny wafers of blackened ash rose in the swell of the heat before resettling. Larkin watched, waiting for the last of the secrets to smoulder.

Acknowledgements

Many thanks to Chris Needham and the team at Now Or Never Publishing for their ongoing support and for all that they do to promote Canadian writing. I am grateful to my writing sisters Laura Francis, Hejsa Christensen, AnnaLiza Kozma, and Hollay Ghadery for their steadfast encouragement, and love and appreciate the gift of each of them in my life. With thanks also to the amazing Shelley MacBeth and the Blue Herons for their work promoting and celebrating the importance of stories. Special thanks to Donna Morrissey who story-edited an early version of the manuscript and to Karen Alliston for her skillful editing. With much appreciation to historian Paul Arculus for his inspiring example amplifying Ontario history, and for all of his support. Kyle Brough was a thoughtful early reader and I am grateful for his friendship and gentle feedback. And thanks also to Vicky Earle and her love of horses for her helpfulness. To Michael and Andrew, thank you for always being so loving and indulgent when I disappear into a book.

"Lucy E.M. Black's aptly named *A Quilting of Scars* is written with grace and depth of character. As with all of her moving historical fiction, Lucy immerses her reader in details. In this early 20th century Canadian story, she touches on animal husbandry, small town life, illness, religious zeal, guilt, shame, and the burden of secrets. The novel moves back and forth in time at a moving pace and yet with delicate sensitivity. There is profound loneliness in protagonist Larkin, ashamed of who he might be, and yet somehow, throughout his life he held his ground, 'lest he disappear into the blackness.' Larkin contemplates how a life might have unfolded differently if he'd been able to trust and share closely guarded secrets and not rub sadness deeper into his pores."

~ Gail Kirkpatrick, author of *Sleepers and Ties*

"Lucy Black has done it again. In *A Quilting of Scars* she has created a delightful novel set in the late Victorian and early Edwardian era. Running through this skillfully crafted historical novel, are unobtrusive, yet relevant mysteries and secrets that keep the reader closely attached to the narrative. Even in the dialogue, with its vocabulary, colloquialisms and phrasing from more than a century ago, we are spirited back to that seemingly less complicated era. But it was still a time of hidden stresses. Throughout the work we are constantly reminded that, in spite of our present-day advances in technology and communication, human nature remains a constant throughout history. A delightful read."

~ Paul Arculus, writer and historian

"In *A Quilting of Scars*, Lucy E.M. Black weaves a murder mystery through the threads of farm life in the early twentieth century, expertly and delectably unfolding the intrigue with the everyday. Black uses cadence, dialect, and honed insight to immerse the reader in the life and psyche of Larkin Beattie—farmer, friend, and secret holder. We get poignant and fascinating glimpses into the hardships and joys of rural existence in Ontario's past through the eyes of a man wracked with guilt, betrayal, and remorse."

~ H&A Christensen, authors of *Stealing John Hancock*

"Lucy E.M. Black's mellifluous prose conjures a lost world, steeped in love of family, memory, and the quiet echoes of regret. In Larkin, she crafts a character who carries the weight of grief, loss, and guilt, each shaping him in ways he cannot comprehend. His solace in the rhythms of farm life—its hard work, its quiet joys—cannot erase what has happened, nor the secret he keeps close: his love for a friend implicated in a murder that shattered his rural community. Among Black's unforgettable creations, Larkin stands as both burdened and transcendent, a figure who lingers in the reader's mind, refusing to be forgotten. This is a story of reckoning, remembrance, and the fragile hope found among the shadows of the past."

~ AnnaLiza Kozma, Journalist and
Senior Producer, CBC Radio